Totally Bound Publishing books by Mimi B. Rose

The Laurentian Mountain Clan
Heart's Ease

I0680949

The Laurentian Mountain Clan

HEART'S EASE

MIMI B. ROSE

Heart's Ease
ISBN # 978-1-83943-786-1
©Copyright Mimi B. Rose 2022
Cover Art by Fiona Jayde ©Copyright March 2022
Interior text design by Claire Siemaszkiewicz
Totally Bound Publishing

HEART'S EASE

Dedication

To my family, for always believing in me.
And to the ladies for feedback and support — you
girls are awesome!

Note about Québécois French

This novel uses some Québécois expressions the
reader may not be familiar with. Most are
profanities or exclamations that do not translate
easily into English, but their use can be understood
in the context. Others are explained when they
occur in the story.

Chapter One

Chantelle Mizuki didn't want to die today.

I'm wearing old underwear. With holes. Nobody is going to see them. No nurse, no doctor, no coroner. Nobody.

Chantelle's footsteps crunched in the autumn leaves of the mountain forest. Night was falling. Wolves were howling.

Real wolves.

Granny Ceci's voice rang in her ears. "Don't go in the forest at dusk, *mon chou.*"

Too late, Granny.

She hadn't planned to be out this late. It was light when the After-School Art Club finished at the library. She had asked her student Alfonso to stay and talk about his application for art school. By the time they were done, the sun was low in the sky. Only after Alfonso had left did she discover she'd locked her keys in the car.

In the daytime, everyone used the path through the woods to get to the other side of the village in the Laurentian Mountains of Quebec. She loved the soft pine needles underfoot, tall trunks stretching their branches to the sky, soothing fragrances of moss and fern. During the day Chantelle expected to stumble across Snow White singing and dancing among the trees.

Night-time was different. Every noise was menacing, every shadow a predator waiting for her to stray off the path.

Chantelle kept to the darkened trail, wishing those howls and barks were getting fainter. The sounds of the forest were soothing when she was tucked into Granny Ceci's gingerbread cottage—her cottage now. This evening, those sounds took on ominous undertones.

She remembered Granny Ceci telling her, "*Ma cocotte*, the Laurentian Mountains are home to many creatures, some fair, some foul. Be prepared for both." Tonight, it was the foul creatures. Why couldn't it be chipmunks or raccoons?

Another howl wailed over the tops of the trees. The hairs on the back of her neck stood up. *One step in front of the other. You can do this.*

Soon she reached the edge of the village. Only a quarter of a mile left. Past Marie's big house on the hill, through the ravine, then up the path to the top of her street.

No problem. She had survived book signings with dozens of cranky children and their bad-tempered parents. She had run off her cheating no-good boyfriend. A wolf or two? No sweat.

She picked up her pace to a jog. Her legs were aching, her chest heaving. At the very least she'd have a funny story to tell Yvette and Kat. Well, it would be funny if she made it home in one piece.

The recent wolf sightings had everyone in town worried. The wolves were larger than usual, more vicious. They had even killed some dogs. Villagers were warned to stay away from the woods at night. She knew her woodcraft and carried her multi-tool at all times, but that wouldn't be enough to stop a feral wolf.

Of course, today was the day she'd locked her keys in the car. She'd forgotten to take her ADHD medication. And her publisher called in the afternoon to say they were passing on her *"passion project,"* as they'd called it. Illustrating Granny Ceci's stories and having them published were a way to honour her grandmother's legacy. But her reputation as a children's story illustrator was not opening doors for the collection of folk tales. Her usual collaborator hadn't helped at all. He didn't want his favourite illustrator distracted from his own book projects.

Was the howling closer now? Or was it her imagination? She crouched by a small cluster of sumac bushes. Her heart raced. The wind whistled through the treetops, clattering in the dying leaves.

There was a clearing ahead. What a relief! It was the small field behind her neighbour's house. Marie, a dear friend of Granny Ceci's, lived on the edge of the village. The little meadow divided the forest from her garden, which was enclosed by a stone wall.

There would be a large blue spruce at the northern edge of the clearing. The conical silhouette of the tree stood tall against the dying light. Three shadows, large and shaggy, skulked at the base.

She spared half a breath for one of Granny's favourite curse words.

Could she make it to Marie's house? She should move slowly, deliberately, not run. But rabid or savage wolves would still attack. If they came for her, she would have to run along the perimeter.

She was stuck. Sweat trickled down her back.

I need a plan. If she got out of this, she could move back to Montreal. There was nothing keeping her here. Granny had died last year. Why was she still here? *Pull yourself together, girl!*

The moon burst out from behind a cloud.

One of the wolves looked up, the cool light illuminating his outline. He cocked his head and looked in her direction. He howled, long and low. The other two wolves nosed him, turning towards her. Could they see her?

She sent a silent prayer up to Ceci. *Wherever you are, please help me.*

The wolves paced at the edge of the clearing, whining and sniffing the air.

She had to move. Maybe make a commotion once she got closer to the garden wall. Marie might hear.

She breathed in and out. *Now.* She took a cautious step.

One of the wolves inclined his head. Had he seen her? Another step.

He pointed his muzzle at her, his tail arching over his back. Two steps.

The lead wolf pushed off on his hind legs, padding towards her position. The others followed on his tail.

Ben l'on! Granny would have said. *Oh, come on!*

She sprinted towards the wooden gate in the middle of the stone wall.

They reached her in the clearing. The largest one growled, ears and tail erect. His eyes looked odd — orange, almost glowing. Impossible. It must be a reflection of the moonlight.

These wolves were big. And their faces looked funny — no, not funny, just strange. Almost human-like.

Heart racing, Chantelle took a step back.

The wolves advanced, circling her. They weren't acting like regular wolves. What was going on?

The leader surged forward, snarling. She backed up and bumped into another wolf. The wolf behind her made a huffing noise that sounded almost like a laugh. Goosebumps broke out on her arms. Was this the end?

The largest one snapped at her leg. As she stepped back, her knees buckled and she fell to the unforgiving ground beneath her. Tears stung her eyes as she scrabbled in the grass and dirt. He descended on her and sunk his teeth in her calf. She batted at him, a shrill scream erupting from her throat. She had to get away.

The other wolves nipped at her arms as she pulled back, dodging their snouts and paws. She searched for purchase on the ground. They dragged her across the ground, away from the wall.

Fear churned in her stomach. Her heart beat fast as she struck at the wolves. Then something changed, fear turning into anger in her chest. Tingling sensations erupted into a warmth across her chest. Her ears buzzed.

What's going on?

Some kind of energy bubbled from her middle. Rising up, it surged from her core out towards her arms and legs. It felt strange, yet familiar somehow.

The buzzing increased, changing into a burning sensation. A shooting pain in her leg snapped her attention back to the wolves. Sliding along the ground, she reached for the wolf attached to her leg. She smiled as she caught hold. His fur was matted, his bulk solid beneath her fingers.

The low droning made her ears itch and blocked out the growls of her attackers. Her field of vision telescoped into her hands, legs, and torso in front of her.

Anger surged within her. She pushed out from her diaphragm. Energy tingled and sparked, hot and strong. It poured down her arms and into her hands. When she shoved against her attacker, something blue zapped out of her palms.

The wolf let go when the blast hit him. Falling back a few inches, he shook his head and coat.

Growling, ears back, he pushed forward. The lights in his eyes glowed. The wolves regrouped and closed in.

I'm going to die here. With no one present to hear a snappy parting line.

A spotlight came on, almost blinding her. A rifle shot rang in the air and the creatures froze. Out from the garden gate stepped a small figure.

Marie!

The ancient woman leaned forward, hefting a rifle that was almost as tall as she was. Her red plaid jacket was three sizes too big and hung down to her knees. She peered out from thick glasses beneath a dark green hunter's cap.

"*Allez-y vous, sales chiens!*" The old woman's Québécois accent was thick but her tone was unmistakable.

Chantelle sucked in a big breath. She shuddered and turned to her attackers. The larger brown wolf swung his head towards her.

Another shot grazed the attacker's mud-coloured fur. Yelping, he jumped out of the ring of light. He whined, pawing the ground, the other wolves huffing beside him. He glanced over at the old woman.

A new growl, low and menacing, rumbled by the gate. Beside Marie was a large dog, ears back, tail up. They moved forward in unison. The wolves backed away from Chantelle.

The lead wolf slunk towards the trees with his two companions. Looking back, he howled once before the trio disappeared into the night.

Chantelle pushed up from the ground, relief warring with the fear and pain. She tried to stand but her leg throbbed. The bite marks oozed blood. Her feet shuffled forward as she held her elbow against her side. Had they bitten her arm too?

She reached towards Marie by the gate.

Then she was falling.

Strong arms wrapped around her. A low voice murmured and Marie's voice answered. She was being lifted up, arms carrying her to warmth. The voices faded away.

Her fingers touched a soft blanket. How long had she been out? A fire crackled nearby. Gentle hands prodded at the bite.

She faded out again.

* * * *

Charles Ducharme sat in his large corner office at the flagship ski resort in the Laurentian Mountains. He spread his hands on his heavy wooden desk and looked down.

Ostie! The land deal's tanking.

He stood up and strode to his office door.

"Ken, where's my brother?"

"Henri?" his assistant asked.

"Thomas."

Charles returned to his desk and drummed his fingers until the phone rang a minute later. "Thomas, what happened to the deal?"

"Another bid. The team's prepping the counter-offer now."

"Who's this Frères Gris Consortium?"

"They're buying up property in the area. Name's from a missionary group from New France. They owned a city block in Montreal a century ago, then dropped out of sight."

"Supernaturals?"

"We found scattered rumours about them. Settlers called them cannibals and devils. Stories of eating children and women alive."

"Those are just tales. Humans think loups-garous are stories too."

"It could be humans using the Frères Gris name. Nobody's seen them."

Charles raked a hand through his wavy hair. "What do I tell our indigenous partners? This project is about reconciliation with our neighbours."

"We'll work through the night if we have to. I don't like losing."

"I'm going to stay. We need this parcel of land to start the geothermal pipelines." Charles stood up and grabbed the files Ken had left on his desk.

"You need some time off, Charles. Yesterday you flew off the handle in front of the kitchen staff."

"It's bad timing—"

"You missed Grand-maman's one-fiftieth last week. Go. Have a visit with her." Thomas had his best interests at heart.

"Yeah, yeah."

"If Henri were here, he'd tell you to get laid."

"Of course our baby brother would. You know I don't like hook-ups."

"Have you been with anyone since Alice left?" Thomas asked.

Charles didn't answer.

"That's twelve months. You can't blow off all that steam in the gym. Something's got to give."

"It's just—my wolf's restless. Nothing helps." Charles put the files in a drawer and closed his laptop.

"You've got a lot on your plate. We've been on high alert since you became Alpha. And with the Trois-Rivières pack nipping at the border of our territories—"

"Another family arrived yesterday fleeing from Roland and his pack. And with the land project stalling, everything's spiralling out of control. I can't keep it together."

"Let your pack help. Don't shoulder it by yourself."

Charles shrugged. "How? I'm stuck in a corner. I can't get out."

"Spend a few days with Grand-maman. Then we'll talk about making changes around here."

They hung up. Charles grabbed his leather duffel bag and left the contemporary suite of offices, walking past the indoor pool and sleek workout rooms. He continued through the main lodge and stopped at the reception desk. He pasted a smile on his face and asked how the reception team was doing. *I have to make more of an effort, show my employees I am approachable.* The front lobby was empty as he exited the main doors and walked to the parking lot.

Stop micromanaging everyone. Thomas was right. He needed to get away for a few days. But with the counter-bid, he couldn't step back, could he? And his uncle had showed up last week talking about a seat on the Board. That would be another nightmare.

He sighed, got in his SUV and turned out of the ski resort property. He drove slowly through the ski village, keeping an eye out for pedestrians, then turned onto the mountain highway. It was a forty-five-minute drive to Grand-maman Marie's village. Time enough to think about his brother's request. Get his head on straight.

A lot had happened since his father died three years ago. A pang hit his gut. It still felt like yesterday when they'd got the news that he'd been killed on the highway. Slid off an icy road and over a cliff, his oldest son in the car with him. It had been such a shock to become Alpha that way. He had relied on his pack's support. His brothers, Thomas and Henri, and his cousins—Michel, Clementine and Bertrand—were always there to help. He had to figure out how to take a step back and let them help more.

He barely noticed the brilliant fall colours around him on his drive. He took the hairpin turns and narrow passes on autopilot. Luckily, it wasn't busy. They still had a few weeks before the snow fell and the tourists descended.

Charles drummed on the steering wheel. There was always something to worry about. If it wasn't the Trois-Rivières pack, it was the Elders in the village. And yesterday the mages had reported disturbances in the ley lines, unusual adjustments to the moon cycles and curious variations in the local flora and fauna. His Elder Mage, Gwen, asked him to keep an eye out in Lac St. Patrice—his Grand-maman's village—since she had identified a problem there.

He would look around a bit while he was visiting. But he would try to relax. Just forget everything for a few days.

Chapter Two

Chantelle woke up in a small bedroom, not her own. Light fluttered through gingham curtains. A well-loved quilt was tucked around her. Her head felt stuffed with fluff.

She rolled on her side and planted a hand on the mattress. When she pushed up, pain shot through her arm. She groaned and lay back down.

The friendly old woman sat down beside her. "Good morning, *mon chou*. How are you feeling?" Marie's glasses magnified the kind grey eyes in her wrinkled face.

"Okay, I think. What happened?" Chantelle asked.

"Last night, wolves attacked you."

Had she almost died? "You saved me, Marie. You had a big rifle. And a giant dog?" Hurting all over couldn't stop her from chuckling at that image.

"Hmm, he's not here now."

"Is Bertrand still here? I think we talked this morning." Bertrand often came to stay with his grandmother.

"He had to leave. My grandson Charles is here now. He can take you home."

A younger pair of grey eyes looked down at her. "Can you sit up?" The male voice shot right through her.

She blinked and nodded. When she leaned on her left shoulder, she winced.

She reached for the strong arm that he held out, the smooth skin lightly dusted with dark hair. When she took hold, a spark of electricity zinged through her, right down to her toes. She grabbed on and hoisted herself up. She was holding on to muscled biceps that led to sculpted triceps. A powerful neck and rugged face topped his massive shoulders.

Hoo-mama! Sexy lumberjack, anyone?

In his face she could see a hint of Marie's kindness, but the jaw was tense and set forward. His dark hair was longer than Bertrand's, a shaggy beard on his chin and cheeks. He was much better looking than he had a right to be.

He picked her up as though she were light as a feather and placed her gently on the floor beside him. She caught a hint of pine and moss from his sweater and fought a sudden urge to bury her face in his chest.

When her knees buckled, the man wrapped a large hand around her waist. Dark grey eyes, angular cheeks and chin, rich olive skin. Yes, he was too good-looking.

"She lost some blood, Grand-maman. Are you sure she can leave?"

"I'll be fine!" Chantelle protested. "I should get home. My friends are coming over tonight and they can check on me."

Chantelle's eyes drifted across his wide shoulders and muscular chest. How did he find the time to keep so fit?

Stop ogling your neighbour's grandson.

When Charles looked at his grandmother, the expression changed his face completely. Where before his good looks had a coldness to them, the ice dropped away. In its place was warmth, love and caring.

I'd give anything to have someone look at me like that.

Charles helped Chantelle down the little staircase. They took it slow. He smelled good but it couldn't make up for the pain she was in. The wound on her leg ached and she had to put most of her weight on the other foot.

By the time they reached the main floor, she was winded.

Charles captured her in his electric gaze. "Chantelle — that's your name? Do you want to sit down for a minute?"

"Yes," she said. *I didn't know it could take so long to get down a set of stairs.* She scowled, worrying about how much she prided herself on her independence. When she was seated, she thought she could sleep for a week. Wait, what about her responsibilities? "My After-School Club, Marie!"

"When is it? Tomorrow?"

Chantelle looked at Charles. "It's for at-risk youth Tuesdays and Thursdays. We meet for art classes at the library. I have to go —"

Charles pulled out his phone. "Kenneth, tell Tori to cover an art class for youth in Lac St. Patrice," he said. "Tomorrow and next week, Tuesday and Thursday. It's at the library — can you get the details from them? And order art supply kits — you know the ones we stock in the recreation centre. But the bigger version." He looked at Chantelle. "How many?"

"Twelve or thirteen." What was he doing? This was ridiculous. He didn't know her or the youth. But it was very thoughtful.

"Send twenty. By courier to the library tomorrow morning so they'll be there before the club meets." He turned off his phone. "It's all arranged. The art teacher at our village recreation centre will take over your classes for this week and next."

"Thank you. And the art kits. They have so little of their own. It will make their day—their week!" Her eyes welled up.

I just have a speck of dirt in my eye. That's all.

Charles nodded curtly and stood up, staring at a wall.

"Time to get you to bed." Marie helped her up. The old woman was stronger than she looked.

Bed. Chantelle had an image of this hunk of a man in her bed. Naked and using those smouldering eyes to devour her. Oh boy!

Shake it off, like the blonde pop star sings.

"Uh, thanks." She made her way to the door, leaning on Marie, one eye on the handsome grandson.

Charles helped Chantelle into his SUV, hoisting her up to the seat. It was nice to hold someone. *Geez, it must be bad if I'm this starved for contact.* He hated to let go of her, but got himself under control and drove through the village. She was beautiful, though. Her dark eyes and hair were just his type.

"What got you into the After-School Club?" he asked.

"I want to support at-risk youth. I didn't have a lot of grown-ups in my life when I was their age."

"You were raised by your granny, right?"

"I lost my parents when I was young." Her voice broke.

"My mom died when I was little, but I still had my dad. I don't know what I would have done without him," Charles said, thinking of his loss. *It must have been lonely with no family.*

When they arrived at her house, Charles helped her out of the car. He liked being near her. When he caught a whiff of flowers from her hair, his wolf snapped to the front, snuffling.

Stop smelling Marie's neighbour.

His wolf wouldn't listen — he wanted to stay as close to her as he could. He had an inexplicable urge to protect her. Why? With a little effort, he shook it off.

The little cottage was cute. Gingerbread moulding painted a creamy yellow, a dark green wooden door. Bright and vibrant, just like her.

He held her close — maybe a bit more than necessary — and walked with her to the living room, helping her down onto the sofa. The space was soft, inviting, with a faint hint of freshly baked bread coming from the kitchen. He took the wood stacked beside the fireplace and got to work taking the chill out of the air.

His eyes ranged over her form, taking in her petite frame, the swell of her breasts, her graceful neck. Her clothes were too big for her — much too shapeless for him to get a good sense of her body.

Charles brought his gaze back to her dark-brown eyes. They held him.

There was something there — his wolf sniffed. *Play?*

"Thanks for your help," she said.

"Oh, Bertrand asked me to bring you something from home." He rushed to his car. This was stupid. Why had his cousin asked him to bring CDs? He returned to the room and handed her a box set. "It's the complete recordings of Ella Fitzgerald and Louis Armstrong. So, you like jazz?"

Chantelle's fingers touched his when he passed her the CDs and a spark of electricity jolted through him. "Oh, right. I told him this morning that I love Ella's voice."

"I have all her albums on vinyl." His body flushed. It must be the fire.

"What?" Chantelle stared. "There's like…" She started counting on her fingers.

"Fifty-nine of them, not including the live recordings. It took me a while to track them all down." At least he had a couple of interests not related to work.

"That's amazing!"

"I don't know many people who would appreciate my jazz record collection. If you want to hear them sometime…" He trailed off. "Sorry, that sounded like a bad line." He didn't want to be a jerk. But he would like to see her again. Should he ask her out?

His wolf said, *Yes. Smell her. Keep her safe.*

Chantelle smiled. "Your family has been so kind to me. Here, wait." She put down her arms and tried to stand up. She sat down again, wincing.

"Anything I can get for you?"

"Yes, in my studio—the dining room, beside the kitchen." She waved him to the left. "There's a sketch of your grandmother. It's in the pile closest to the easel."

He found the room. He looked around at the piles of sketches, watercolours on three different easels, glasses with paint brushes in dirty water.

"Umm, where?" he asked.

"Sorry it's a mess. Comes with my ADHD. Look on the table by the window. There's a pile of papers."

He looked around again, stopping at a recent sketch modelled on herself as a teenager. She had fairy wings and was kneeling in a field. It reminded him of something, but he couldn't place it.

"You're very talented," he called to the other room, leafing through a pile of papers.

His phone rang. It was his cousin Michel's number.

"There's a body in Lac St. Patrice. The police want us to take a look at it."

"Wolves?" Charles asked. Chantelle gasped from the other room.

"Yes. Same as before. A young woman."

"*Ostie!*" This was bad. The pack's relationship with local police was strong, but with all the recent wolf attacks, it had become strained. "Do you need me there?"

"Since you're in town."

"Right." He ended the call.

He returned to the living room. Chantelle looked so beautiful lying on the couch. Her black hair framed her sweetheart face so perfectly. "I'm sorry, but I have to go. The police have found a body."

"A body—where? In Lac St-Patrice?" Chantelle's face drained of all colour.

"Yes."

"I have to come with you. One of my youth went missing last week and…"

Oh, no.

"You're in no shape to go gallivanting across town."

She crooked an eyebrow, saying, "Gallivanting?"

"You know what I mean. You've been attacked—"

"By *wolves*. I know. That's why—"

"No."

She hung her head and sniffed.

Dammit, why did she get to him? "You can't come with me. But I'll drive back here when I'm done and fill you in."

"Okay." *If she asked me for anything right now, I would say yes.* Her eyes were shining.

Oh boy, he was in trouble, big trouble.

* * * *

Chantelle wiped her eyes after Charles left. She had a feeling in her gut—a bad feeling about the body.

She was worried about Christine. She hadn't shown up for the After-School Club on Tuesday. Alfonso had said her dad was back at the reserve last week. Chantelle hoped she was spending time with him. But it wasn't like her not to come to the group.

Chantelle closed her eyes, mind still racing. *Don't spiral.*

She and Christine had a lot in common. They had both grown up biracial in rural Quebec, with people touching their hair without permission and asking where they were from—among other, worse things. It wasn't the most tolerant environment.

Wait until you know for sure.

She ran through the box-breathing exercises Granny Ceci had taught her. *One breath in – count to four – one breath out.* When her heart stopped pounding, she did her body scan visualisations. Calm enough to lie still but not sleep.

Charles had put on one of his CDs before he left. She concentrated on Ella's and Louis' voices, breathing deeply. *In. Out.* It seemed like hours before she heard a knock on her door.

"Come in," she called.

The door opened and closed. Footsteps, then Charles appeared beside her. He sat on a chair kitty-corner to the couch. She pushed herself up, setting her feet flat on the floor.

His jaw was set tightly as he massaged the back of his neck with one hand. He held his phone loosely in the other hand, tapping it against his thigh. Her heart raced.

"I have something to show you. Just a photo of a face."

She bit her lip.

It was Christine. The face in photo looked peaceful, but the colours were wrong — too blue and purple.

She closed her eyes. "Yes, that's her. Wolves?"

When he touched her shoulder, a shock of electricity shot through her. She had felt that before. When? "Wolves. They think it happened a couple days ago."

Sobbing, she told him the little she knew. A life, so small, so insignificant. But it flared inside her — Christine was important. To her family, to her friends, to those she had touched in her short life. Something had to be done.

Chapter Three

Charles watched this strong woman crumble in front of him. She'd been through a lot in twenty-four hours. *She must be exhausted.*

His eyes kept roaming over her form. She was beautiful — petite, lithe, sexy. Her yoga pants and baggy T-shirt couldn't hide her curves. But she was his grand-maman's friend — he had to leave her alone. He touched the top of her head, soft hair underneath his fingertips. "Just rest. I'll make some tea."

She closed her eyes as he left the room.

Poor thing. His granny had told him about Ceci's granddaughter — how she had returned to the village to care for the woman who had raised her. Why hadn't she sold Ceci's house and gone back to her life in the city?

In the kitchen, he filled the kettle and turned it on. He washed the dirty dishes piled beside the sink as he waited for the water to boil. Her tea cupboard had piles of half-empty boxes of teas — herbal, black, chai. A soothing chamomile-mint blend seemed best. A dozen teapots were stacked on the counter. Animal shapes, floral patterns on china, and one with all the wives of Henry VIII. Chuckling, he selected one with a Rupi Kaur poem on its side. Clem had made him read her first collection of poetry. She captured so well the experience of being a woman of colour caught between cultures.

Charles thought fondly of the arts courses he had taken while getting his business degree. In another lifetime, he would have studied music, literature and art full-time. But he had family responsibilities. Maybe when he retired — whenever that would be — he could explore that side of his personality more.

Chantelle still had her eyes closed. His hackles raised as he thought about wolves touching these innocents in his territory. Two women last month and the young teen discovered today. And this gorgeous beauty. Smooth, black hair that asked to be stroked. A heart-shaped face that begged to be kissed. He felt his cock starting to stiffen and told himself to calm down.

Someone was going to pay for injuring her — them — on his territory. Especially so close to his grand-maman's home.

He put the teabags in the pot and poured the boiling water, thinking about the attacks. They didn't encounter a lot of rogues in the Laurentian Mountain territory. The winters were cold and his patrols looked after their region well. It was likely the wolves came from Trois-Rivières pack.

When he was done arranging the mugs and pot on the tray, he found sugar and honey in the tea cupboard. Were the wolf attacks unplanned or premeditated? Either way, it was concerning. They were willing to invade his territory, undermine his leadership. He couldn't let it go to full-out war.

He heard small noises in the living room. Chantelle stirred.

When he brought the tea tray out, she sat up, taking the mug from him. Her lashes fluttered around gorgeous dark-brown eyes. He sat down, feeling his body respond to her.

After she had finished her tea, he put down his mug and kneeled in front of her, resting his hands on her knees. "Grand-maman insisted I check your bandages."

She pulled up one side of her yoga pants. Her creamy beige skin, the lean curve of her calf begged to be touched.

Chu dans marde! I'm in trouble. Just concentrate on your first-aid training.

Her hand reached out, touching his shoulder. Electricity sparkled between them, the frisson shooting through his chest.

"Who are you?" she asked. "You send art supplies and a teacher to help local youth at a moment's notice, you're invited to crime scenes, and you change dressings. Plus, you collect jazz records."

A faint hint of flowers swirled under his nose. "I run a ski resort near here. Our employees live in the ski village." He fixed the bandage and pulled down the hem of her pants, caressing her calf softly. "It's prudent to stay on good terms with local law enforcement." He was still rubbing her leg but she didn't pull away. "And everyone needs hobbies."

"You have a big family."

He could get lost in her brown eyes. "Two brothers and three cousins. We all work together."

"It must be a big responsibility, running your business."

"It is. And my family's not much help. Things always fall on my shoulders." This needed to change.

"What about your free time? The little you have?"

How did she know what he was thinking? "I play the fiddle. I don't do that very much these days. And since my father died—" He broke off.

He stood up. *Too close to the bone.* "Thank you for letting me visit. I should go now." He strode to the door.

What did I do? wondered Chantelle. She pushed herself forward and tried putting her weight on her legs. She wobbled. Her injured leg ached.

She turned towards the door but Charles was already beside her, reaching out and helping her sit down.

He swore under his breath again.

"Look—" He sat down beside her, snared her in his gaze again. He breathed in and leaned closer as she turned towards him. He stroked her cheek. Light fingertips brushing against her skin. His intoxicating scent drifted around her—moss and pine.

His fingers traced her jaw, then held her chin, tipping it up. She resisted the urge to nibble his fingers, draw them into her mouth. He pulled her mouth to his, brushing his lips against her. Then he kissed her, long and searching.

Mint and something dark—chocolate? Whisky? He swept his tongue over her lips and she opened her mouth, tangling her tongue with his. It was like falling down a well. Deep, dark and wet. She wanted it to go on forever.

When he moved to kneel in front of her, blood rushed to her core. Skimming his hands along the contour of her back, he pulled her fast against his strong chest. She shivered from his touch. As he gripped her hips, she slid her arms up his sculpted back, seeking the feel of bare skin on her hands. It had been so long since someone had touched her like this. Desiring her, wanting her, craving her.

Kissing her again, he reached down to squeeze her buttocks, pressing her aching centre against his erection. She sighed and wrapped her legs around the indent of his waist, revelling in her hunger for his body. He growled and she drew him tighter, inhaling his all-male scent. This was what she needed. Him. He nuzzled the smooth column of her neck and ran his hands along her outer thighs. His mouth-watering muscles felt so good against her all-too-willing body. She'd missed being so close to someone. He reached forward to massage the heavy mounds of her breasts. He squeezed lightly, moaning in her ear, his breath tickling her skin. She arched her back as he bent down and nuzzled her aching nipples through the thin fabric of her shirt.

She wasn't wearing a bra, hadn't thought she needed one at home. Now she was glad she'd left it off, as he licked the pebbled tips of her peaks. She brought her hands up to tug his hair, breathing in his scent and melting into him.

Her pussy throbbed when he ground his swollen cock against her centre. Too good. Too much. Or maybe not enough.

What am I doing?

She pushed his shoulders back. "Mmm," she moaned. "We should stop." She licked her tingling lips and willed her hands to stop squeezing his pecs. Maybe she should make an exception and strip this hot stranger naked for some wild sex.

He cupped her face in his hands, his dark eyes staring at her lips. God, if he kept looking at her like that, she didn't know what she'd do.

He blew out a big breath. "Stop, give me a minute." He leaned back, separating them, leaving his hands on the top of her thighs.

She knew they should slow down. If only her body would listen to her brain.

He closed his eyes for a moment. Then he stood. "I should go."

As she tipped her head towards the ground, her curtain of black hair fell in front of her face.

She felt his hand reach down to touch her hair —

Then the world stopped.

A fuzzy memory half-surfaced. A hand reaching to her hair. A younger man with shaggy, dark hair, the same steel-grey eyes. When had this happened? Ten years ago?

She was younger, a teen? Something had happened to this young man, but she couldn't remember what. She couldn't summon it up. She touched his leg, then he wrapped himself around her as they fell to the ground.

White fog swirled around them and suddenly they were in the woods. The same steel-grey eyes were in an older face. Wise, regal, glorious. He took her breath away.

Nuzzling his face in her hair, he murmured, "*Rouanez.*"

Yes. She wanted him. She didn't know how or why. She looked up, seeking his lips but he slipped away as a white mist surrounded them…

The spell was broken.

—She shook her head. He was kneeling in front of her, and she was sitting on the couch. The electricity had fizzled out, but remnants still sparked in his eyes.

What had happened?

Her legs were wrapped around this handsome stranger. His lips were kiss-swollen and it looked like she had dragged her hands through his hair with wanton abandon.

Mmm, wanton abandon? Focus.

"Okay." She sucked in air like she hadn't breathed all day. "What is—"

He reached for her lips, brushing his fingers along them. She opened her mouth, but suddenly he pushed her back on the sofa and stood up. He sprinted for the door and slammed it behind him.

Talk about mixed signals. One minute he was hanging onto her like a life preserver and the next he was out the door.

Her heart crashed in her chest. She hadn't felt like that in a long time. Not since she left Montreal—well, not even then. Frankly, she'd been in a long dry spell. Lac St. Patrice was a nice place but there weren't a lot of dating options. That must be why he had affected her so much. Or was it something more? Something had happened when he touched her, but she couldn't remember it. It shimmered just out of her grasp.

Oooh, boy, I need to get out more.

When he had gotten close, she wanted to kiss him all over. Breathe in the pine and moss and earthy scents of his all-male body. Caress his chiselled form.

Get a grip, girl!

She didn't go around kissing strange men. Even when they were really hot. And built. And they looked at her with those smouldering, bedroom eyes.

No. She didn't need a man to make her complete. She didn't need the complications and lies men always created. She was perfectly happy the way she was. She had her friends, her hobbies and her cabin. That should be enough.

Chapter Four

Charles parked his car outside Grand-maman's house. He had so many good memories of family dinners here—everyone gathered together, playing, feasting, laughing. After his father had died, the laughter had died, too. He missed it. Maybe it was time to bring it back.

But how? And when? He had wolf attacks to contend with. Corporate restructuring. Clan politics. There was always something in the way.

And Chantelle. She could definitely get in the way. Something about her reminded him of Grand-maman. He couldn't put his finger on it. Was it the mixture of strength and warmth?

Her brilliant energy had hit him like a clap of thunder when they collided. He looked into her beautiful eyes and almost lost himself in their pools of brown. Half of him wanted to run back and scoop her up in his arms, while the other half wanted to get as far away as possible.

Charles opened Marie's door. *"C'est moi, Grand-maman."*

Finding her in the living room, he kissed her on the forehead.

"How was your afternoon?" she asked.

"The police found a body. Mauled by a wolf."

"Loup-garou? Like last night?"

"Mmm-hmm. Too big to be a regular wolf."

"What are you going to do?"

"I'm benched. Thomas is going to look into it, with Michel's help. I've been told I have to take the rest of the week."

"Are you still working twenty hours a day?" She patted his arm.

"Mamie, I make sure to shift and go for runs every day with the boys and Clementine. We look after each other."

"Still, I worry about you. You don't want to end up in an early grave. Like your grand-papa. And your father."

"I know you're right." He hugged her and sat down. "But it seems like every time I try to take a break, something happens. It's exhausting."

"Are you seeing anyone?"

"You know very well I'm not. Clementine said you asked her that same question last time she visited. I know you worry about me, but I'm all right."

"That Chantelle is a lovely little thing. She was so devoted to her grandmother — it broke her heart when Ceci died. She's seemed so lost ever since."

"You know how important family and work are to me. There's no time to date right now." He stood up and walked the length of the room.

"I know it still hurts, but I don't want you to spend your life living like a monk."

Charles stopped pacing. "What does *Rouanez* mean?"

"When you were little, I would tell you a story about a Fae Queen who meets a Wolf Prince and they save each other." Marie picked up her knitting.

"Have I met Chantelle before?"

"Her family used to live near us when she was little. When she finished grade school they moved away. Ceci came back to her house in Lac St. Patrice after Chantelle moved away for college."

"I have something like a memory…" He shook his head.

Marie skipped a stitch and had to start again. "You might have seen her once or twice when you were little."

"It's something else, I think. It's probably nothing."

Marie dug for another ball of yarn in her knitting basket. "How are your brothers?"

"Michel is impatient to move Henri into his division. He could use some help in acquiring new properties." Charles sat down.

"I thought Henri was going to work in security with Thomas?"

"Juana doesn't want Henri to work in security. Says he's acting too irresponsibly. She can't rely on him."

Marie snorted. "Those two have always argued. Don't provoke your Pack Protector — Juana's work is too important."

"I'm glad I have my brothers. But they'll never replace you."

"Someday you'll have a partner of your own to work with you."

"Oh, Grand-maman, you never give up, do you? Maybe in a few months I'll be ready."

"Don't wait too long, *eh, chérie*?"

Charles stood, towering over her chair, and bent down to give her another hug.

"*Ben*. What did Chef Martin send for supper?" she asked.

"He said he was sending you some sugar pie and game stew."

"My favourites! Thank you, *chérie*."

Charles went to the kitchen to fix some plates.

* * * *

Chantelle sat in her little studio going through the piles of papers on her table. She looked out the window into the backyard. Light rain pitter-pattered against the brilliant autumn foliage. Shivering in the fading grey light, she reached for a sweater. She ran her hands over the embossed green leather cover of Granny Ceci's notebook and thumbed the well-worn pages to the bookmark.

The notebook held marvellous tales about fairies, loups-garous, magical swans and other fantastic beings — stories Ceci had spun to Chantelle when she was small. Chantelle had always credited her grandmother's vivid imagination with sparking her own interest in drawing. She had made countless drawings of fantastic creatures when she was a child and still drew on those early impressions for inspiration in her work.

Chantelle placed the notebook on her desk and got out her watercolour brushes. She was working on mock-ups for some of the tales to shop it around to other publishers. She had talked to one of her authors today. Even though she had illustrated several of his books, he was reluctant to help her out.

It was so frustrating! Couldn't they understand how important this was to her?

Four of the twelve tales were typed in already. She glanced at the mock-ups for the last tale. It was about a foundling fairy child who had been raised by a fairy godmother. Ceci had often told her this tale when she was little. It was meant to take the sting out of her parents' early death. And it had helped a bit. But retreating into a fantasy fairy world did not make up for being orphaned.

In her grandmother's version, Chantelle was born from a beautiful fairy princess who had been imprisoned in a tower by an evil sorcerer. Her mother escaped with her baby, running fast and far through the forest. When her captor caught up with them, she sacrificed herself and hid her baby in a tree. A fairy godmother found the baby crying, a wolf family closing in — to help or hinder, it was never clear — and she took her home to care for her.

This tale had given her comfort when she was small. Ceci really had been like a fairy godmother to her — stepping in when her parents died in a car accident. Granny Ceci had been so full of joy and love. Chantelle's life felt so empty now that she was gone.

The doorbell rang. A young voice rang out. "Chantelle?" Footsteps pattered to the studio. A ten-year-old girl ran into Chantelle's arms.

"Hey, beautiful!" Chantelle said. "Are you being good for your maman?"

"Yes!" Nadiya's eyes twinkled. "What are you working on?"

"I'm starting the next story—a tale of a seigneur from New France who fell in love with a beautiful Fairy Queen. He was betrayed by a witch and turned into a loup-garou."

"A werewolf? Oh, I love those Québécois stories. We read them at school." Nadiya looked at a sketch of a man turning into a wolf. An older woman with short hair came in the studio. "Mom, look! A loup-garou!" Nadiya waved the paper. "What happened to him?"

"He was cursed to wander through the forest until true love's kiss freed him," Chantelle said.

"Oooh! Can I be the Fairy Queen in this one?"

"*Chérie*, I want to make you the powerful witch—is that okay?"

"Can I be really scary? Warts and ugly teeth?"

"Own it!" Chantelle said.

The doorbell rang again. She heard their friend Kat's voice. "Hey, squirrel friends!"

"You look great!" Chantelle said.

Kat was wearing one of her favourite flowing dresses, bright colours against her dark-brown skin. "I always do. Marie said you got hurt."

"I'll be fine," said Chantelle. "Just a scare. When did you talk with Marie?"

"This afternoon. She was ordering pies, but I think she was just making sure the good ol' boys weren't bothering me."

"She's been your biggest support since you came out."

"I know. She said deep down we're all the same and she was glad I knew who I was."

Nadiya's mom, Yvette, called them to the living room. "Pizza's ready!"

Chantelle started the latest Disney movie for Nadiya. Yvette brought out three glasses of wine and a glass of milk. They toasted and dug in to the gooey slices festooned with pepperoni and veggies.

When everyone was settled in, Chantelle turned to Yvette. "I met Marie's grandson — do you know who he is?"

"What does he look like?"

"Dark hair to his shoulders, gorgeous grey eyes, olive skin. Cute and dangerous-looking. Well, not dangerous. Just big! Way over six feet tall and bursting with muscles. And he scowls a lot."

"Sounds like your type."

"I thought pasty nerds were my type."

"We should change that. Maybe this is your chance." She waggled her eyebrows.

"Don't be silly! I just want to know who he is. His name is Charles."

"Oh, congratulations!" Kat said. "You just met Lac St. Patrice's most elusive billionaire."

"*Most* elusive. You mean there's more than one?"

"His brothers help him run the family business."

"He said it was a ski lodge near here," said Chantelle.

"Well, I guess so. But he should have said they own a dozen ski resorts across the country. And they have other property investments."

"Why does he live in the middle of nowhere?" Chantelle asked.

"Their family grew up in the Laurentians. They have their head office at the ski lodge an hour from here," Kat said. "What was he like?"

"Like a CEO. Bossy, opinionated and self-important. But he was also sweet to his grandmother. And we like the same music. Then we shared a moment and he ran away."

"A moment?" Yvette leaned forward. "Did he kiss you? Was it good?"

"Yes and yes. And confusing and hot and over too fast."

Kat whooped. "Yes, girl."

"Charles is the captain of the lacrosse team type," said Yvette. "His youngest brother, Henri, is more sociable. Thomas, the middle one, is a serious nerd but nice."

"After their dad died, they retreated from the public. They concentrate on their business twenty-four-seven," Kat said.

"That sounds lonely," Chantelle said. *We have more in common than I thought.*

Yvette got a gleam in her eye. "Maybe you could cheer him up?"

"No way! He's too much—in every possible way. And I don't need anybody. I'm happy the way I am."

"Just because you've dated some bad ones doesn't mean there aren't any good ones left," Yvette said.

"You should get back out there," Kat said.

"I'm not ready yet."

"I will if you will."

"Let me think about it." *Yeah, right. I'll chicken out.* "Pass me another slice of pizza."

She asked Nadiya about the latest tween trends and they chatted about pop stars and social media.

Then Yvette told them she had good news. "I've finally persuaded Tanya to move up here. There's an opening at the police station and she's going to apply."

"That's great news for you two! It's about time you lived in the same place," said Chantelle.

"Will she be able to keep working on the Missing and Murdered Aboriginal Women and Girls Project here?" asked Kat.

"I've been talking to the aunties on the Rez. The community could use more allies. There's been little progress on the local disappearances."

"Christine's death was wolves, not humans, but still I'm worried," Chantelle said.

"It's all part of the same disturbing trend of violence against indigenous communities. And maybe it was humans who made it look like wolves. Who knows?" Yvette said.

"So many women lost and not found," Chantelle said.

They finished their glasses of wine in silence. On the television, a girl sang about finding her prince.

Chapter Five

Charles had his pack—brothers, cousins and grandmother—together for the first time in weeks. Sunday dinner at Grand-maman's, a fire crackling in the living room, pot roast cooking in the oven. His brother Thomas was cooking vegetables with Grand-maman in the kitchen. In the living room, Clem was ribbing Bertrand about the young women and men he had dated in high school. Henri set the table in the dining room.

This was the perfect ending to his time off. Then it was back to work on Monday.

When there was a knock, he answered the door. It was Chantelle. She looked like she had stepped out of a fairy tale—luminous dark eyes and luxuriant hair under a green cloak kissed with a layer of mist. He sniffed—flowers? Rain? Meadows? She reminded him of soft greens and pinks twining together in sultry spirals. *Play?* his wolf rumbled.

"What are you doing here?" He scowled. So much for a quiet evening.

"I — your grandmother invited me. I brought wine." She brandished a bottle.

He opened the door slowly and took her coat. When the floral scent wafted up from her garment, his body responded.

Mine, said his wolf.

Down, boy, she's not yours.

His wolf just laughed and sat, waiting.

Henri came to the door to see who had arrived. They brought Chantelle into the living room and Bertrand introduced her to the remaining family members.

Henri offered her a seat on the couch beside him. He turned on 'the charm,' as Henri called it. Lots of women fell for it — supposedly.

Charles' wolf's fur bristled. *Somebody needed to back off.*

Charles tried to shrug it off. His brother was just being sociable, making Grand-maman's friend feel comfortable in the group. Maybe he was reading too much into an innocent conversation.

I need a drink.

He walked to the dining room and poured himself a scotch. This was better. After taking a sip he returned to the other room and looked at Henri on the sofa.

Henri reached out and touched Chantelle's hair. *No, not good.*

His wolf leapt to the surface before he could stop it.

He waded into the centre of the group, clenching his fists at his sides. Pushing forward, he loomed over Henri on the couch. Low growling noises emanated from his throat. His eyes glinted with specks of yellow. *Back off, brother.*

Charles stood above Henri, hunching his shoulders and staring down in his face. He couldn't relax, couldn't drop it. Something had triggered him. He wasn't going to back down.

Henri looked up, the faint hint of a smile on his lips. When he saw the yellow glint of the wolf in Charles' eyes, he blinked. Henri jumped up and to the side, reaching out his arms in a defensive posture.

Charles growled low and bared his teeth, moving in so he was only inches from Henri's face.

Realisation dawned in the younger man's face. Henri splayed his hands, palms up, in front of him. He sidestepped away from Chantelle on the couch.

It was over. *No more threat.*

"What's going on, Charles? Are you okay?" Chantelle looked confused.

Henri piped up. "Hey, bro, do you remember meeting Chantelle when we were little? It was at my birthday party and I told her I loved her." He laughed and ducked his head, putting his gaze on the floor.

Charles remained standing for another second, glowering. Rousing himself, he looked around at everybody staring at him. "Oh," he stammered. "I thought we'd met her before." He looked at Chantelle. "Sorry, I had a long day and I'm not myself."

Clementine reached for Chantelle's arm, pulling her up and out of the group. "Help me with the potatoes?" she asked, arranging a bland look on her face. The two women left the room.

Charles watched Clementine leave with Chantelle, then took a deep breath and turned back to Henri. "I just met her the other day and I didn't—"

Henri punched him in the arm. "Awww, my big bro is in love!"

"Keep it down! No, I'm not," protested Charles.

"She's pretty classy. Are you sure she likes you?" asked Henri.

"No, uh, I—I don't even know her really." He could feel his face growing hot.

"Well, you'd better lock her down before someone else does."

Charles turned and scowled at him, a low growl rumbling through his chest.

"Ha, I'm just kidding!" When Henri put his arm around him, Charles pushed it off.

"Wait, are you serious about her?"

"How can I be? We just met!" Charles snarled.

Henri exchanged a glance with the others. "Maybe it's—you know…"

"I don't believe in Fated Mates."

"Well, maybe—" Henri began.

"She's just a woman I met the other day. That's all."

Henri raised his hands, "Okay, I surrender. But I'll stay away if it makes you feel better."

Charles grimaced at him, showing all his teeth.

Chantelle followed Clementine into the cosy kitchen space. Clementine gave Thomas a look. He helped Marie up from the wooden chair at the small table and walked with her to the living room.

Clementine checked the old stove. "The potatoes are almost ready. Let's get out the milk and butter." As she rummaged in the big fridge, she asked, "How are you feeling since the attack?"

"Much better. If your family hadn't been there…"

"Grand-maman was close to your grandmother, wasn't she?"

Chantelle nodded, then frowned. "I can't figure Charles out. He's angry and intense. But he smiles so sweetly at your grandmother. And then he almost kissed the life right out of me the other day."

Clementine looked at her, eyebrows raised. "The Ducharme boys are...complicated."

"Why was he so mad at Henri?"

Clementine studied her for a moment. "He's very protective. He's old-fashioned and doesn't like his brother taking advantage of women."

"Henri?" Chantelle scoffed.

"Charles misjudged the situation, that's all," said Clementine.

"He seems to overreact a lot."

"He isn't always like that. It happens around certain people more than others."

"Like his brother pushes his buttons?" asked Chantelle.

Clementine paused. "Something like that. The potatoes are cooked. Can you put them in the colander?"

The two women busied themselves with their task and Thomas returned to take the roast out of the oven.

* * * *

Chantelle was so full she thought they'd have to roll her home. She thanked Marie and Thomas for a wonderful dinner. When Charles insisted on walking her home, she tried to turn him down.

"Don't argue!" he snapped.

Clem said, "After the other night, I'll feel better knowing you got home safe."

"All right." Chantelle bit her tongue and put on her cloak, saying goodbye to the group.

It had been a fun evening. So much noise—laughter, teasing, arguments. All in good fun. She envied how comfortable they were with each other.

She and Charles walked in silence through the quiet little village. The wind whisked some leaves down the street. She trembled in the breeze and looked up at the gibbous moon. Full of promise, bursting with opportunity.

Charles wore a suede jacket. It looked so buttery soft she wanted to touch it and rub her cheek along it. His khaki button-down shirt was tailored to hug his muscular frame. They probably had to do something to the shirt to make enough room in the shoulders for him. Bespoke tailoring—was that what it was called?

He was quieter and less arrogant than she had assumed when they first met. But he still had some issues. It was a good thing he was going back home tonight.

When they turned onto her street, he stopped. "Look, I want to apologise for the way I acted the other night. I don't usually make out with strangers."

"Me too. I haven't dated much since I broke up with my boyfriend three years ago."

"You should."

"Should what?" she asked.

"Start dating." He fixed his steel-grey eyes on her and the hairs on her arms stood up.

Ooh boy.

"Well, my boyfriend cheated on me…"

"Is that why you're hiding here in the village?"

"My grandmother died and I'm working from her house—my house now."

"I'm sorry." His eyes were smouldering, putting her body on high alert. Chantelle's nipples were hardening and tingles were skittering across her chest and shoulders.

Calm down, girl!

"I'm not ready to go back to the real world yet."

"You're gorgeous and enchanting and way too alive to be stuck here. You should be having adventures in Paris or New York. Not trapped in the mountains of northern Quebec."

"I don't belong anywhere," she said in a small voice.

He put a large hand on her shoulder. Her heart raced as the warmth spread through her.

"You are a surprise," she said. "As soon as I think I have you figured out, then something else happens."

"What do you mean?"

"You come on strong—bossy and controlling. But then you have this passionate side, sexy, funny. When you let that out, I don't think anything could stop you."

She heard a low rumble in his chest. There were some little yellow spots in his irises. Had they always been there? He closed the distance between them and touched her face with his hand. The blood rushed to her face as she rubbed her cheek against his palm. His rough skin gave just the right amount of friction. She almost purred.

"Stop doing that," he growled, jumping back.

"Doing what?" What was going on?

"I don't know. Just stop it."

"This is what I mean. Unpredictable." *I wish he could keep his hands to himself. It would make this easier.*

"Oh." Charles looked taken aback. Maybe he did have feelings?

"You're angry and accusatory one minute, then you look at me with your bedroom eyes the next."

"It's confusing for me too. I pride myself on my self-control."

She scoffed. *As if.*

"Damn it, woman. I'm the epitome of control. Everyone usually complains that I need to relax."

"Really?" She looked at him. He was practically vibrating. He needed to get a grip.

"I said usually. But you leach all restraint out of me. I can't have you doing that."

"I'm not doing anything!" He was so infuriating.

She spun away from him and started walking quickly to her house. He followed behind her, not saying anything. When she stepped on her porch, she halted and turned towards him. His face was hidden in the shadows. He came a step closer and the porch light illuminated the angles of his face. She itched to touch him, trace the bones and hollows of his cheeks, snare his chin in her hand. When he reached the steps, she caught his scent and her core started to melt.

She knew whatever this was between them might be wrong. Suddenly she didn't care. She bit her bottom lip. "Do you want a coffee or anything?" She opened the door and gestured for him to come in. *Say yes.*

He bounded up the steps and crossed the threshold. "I want…" he trailed off. His eyes almost glowed as he raked his gaze over her whole body, licking his lips. It felt like he was running his hands all over her. She shivered.

She didn't know what possessed her to close the door behind him and reach out. She just couldn't stand not holding him for another second.

Charles had entered her house without thinking. What was he doing? He didn't know. But he wasn't going to stop. When the door closed, he stepped forward and put his hands on her waist. Charles' wolf snapped to the front. *Play.* He felt the urge to pounce on Chantelle and pin her to the floor. Or against the door — it was closer and more convenient. He would pull her delicious jeans down, rip off her tiny lace panties — he hoped they were tiny and lacy — and pump into her so fast with his aching cock they would both be climaxing in seconds. Not that he didn't want to enjoy her and take his time too. But that would come after, when his wolf was calmer. He would eat her right up, bringing her to orgasm, then plant himself so deep within her he might never come out.

He moved forward and enveloped her in his arms. At the back of his mind, he knew he should slow down, but his wolf didn't agree. *Mate.* Grabbing her hips, he inched the two of them backwards until she was against the door, his whole body pressed against hers. She gasped and melted into him. His wolf rumbled through his chest. *Good.*

His mouth met hers as he slid his hands along her torso. She was slender, but her slim curves were enticing. She snaked her hands around his waist, exploring his back. He could hardly think as he pulled her closer to him, grinding his throbbing erection on her middle. He thought it might be too much but she moaned and gyrated against him, too. She was so supple and pliable... He just wanted to take all of her.

He slipped a hand under the waistband of her jeans, sighing into her mouth as his fingers brushed over her silky skin. He reached for her zipper and slowly pulled it down. Gripping her waist, he pushed her jeans down roughly, working fast. After she stepped out of them, he returned and ran his hands down the curves of her luscious waist and hips. Finding the string of her panties—yes! Lacy and tiny!—he moved his hand around behind to grab her ass cheek and knead it.

Somehow, he managed to find the condom in his wallet before she pulled down his trousers and wrapped her lush legs around him. He held her with one arm while he ripped open the condom packet with his teeth and the other hand. She was moaning and pressing her wet pussy against the front of his boxer shorts as his hard shaft rubbed against her centre. He pulled back long enough to pull down his shorts and put on the condom, while she stroked his rigid length. When he brought his sheathed cock to her entrance, she moaned and urged him on.

He pushed deep inside and she sighed, starting to gyrate as he held her smooth buttocks. He couldn't wait—he needed to thrust in her wet channel so deep, over and over again, feeling her walls clench around him. She fit him like a glove and he wanted it to never end.

He shifted position so that he could reach her swollen clit with his fingers. She moaned as she rode his hand and cock, moaning and gyrating as she climbed towards her climax. His body was coiled tight, seeking release. When she began shuddering around him, he thrust deep inside and found his own orgasm, crying out in pleasure. They held each other tightly as they rode the waves of ecstasy.

When they came down, Charles eased out of her tight walls, swung her into his arms and took her to her couch. Panting, he sat her down on his lap and caressed her curves with his rough hands. He put his head on top of hers, smelling her scent. Her hair tickled his face.

She leaned against his chest. "Charles," she murmured. "What was that?"

He plucked one of her hands from his back. "I can't say." Setting his nose at the pulse point of her wrist he breathed in. Flowers—lilies and honeysuckle, grass and rain. The scents nearly undid him.

She whispered, "You can't say or you won't say?"

"Can't, won't…" He dropped her hand and leaned forward, nuzzling her neck and crushing her against his hard chest. When he put his lips on her ear she sighed and turned her mouth towards his—

The world stopped. The air shimmered and her house faded away.

Wisps of mist swirled around them. As they dropped away, he saw the moon ahead, full and ripe. The acrid smells of pine trees and wood smoke hung in the air. Dried leaves swirled in the breeze. A creek trickled nearby.

Charles still held Chantelle in his arms but she was older—tall and proud, her eyes clear and shining. She wore a long cloak the colour of the pines, her dark hair spilling out of her hood on the side. She pushed him against the bark of a tree. Were they arguing? Fighting?

Yes. She put a blade to his throat. He caught his breath. But was it in fear or desire?

His wolf reared his head and came to take a look. He huffed. "*Rouanez? Caradec?*" Queen or Beloved?

"*Caradec.*" Charles pulled her towards him and she dropped the knife, raining him with kisses.

Then white light and silence surrounded them. The mist whirled around and they were back at her house.

—Something had changed.

"Did you—" Chantelle rubbed her temples.

He pulled away. What had happened? One minute they were talking and the next they were having sex. This was too much—he didn't do things like this. "I have to go." He pulled on his clothes and rushed to the entryway.

Opening the door, he heard a sound. A growl. Whipping his head around he saw a dark form in her front yard, skulking near the hedge. It was large. Loupgarou. Shifter.

He turned back to Chantelle. "Shut the door behind me! Then back away from the windows."

He advanced on the wolf. The creature turned to him, snarling. Should he shift? Chantelle didn't know what he was. Would he need the strength? His teeth and claws?

The wolf stood his ground for a moment, lowering his ears and pawing the ground. When Charles stepped forward, the wolf growled then whined. It backed up, creeping towards the back yard, following the line of bushes. The wind whipped up, clattering through the branches.

Charles followed the shifter, but he was too late. The wolf had already slunk into the forest. He gazed around, but it was too dark to make out anything in the trees. He listened, heard paws retreating, breath huffing. Nothing coming towards them. The danger seemed to have passed.

Returning to the front door, he let himself in. Chantelle stood by the window.

"Didn't I tell you to stand back?" He growled.

"What was it? I'm fine."

"I can't look after you if you won't listen to me."

She bristled. "You don't have to look after me. I'm fine on my own." Fiery and feisty. Why did he find it a turn-on? *It should be driving me crazy!*

"Then why was there a wolf in your yard?" Charles asked.

"What?"

"There was a wolf. Just now."

"Not the same ones from the other night?" Her eyes grew wide. He took her by the arms and led her to the couch. After he sat her down, he pulled out his phone and made a call.

"Thomas," he said. "Send a team to Chantelle's house. There was a wolf. Yeah, could be." He gave the address and hung up.

He turned back to Chantelle. "My brother is sending some people to look. Don't go out until we know something more. And stay inside at night-time—no more midnight rambles in the woods." She was so adorable when she blushed. "I mean it, Chantelle. Will you listen for once?"

"Okay." She was trembling. But she still had that fire in her eyes. He didn't know if he should kiss her or spank her.

He fixed her some tea, trying to keep her mind off the situation while they waited. Grand-maman always said tea helped any situation. Within fifteen minutes, there was a knock on the door.

"Mr. Ducharme? It's Beta Team two. Permission to enter?"

Chantelle sat up and looked at him with her big eyes. *What am I getting myself into?* Charles stood up and went to open the door.

Charles saw the team out when they finished. It was late and Chantelle was half-asleep. The team would keep surveillance on her for a few days. When she had tried to say no, Charles told her that Marie insisted on it. Nobody could say no to Grand-maman. And he didn't want her unprotected.

After doing one last check on the doors and windows he came back to where Chantelle was sitting on the couch. "I'm sorry if I got carried away tonight. I don't usually do casual sex."

"Me neither," she said, looking at the floor. "Sometimes it's good to do the unexpected."

"Do you want me to call?" he asked.

She shook her head. "It was just one night. That's all. Go back to your life, I'm okay."

He hesitated. It didn't feel right. But she was right, they didn't know each other. He kissed her, said goodnight and left. He looked back at her gingerbread cottage as he climbed in his car. He sighed, knowing he wouldn't be coming back here again.

It was a bad idea to get involved. Even though it had felt so good. What was going on with him? He had to stay professional while they figured out how she was involved in the attacks and if it was linked with the other incursions by Trois-Rivières pack. He didn't need any distractions. It would just make it harder to do his job.

He drove back to Marie's to pick up his duffel bag and say goodbye to his grandmother. *Back to work. I need to get away from this place.*

Chapter Six

The next day Charles met with Thomas and Clementine in the boardroom. His assistant, Ken, had brought coffee and croissants from the dining hall. They sat in the comfortable executive chairs at the long table.

"Buttering me up with pastries?" Charles asked.

Ken shot him a look and scooted out of the room.

"You know it's time to make some changes," Clementine said. "We need a West Coast office soon. And a proposal for the next community meeting."

"The Elder Council."

"Joshua is pushing it through. We have to be prepared."

"It's a good idea," Thomas said. "We can't rely on informal discussions to canvass opinions. We're too big now. Having some trusted community members to advise the village and the company would ensure we hear from everyone."

"I've tried to honour Father's commitment to democracy and fairness. I just don't know if it's the right time." Charles ran a hand through his hair.

"When will be a good time then?" asked Thomas. "We can't wait until it's too late."

"What if I can't keep them safe?"

"That won't change. You'll have a group of trusted elders to help you protect them," Thomas said.

"I don't know."

Thomas took a big breath. "I've been offered a job in Switzerland."

"With the Geneva clan?"

"Yes."

"But I need you," Charles said. *This can't be happening to me.*

"Then listen and make some changes."

He was stuck. "Can you put together a plan and we can discuss it tomorrow?" Charles asked.

Thomas nodded and smiled. "Now, Clementine, what are your ideas for corporate restructuring?"

"We've identified some key employees for promotion. I've got a short list for a new Lieutenant and two more Commanders. Juana and I have also discussed succession-planning for the Protector."

"Juana's not going anywhere, is she?"

"She can't be everywhere at all times," said Clementine. "She's going to need two or three Lieutenant-Protectors who report directly to her. They'll oversee some of the day-to-day operations."

"Henri wants to work with her," said Charles.

"Not yet," said Clementine. "He could liaise with Juana and me to discuss these hires. Maybe next year."

"He's grown up a lot in the last twelve months. Another year could make a big difference," Thomas said.

"So, what do we do with the Magecraft Division?" Charles asked.

"Edwin and Erik are ready to assume leadership responsibilities," said Clem. "Gwen can step back then. She doesn't have time to do everything herself, but it'll take time for her to adapt."

"You're talking about me, too," Charles said. Clem and Thomas looked at each other. "What will I do, then?"

"You will stay on as president but we'll move someone into the CEO position when we add the additional management layer," Thomas said.

"Thomas, I want you to stand as Pack Lieutenant," Charles said.

"Is that what you want? Or is this just because of the job offer?"

"It's what I want."

"Uncle Jean has been nosing around. This might keep him from getting his foot in."

"What do you think, Clem?" Charles asked.

"It's a win-win then. Let's float Thomas' name and see where it goes."

When Clementine left to put their plans in motion, Thomas asked Charles to stay. He looked at him. "Have you thought about dating again?"

"Too many complications. I just want to keep life simple," Charles said.

"What about Chantelle?"

"It's just... I can't." Charles put his head in his hands.

"You are so full of love and passion. Don't hide it away because you got hurt."

"I don't think I can handle a relationship right now."

"The right person can come along when you least expect it," said Thomas.

"All right, I'll think about it." Charles finished his croissant and returned to his office.

* * * *

Chantelle put the watercolour brush in the can of water when her phone buzzed. It was her agent. She wiped her hands on a rag and picked up her cell.

"Jamie?" she said.

"How's my favourite client?"

"Much better, thanks. What's up?" She readjusted her hair in its barrette.

"I've had a nibble for your grandmother's story collection."

"Really?"

"Montreal Island Press wants to see the mock-ups and prospectus. They're thinking of publishing the collection in French. If they take it, they'll assign an editor to prepare the stories and you'll illustrate it. They also want to produce several stand-alone tales as picture books in English. You'll illustrate those as well."

"That's everything I wanted!" said Chantelle. "Are they serious?"

"I think so. Do you have any updates before I send them the package?"

Chantelle walked back to her desk and leafed through some of her sketches. A golden fairy child—

tears in her dark-brown eyes — caught her attention and she started a pile on her desk.

"I'll need a few days to pull some things together."

They signed off and Chantelle wiped a tear from her cheek. She couldn't take another rejection. She'd just have to make sure the package was excellent.

She leafed through the notebook again, glancing at the next tale, "The Fae Queen and the Wolf Lord." *A princess flees her kingdom after an evil prince attacks her family. Disguising herself, she rides through the forested mountains to escape. When she meets a stranger at night, the Wolf Lord, she fears he has been sent by the prince. But he is on his own quest to save his people and she knows in her heart of hearts that he is her true love. As the evil prince closes in on them, they part and the princess goes into hiding. Upon discovering that the prince is responsible for the attacks on both of their people, they work together to defeat their common foe.*

She had just finished an illustration of the pair's happily ever after. Crowned as the May Queen and King, they celebrated with their subjects. The Fae Princess looked out to the viewer and the Lord was facing her, his back to the readers. She took out her sketchbook and scribbled some ideas for the scene in the woods. Something was in the back of her mind. She tried to coax it out onto the paper.

Taking a new canvas, she placed it on her easel. She mixed dark greens and browns for the conifers, silver for moonlight and reflections. A female figure stood in a clearing with her sword drawn, lit by the moon. A male figure emerged from the shadows, hands held out in a gesture of peace. His smoky grey eyes pierced through the gloom. The strokes on the canvas weren't right yet. But she was on the right track.

She sketched on paper before moving back to the canvas. Painting always calmed her. Chantelle and Granny Ceci had moved a lot after her parents died. It had been difficult for a shy, dreamy, scatter-brained girl to fit in. She spent a lot of time with her paints and pencil crayons. Granny Ceci had encouraged her to get lost in worlds of her own making, but she had always brought her back to the present with her kind affection. What would have happened to her without her grand-maman? Would she have ended up lost and alone? Wandering through the woods in the mountains, searching for her Wolf Lord?

She laughed. There was no such thing as magical princes and princesses, wolves and lords. But she was glad her granny had woven those fantastical tales. It was Ceci's special gift.

Would she find her own gift? Her agent said it was her illustrations, and she loved the work. But being artistic wasn't necessarily a gift. She used it to bring her love of reading to others. The After-School Club provided a safe space for creative expression for youth. It was important to her, but it wasn't a special gift. That nameless something shimmered just out of her reach.

Maybe she was too impatient. It would arrive when it was meant to be. She rummaged through a pile of papers looking for the May Queen drawings. The sketch of Marie she had asked Charles to find the other day fell into her hand. She looked again at the kind face outlined in pencil. She should deliver the sketch to Marie's family this week and say thank you for their help when she was laid up.

Not to see Charles again. He was too hot and cold. When he was hot, she liked the attention, but it wasn't worth the trouble. Yet they were such a lovely family. She wanted them to know she appreciated them.

She turned back to her easel. In the meantime, she had to figure out how to make this scene work. How to paint a believable connection between two lost and lonely people. She picked up her brushes and set to work.

Chapter Seven

Chantelle drove up the winding road to the Ducharme ski resort. When she'd contacted Clem — no use bothering Charles with this, he was so busy — she had insisted Chantelle come for morning coffee and drop the sketch off in person. Chantelle owed it to the youth in the After-School Club to put on her big girl panties. She had collected a homemade gift basket to say thank you and added the sketch on top. The Ducharme family, all of them, should know how much their support of the youth mattered to her.

Looking out the windshield, she understood the attraction of living in the mountains. Aside from some hairpin turns, the drive was spectacular, especially at this time of year. Scarlets, russets and golds shimmered in the leaves, set against the dark greens and browns of the fir trees, rocks and moss. *All I need is a little mist to make it a fairy-tale setting.*

Approaching the ski village, she marvelled at the quaint houses and cobblestone streets. They shone in the sunshine, illuminating the happy townspeople going about their business. She started humming that song from *Beauty and the Beast*. Through the village and up to the resort she drove. She had read up on the Ducharme family on their website. They were descended from *coureurs de bois* in the early European settlement of New France, the French traders who often intermarried with the indigenous peoples. This early history gave the family—and many of the European descendants in the area—ties to the land and its people, but it was not a happy history in several respects. The family had recently published a mandate to work with local reserves to pay some small restitution for the ravages that colonisation had wreaked on the indigenous peoples. The early results of war, disease and violence had turned into later horrors. Residential schools, so many indigenous women and girls lost and killed, numerous land claim disputes and a lack of basic infrastructure on reserves—the government and the settlers had devastated indigenous communities. There was no way to make it right. But things still needed to improve.

She drove through the resort towards a large parking lot. Small chalets were arranged around a central lodge. She could see several medium-sized buildings behind the main building and up a slope. She pulled into one of the visitor parking spots. The main lodge looked like a postcard from the Alps. Wood beams across the front, enormous field stone pillars, balconies across the second and third floors. Bernard had told her about the family's commitment to renewable resource use and sustainable reforestation practices. Were the materials used at the ski resort part of this commitment? Gawking, she grabbed the basket from her back seat and walked up the wide steps to the large double front doors.

She put down the basket and smoothed her hair, her pulse pounding. *Don't be a coward. You won't even see him.*

Clem burst out of the doors, greeting her with a big hug. She had forgotten how warm and generous the woman was. Chantelle kept hold of the basket as she followed Clem into the front lobby. The large open-concept area showcased an enormous wood-burning fireplace at the back. Comfortable overstuffed chairs and couches were scattered tastefully around. A small coffee and tea station was set up near a reception desk.

Clem made small talk as they walked towards the fireplace area. Bertrand waved from a seat across from the fireplace. Chantelle manoeuvred past the back of a tall armchair so she could put the basket on the coffee table in front of Bertrand. Then she shook hands with the smiling young man. He was so much like his sister, Clementine, that she felt right at home.

Bertrand gestured at the chair behind her. "Look who's here, Charles." Chantelle gripped Bertrand's hand, not turning, her heart racing. Bertrand nodded at her.

He stood up at the same time that she turned around. She stumbled and fell into his arms, feeling the familiar electricity zap through her from his touch.

"Hello?" said Chantelle. Charles trapped her with his smoky eyes, almost scorching her with their intensity. *Câlice! Why does he have to be so hot? And always scowling? It's so confusing.*

He started to draw her in closer, then shook himself and helped her get steady on her feet before releasing her. Slowly, he withdrew his hands and she immediately felt empty, his heat retreating from her skin.

They sat down. Bertrand placed her on the couch so that her knees were almost touching Charles, whose form took up the large-overstuffed chair. *Too close, not close enough.* She stifled a nervous giggle. A server appeared with a tray of coffee and muffins.

Chantelle cleared her throat, willing her nerves to stop tingling. "I just stopped by to say thank you for the art supplies and loan of your art teacher. We hope we can invite Tori back sometime to thank her in person too."

Bertrand opened the cellophane on the basket and ran a hand over the contents. "Thank you," he said.

"I made the jams and salsa myself, but the honey comes from my neighbour. And I put something else in there. It's nothing important, just a little sketch I made of your grand-maman."

Bertrand pulled it out from the back of the basket. "Chantelle, I didn't know you were so gifted!"

"Really?" Charles said. "It's obvious how incredibly creative she is."

Chantelle's face grew hot. *Must be the fire in the fireplace.*

Clem handed it to Charles, who peered at the paper.

"You captured the light in her eyes. You can see the kindness and love she pours out." Charles bestowed one of those rare smiles on her that lit her up from the inside.

She smiled in return, feeling her core start to heat up. Her stomach did cartwheels. How did he affect her so much?

It grew silent. Everyone had stopped talking.

Clem turned to Bertrand, saying, "We forgot about that important meeting in the dining hall."

"Oh yeah, that meeting," Bertrand said, standing up. "Sorry, we have to go. Charles, can you please show her out for us? Ken cleared your schedule for another twenty minutes or so. Thanks!"

Chantelle cursed inwardly as Bertrand and Clementine made a hasty exit.

Charles fidgeted in his seat, his eyes burning into her. "Would you like more coffee?"

"Sure." She held out her cup, keeping it steady and trying not to think about having more of him. That had been the best sex she'd ever had.

"How are you feeling?" he asked, eyes on the coffee pot.

"Much better, thank you." Chantelle shifted and took a sip from her cup. He meant from her injuries, didn't he? Not from fucking her against her door? She shook her head, clearing out the enticing images.

There was something else about him that she wanted to figure out. Maybe a memory? Like she should remember him from somewhere.

"So," she began, "do we know each other?"

Charles started. "I don't think so. Grand-maman said we may have met when we were children."

"I just have this feeling—" She looked in his eyes. It seemed as though he was trying to remember something, like it was on the tip of his tongue. She felt the same way. *This is ridiculous. Let it go.*

Chantelle stood. "I should head back."

He stood up and walked her through the lobby, holding his hand at the small of her back. A small touch that blazed through her, keeping her on edge.

As they walked to her car, they chatted about the upcoming ski season. "Do you like skiing?" he asked. "You should come back when the slopes were open. We could listen to some of my records then, too." His cheeks reddened.

When she opened her car door he asked for her phone. Programming in his cell number, he muttered, "In case you need anything."

"Next time you visit Marie, come by and say hello," she said. *He wouldn't, though, would he?*

"Sure, yeah." He crossed his arms. Sleeves rolled up to his elbows, he showed off a muscular expanse of forearm with a sprinkling of dark hair. When she licked her lips, he looked at her mouth. She couldn't stop herself from inching closer to him, her nipples hardening under his gaze. His hand grazed her arm as his head crooked towards her. She turned up her face, staring into his eyes, her whole body on fire. There was something about him, wasn't there? If only she could remember.

The lodge doors crashed open and a family came rushing down the stairs. Like lightning, Chantelle and Charles jumped away from each other. Chantelle quickly climbed into her car. As she drove out of the parking lot, she saw him staring after her, not moving. *Stupid, stupid, stupid.*

What did she think was going to happen? He would sweep her up in his arms and they would live happily ever after? He was a hotshot businessman and she was—nothing. He'd probably forgotten her already. She wasn't one of his supermodels or actors. She couldn't hold a candle to them. *Just go home and forget him.*

* * * *

Chantelle stopped on the other side of the ski village. A large branch had fallen across the road. She parked the car on the shoulder and got out to have a closer look.

It was too heavy to move. She could call emergency services here or go back to the resort. She pulled out her phone and contemplated calling Charles — his number was still on her screen. No, she would just drive back to the village and ask someone for help.

Turning back to the car, she saw something out of the corner of her eye. She scanned the trees past the ditch.

Wolves. Her heart jumped in her throat.

They moved silently, jumping across the ditch onto the median, approaching her car. The wolves shot forward, blocking her access to her vehicle. They howled, loud and long, like trumpets heralding a king. *This is bad.*

She counted three wolves, mud-brown like those who had attacked her before. Same mangy fur. That was too much of a coincidence — surely there weren't another three brown wolves wandering around in these woods looking to prey on humans? But how could the same wolves have found her here?

No time to puzzle it out. Do something. Her phone was still in her hand. She unlocked it and saw Charles' number on the screen. She pushed the call button as the wolves surged around her. Her hands shook so badly she dropped her phone. *Did I get through?*

Another bark sounded from the ditch. A new wolf appeared, bounding out from the woods from the same direction as the others and reaching the group. He was tawny brown — bigger than the other three in front of her. The new wolf circled around her. Growling, with his ears back, he looked like he had a sneer on his snout.

This is really bad. She backed away but one of the wolves circled behind her. The largest one sniffed and came closer. He surged forward and she tried to push him back. Her heart raced as she tried to see what the wolf was doing. He growled, reared on his hind legs and leapt at her. She fell to the ground, the wind knocked out of her. Curled on her side, she couldn't stop her chest from heaving as she struggled to get air into her lungs. She needed to fight back, but she couldn't breathe.

The tawny wolf climbed on top of her and nosed around her torso. She gulped in some air as he pushed her on her back. The wolves snapped at her hands and feet. She stiffened, lying prone on the asphalt, the back of her neck prickling. Her attacker nosed at her leg, investigating her old wound.

She whimpered as he set his paws on each side of her and brought his furry head to hers, breathing in and out on her face. A thread of saliva dangled from his muzzle and dripped onto her face. Then he licked her, from her chin to her forehead. Tears leaked from her eyes. *Too much tongue and slobber.*

She couldn't take it anymore. She struggled and flailed her arms. When she tried to push him off, he bit down on her shoulder, sending shooting pains as she fought against him. He crushed an arm beneath his foot, scratching her as he pushed down. Seeing stars, she cried out. He huffed as she scrabbled underneath him. She tried to push down the fear. What had she done before? Something with her hands?

She heard a howl in the distance, from the direction of the ski resort. It was loud and fierce, a cry that jolted right into her chest. The sound was different than the wolves with her. It connected with her — it gave her a twinge of hope. Maybe help was on its way.

The wolf on top of her paused, looking around. She tried to push him off again. What was going on? Was it salvation or more torment?

There was a low, fierce growl near her car. She tried to look, but couldn't see anything. Did she hear sirens in the background? Or was her mind playing tricks on her?

The tawny wolf turned towards a snarl on his right. Growling, he raised his hackles. Another, larger creature came out and confronted her attacker. The new wolf was giant and ferocious — elegance in action. Dark grey fur, powerful limbs and expressive yellow eyes that shone when they caught the light. Even his throaty growl was appealing — it rumbled through her core, heating her up.

What was wrong with her? Maybe her body was shutting down under the stress.

The grey wolf was ready to fight. The tan wolf got ready to spring but the new wolf reached him first, rolling the attacker onto his back. When the tawny wolf broke off, he dove at him, snarling and scratching. They tangled with each other, a blur of brown and grey.

Chantelle tried to stand up but felt woozy. Sitting back down, she crawled towards her car. Inching along the road, she reached her goal and leaned against the car's side. Panting, she tried to apply pressure to her shoulder. Her mind registered that her leg was bleeding but she couldn't do anything about it. It seemed too far away.

Growls and snarls reached her. The tan wolf feinted and danced backward, giving way to the grey one. She noticed that the grey wolf angled to keep his body between the brown wolf and her. He snarled and pushed the brown further back. The tawny wolf was bleeding from a nick in his ear and cuts on his belly.

As the pair continued to engage, the other three brown wolves slunk towards the ditch. They stood back, not getting involved. *What are they waiting for?*

Barks and growls came up the road. Were these reinforcements? For which side?

Five dark grey wolves appeared, fleet and fearsome. They stopped at Chantelle's car, taking in the scene. One of the smaller wolves came to stand by Chantelle while the others moved to contain the ones by the median.

The small grey wolf beside Chantelle barked as the first and largest wolf pounced on the tawny attacker. *Are these two Alphas facing off?* The others hung back, waiting to see what was going to happen. After more growling and scuffling, the tan wolf backed up, trailing blood from his side. He snarled then barked at his followers.

The rest of the grey wolves advanced, growling. The brown wolves ran towards the trees and stopped on the other side of the ditch. The tan wolf pursued them. Then all four disappeared into the woods.

Chantelle got dizzy and slumped over on the asphalt. It was cold, but soothing. Her wolf companion nosed her, licking her face. It seemed like the wolf was asking her if she was all right. Her furry guardian approached the Alpha. He barked and brought the large wolf back to Chantelle.

The Alpha sat in front of her, cocking his head. He came forward slowly, looking at her with his yellow eyes. He reached in and snuffled around her head and neck and shoulders. She wasn't afraid of him. He started licking her face just like her family dog used to do.

"Not what I was expecting. Nice doggie?" She reached her hand up but held it back. "My, my, what big teeth you have." She tittered. *What's wrong with me?*

Still lying on the ground, she reached up and touched his neck. He whined and licked her again. He was so beautiful she just wanted to dig her hands into his fur. That was probably a bad idea. She saw that his leg was bleeding. When she reached out a hand gently, the wolf stilled and let her touch him. Gratitude and affection welled in her. She felt a kind of tranquillity that had eluded her for months.

What is happening? I should be freaking out.

An energy started buzzing in her middle. Heat built up from her chest and stretched out to her fingers. When she put her hands on the wolf's leg and pushed from her core, she could feel warm tingles flowing down her arms. She directed them out from her palms and fingers, remembering she had done the same thing the other night. This time the energy had a different quality—a calm feeling instead of sharp and shooting shocks. She saw colours—were they real or imagined?—green and pink and brown swirling from her hands onto the wolf's leg. Had there been colours last time? Dark grey? Red sparks, maybe?

The wound was stitching itself back together, the blood stopping. *Am I doing that?*

Then things changed again.

The large wolf in front of her howled, sitting back on his haunches. His limbs elongated, paws turning into hands and feet. Fur shrank and disappeared on the body of the creature. Hair sprouted long on its head. Ears shrunk and rounded, the snout crumpled in and turned into a human face. It happened so quickly it didn't seem real.

She blinked. After a few more seconds, the creature turned to look at her. It was Charles.

"You're naked. And you're a wolf," she said. She pushed up and sat against the car. She couldn't believe her eyes. This couldn't be happening, could it?

He kneeled in front of her, pinning her with his gaze. His throat rumbled and she could feel her core heating up again. It had been a long time since she'd been face to face with a naked man.

She looked at his broad chest. "You have a lot of muscles, you know? And they're glistening." She reached out and skimmed her palms along his bulky shoulder. "And I'm rambling." She tried to stop herself but it was like her brain had a mind of its own.

His eyes peered into hers, turning from yellow to grey. He rumbled low again and the sounds went right through her. She grabbed onto his arms as he leaned forward. She could feel her nipples turning to pebbles under her sweater as she took in this tantalising specimen in front of her. He had just saved her life.

"*Mate*." Charles' voice was still a growl but she understood that word. He ran his nose along her jawline and she shivered, grabbing his face and pulling him closer.

"I am not having sex with you right now. We're outside, for heaven's sake! And there are a lot of other reasons, if I could just think of them right now..." She trailed off, running her hands through his hair. Soft and silky…she wondered if the rest of him felt this good. The muscular columns of his thighs pressed between her legs and she opened to him.

"Mate. In den. Have pups." When he spoke in that sexy voice — husky and throaty — she could almost agree to anything he said. She scooted closer and he rubbed his body against hers. All that delectable muscle pressed up to her arms, her chest, her thighs.

"That's a lot to take in right now. Can I get back to you?" She squirmed and felt his firm cock press against her centre. It felt so good she squirmed some more, feeling the heat of his body flow into hers. He worked his way down her chest, past her sensitive navel to her sex, flicking his tongue out along the way. She ran her hands along his sculpted back.

"Look, we've ended up in some compromising positions," she said, wishing she didn't have her clothes on.

"Positions, yes," he rumbled, making happy puppy noises between her legs.

She writhed under his touch, savouring his hot breath on the seam of her jeans. It was difficult to concentrate. "I find them fascinating. Maybe that's not the right word, but I'm not sure what's going on."

He brought his head back in line with hers. He nipped at her chin, that sexy rumble of his going through her body. She reached for his silky hair again, pulling him close and against her neck and shoulder.

Get yourself together, girl. She should be freaked out. After all, just a few minutes ago she was being manhandled by a wolf. She almost giggled. *Wolfhandled?* Was that a word?

Chapter Eight

Charles fought the urge to let his wolf take over again. *Mate*. He pushed back at his wolf. But it was hard not to agree.

"We need to talk about what happened," she said, still running her fingers through his hair.

He tried to concentrate. She put her hands on his shoulders and untangled her legs from his. He scooted back and pushed his wolf down again.

"You were in trouble. Wolves attacked you," he said.

"And then you showed up. You were a wolf and you fought him off." She didn't look like she was going to bolt. "How is that possible?" she asked.

"I'm loup-garou. My family are shifters."

"That's just folk superstition!" She backed up against the side of the car, eyes wide.

He shrugged and reached for her hand.

"Okay, so how am I supposed to believe it?"

"You saw." He started stroking her hand. Her skin was so soft.

"I'm seeing a lot right now. Do you have any clothes?"

"Someone will bring me some." He was in no hurry.

"My grandmother believed the old tales. I thought she was just eccentric."

He put his arms around her waist. It felt natural to touch her, to hold her. "She was right, it's true." He tried to think. Something else had happened. He scratched his leg – that was it! "What did you do to me – "

"I'm just going to lie down now." Chantelle's eyes started to close as she slumped onto his shoulder. Charles touched her cheeks with the back of her hand. Burning hot. Her pulse was too fast. He scooped her up and called for a car.

Henri appeared. "Let me take her."

Charles shook his head, trying to push past his brother. Henri stood his ground. Charles growled low. "I need to be with her." *Do I have to push my brother out of the way?*

Henri stepped back, understanding in his face. "I'll find out what happened."

Charles hurried to the nearest SUV and gestured to the driver to open the back seat. He put Chantelle in and climbed in beside her. The driver passed him a blanket and some of his clothes. He put the blanket and his jacket on top of the woman, checking her vitals. He'd just found her – he couldn't lose her already.

As the driver pulled around, Charles got on the comms and called their Head Mage, Gwen. "Bring a medic team. I've got a woman in distress – she's been injured."

"Anything else?"

"You and Edwin meet me at the front doors. She crashed after performing a magical working."

When Chantelle stirred and opened her eyes his heart stuttered.

"What happened?"

"You're going to be okay." He tried to put the blanket around her, settling for leaning her against his warmth and wrapping his arms and the blanket around her. Her eyes drooped but didn't close. He tried to swallow and his mouth was dry. "Do you remember what you did?" he asked.

"There was a wolf... I did something."

"You healed me."

Her teeth chattered. "You were naked."

"I've got some clothes on now." He searched for more layers to put around her.

She mumbled, "There's something, like a memory." When her eyes closed his heart dropped. "I can't recall. It's fuzzy. There was a boy once..." She looked into Charles' face, searching.

"At Grand-maman's. There was a girl..." Charles half-remembered. "She looked like a small version of you. Something happened." Where was this coming from?

"There were a lot of kids. And a cake... That's impossible." Her eyes went wide and rolled up in her head. Was it a memory? Or a dream? He had to make sure she was going to be okay. He held her tight.

A minute later the driver stopped the car. Gwen, Edwin and a medic team waited in front of the main lodge. His stomach stopped flip-flopping. Still, he held her close.

The Elder Mage Gwen opened the car door on the far side and leaned in. "Charles, give us an update."

He looked at the tall woman with greying hair. He couldn't speak, couldn't move.

"Charles? Can you pass us the woman?" Gwen moved back and the medics looked in.

He tried to lift his arms. But he couldn't let her go. Instead, he backed up as far away as he could get from the medic team.

He didn't want them close to her. She was his. A low growl rumbled through him as he clutched Chantelle.

The medics exchanged a glance. They backed up and approached the Head Mage.

Gwen poked her head inside the car. "Charles? Are you okay?"

"*Mine,*" he snarled. When Gwen moved closer, he scooted back against the car door, Chantelle still in his arms. He had to protect her. Keep her safe. Gwen tied back her long hair and inched her way onto the edge of the car seat. She kept her hands palms up, her head and eyes below his. Slowly she inched closer, assessing his reaction.

Charles sniffed Gwen's scent. No threat from his mage. She came closer, radiating calm. She reached out a hand and slowly touched his forehead. He felt a small pulse from her hand. Warmth spread to his head, clearing some of the fog. *What am I doing? She needs medical attention.* He tried to let go of this woman. "Gwen? I—I need some help." He couldn't focus. He just needed to protect the woman in his arms. Nothing else mattered.

She placed a hand on his shoulder. "Can you let us examine her?"

"Maybe? My hands won't move."

The mage came closer. She reached down and touched his hands. Warmth spread through them and he let go of his grip. He put Chantelle on the seat beside him. "Okay. You can take her. I think." Gwen leaned forward and put out a hand. He took in a big breath and held it. Gwen put her hands underneath the woman. He held himself still.

"I have to come with you," he ground out.

"Sure." The Head Mage was smiling, like this kind of thing happened every day. "Then when you're ready, we'll want to ask you some questions."

"Once she's okay."

"What are we looking at?" she asked.

"Lacerations on her legs, a bite on her shoulder. And then—and then she healed me. I don't think she knew what she was doing. She passed out after expending the energy." She had to be okay. After all that, he had to make sure she was going to be fine.

"Right," said Gwen, passing Chantelle to the medics. "Let's look at her physical injuries first, then I'll work with Edwin on the psychic ones."

When Charles nodded, Gwen eased him out of the SUV, his heart still racing. They followed the medic's gurney. Gwen's touch kept him grounded. As long as he hung on to her, it was all right.

They followed the team as the medics set Chantelle up in one of the clinic rooms. He waved off their attempts to make him leave. Gwen asked a nurse to find Charles a chair. The mage disappeared for a moment, then returned with coffee and a protein bar. "Take these. Then we'll talk." Hands shaking, he sipped the coffee and started on the bar.

* * * *

Gwen shook him awake. He must have dozed off while the doctors were with Chantelle. His Head Mage looked pale.

"Is she?" His heart fluttered.

"No news yet. Do you feel up to some questions?"

He nodded. He needed some clean clothes. And a shave.

"So how did she heal you? Lead me through it."

He explained what Chantelle had done. "Not as precise as you, but fast and effective."

Gwen looked at his leg. "Remarkable. I can't see a trace of the wound, or even a scar. But I can feel the residual energy of a working. It has an unusual flavour" — she felt around the site — "but it definitely was powerful."

"Gwen, I can't explain it, but when she healed me, I had a flash. Like a memory."

"Go on."

"Like it had happened to me before. And I saw her — Chantelle — but she looked younger. We were at Grand-maman's summer cottage."

"Unusual magicks can touch off synapses or bring back similar experiences. Do you remember an event at your grandmother's? An injury? An altercation?"

They had visited the cottage every summer. The cousins and his brothers would play all day. Swimming in the lake, traipsing through the forest, fishing in the canoe. He had many happy memories and few unpleasant ones. Someone had eaten a bad mushroom once, and Henri had gotten poison ivy. But that was all he could remember.

"Nothing I can recall," he said.

"If we need to, we can do some memory recall. In the meantime, do you think this flash has anything to do with your reaction when we tried to take Chantelle in the SUV?"

He must have looked like an idiot. "I shifted and she healed me. I got her into the vehicle. Then I had an overwhelming urge to keep the two of us in the back of the SUV. Like it was my job to make sure nobody got near us. That I kept us safe." He knew it sounded impossible.

"Do you know this woman?"

"We met a few days ago at Grand-maman's. She's a neighbour."

"Have you slept with her?"

"That's none of your business." His face grew hot. "It's complicated."

"Complicated how?"

"These images. Every time we get close something happens and I see her—us." It didn't make any sense. But they had a connection.

"They happen when you have a strong reaction or intense emotion?"

"Yes." Charles said. It was intense—that was for sure.

"It is similar to an Alpha mating practice."

"But we just had a one-night stand! And she's not my mate."

"I said it was similar. Not exact. It could just be a strong physical attraction to an untrained mage."

"That would make sense. The energies could be pulling us together." This was something he could live with. Gwen could figure out how to stop it.

"Charles, could you do me a favour?"

"Yes, anything for you, Gwen. You know that."

"Keep an open mind. Maybe it's some kind of Alpha claiming."

"But I don't know her. I like her. She's gorgeous and smart and creative. But..." He trailed off. He knew, somewhere inside him, that something linked them together. Could he fight it? Should he?

"Can you do this for me?" Gwen said.

"Yes, all right." He would try. But he didn't like it.

Chapter Nine

Chantelle woke up in a strange room. Her head felt thick, but she was warm. *I'm just going to rest my eyes for a few more minutes. Then I'll figure out where I am.* When she opened her eyes, she saw an IV in her arm. She was wearing a hospital nightgown. The room didn't look as sterile as a hospital ward, no garish fluorescent light panels overhead. It was more like a hotel room, but with medical equipment.

She didn't see anybody. "Hello?" she asked.

A large black man poked his head through the door and came in the room. He looked like a G-man. There was even an earpiece. When he sat down on a chair by the bed, his dark eyes were kind. "Ms. Mizuki?" He had an accent but she couldn't place it. Nova Scotian, maybe?

Where was she? What was going on?

"My name is Dominick and this here is Derrick." He pointed as another man entered the room. They almost looked like twins — tall and muscular, confident and in control. Shaved heads, identical suits. Serious and professional, but they radiated warmth and kindness.

"Where am I?" she asked.

"The family brought you back to the resort after the attack. You're safe here. Nobody's going to hurt you." He looked at his companion. Derrick left the room quietly.

"Why am I here?"

"Do you remember what happened yesterday?"

"How long have I been out?" She rubbed her temples with her free hand.

"Eighteen hours. You had a shoulder wound and some lacerations. Then your blood pressure dropped. The doctors were worried. Mr. Ducharme —"

The door opened. Suddenly Charles was at her side. What a relief. She reached out to take his hands, then she pushed him back. "Why did you bring me here?"

"What? No, that wasn't —" He looked at Dominick and Derrick. They left the room.

"I took you back here after the attack. In the SUV. You don't remember?" he asked, squinting his eyes.

Bits and pieces came back to her. "The road was blocked by a tree. Then these wolves attacked. But some more wolves came and — they were you and your family, weren't they?" She didn't know if she believed this. Maybe her memory was affected or she had hallucinated.

He just nodded his head, like it was normal to shift into wolves. But that was impossible! In her heart, she knew he was telling the truth.

He checked her vitals, his touch lingering on her face and wrists. "I heard the wolves through your cell. When I took off, I alerted the pack. They helped fight off your attackers."

"I thought I was going to die." She wiped at her face.

"Not on my watch. And we recognised the leader. We've taken a big step forward in our investigation."

Chantelle closed her eyes for a moment, blocking him out and trying to concentrate on her memories. "After you shifted, you were rubbing your sexy body parts on me." *And I wasn't complaining, was I? They were some very nice, very sexy body parts.*

He dipped his head. "Sorry. I couldn't stop sniffing you. Other shifters are used to that, but not humans."

"It was a little intense. You make quite a sight when you're a naked wolfman." Her face grew hot and she looked down at the covers.

He sat down on the bed beside her and reached for her hand. "You'll have to stay here for a few days. The doctors want to run some more tests and we want to install a security system at your house before you can go back."

"Wait, what? Slow down." What was going on? Security system?

"We're installing twenty-four-hour surveillance and a panic alarm. There's security posted in your neighbourhood. You or Grand-maman can call and have someone at your house in five minutes."

"This is too much." *Why is he taking over like this? I don't need his help.*

"You can't move back without protection."

"I didn't ask you to do this. I'll be fine." She could take care of herself. She didn't need him to interfere in her life.

He squeezed her hand. "I'm trying to protect you. When your house is secure, you can go home."

"I'm not some princess who needs rescuing. I can take care of myself!"

He looked at her, smiling like a giant, annoying cherub. "Yes, you are independent, strong and capable. But until we can determine who and what the threat is, you stay here. They were going to kill you yesterday." He lifted her palm to his cheek.

She bit her lip. How could he do that to her? One little look and she wanted to be back on the asphalt with him. "What is going on?" Her voice sounded small.

"That's what I'm trying to find out. And I can do that better when I know you're safe."

She put her shoulders back and nodded.

"There's something we need to talk about," he said.

"The wolf thing?"

"Something else. Do you remember what happened right before I shifted back to human form?"

She blinked. "You were a wolf one minute and the next you were human."

"Anything else?"

"No."

"You healed my leg. You reached over, touched me and fixed it."

"I can't do that!" She let go of his hand and turned her face away. She'd had enough impossible things for one morning.

"Yes, you can. I have some people to meet with you. They'll do some tests to figure out what happened."

"That's not necessary. I didn't do that." He wasn't making any sense.

"Why can't you do what you're told?" He sighed.

"Why are you so bossy? I just need some rest." She hid her head in the pillows.

"I didn't mean it like that. I'm asking you to trust me."

"Trust a man? That'll be the day." But she knew, somewhere deep down, that she trusted this surly, scowling, beautiful man. *I hardly know him! It's not right.*

He touched her shoulder. "I need your help, too," said Charles. "We know the identity of the tan wolf who attacked you yesterday."

"Who is he?" Her heart raced. Before today she just thought a few vicious wolves were loitering around the village woods. Now they were shifters and she was a target.

"His name is René Reynard. He's the son of the leader of Trois-Rivières pack."

"Who are they?"

"They're our neighbours, over by Parc La Mauricie, north of Trois-Rivières. We've been at loggerheads for many years now. But they've never come into our territory like this before."

"When I was a child, we used to live near the park."

Charles looked at her. "Did you know the Reynard family?"

"I don't think so. But Granny used to tell me stories about scary wolves to keep me out of the woods."

"Did you live there for long?"

"We never stayed in one place very long. Granny liked to wander."

"We're going to need your help to figure out how you're connected to this." He took her hand again.

She looked in his eyes and fought her rising panic. "I can't stay."

"Why?" His eyebrows hitched up.

"It's just..." How could she explain it? It would sound stupid. *Okay, deep breath.* "That's where I'm supposed to be. I have to stay at the cottage."

"What do you mean?"

"Well, that's my Granny Ceci's house. She was all the family I had. I have to be there so that —" Another tear trickled down her cheek. "I can't explain…" It sounded stupid when she said it out loud.

Charles took her hands. "So you honour her memory."

How did he know?

"I feel the same way about my father," Charles said. "I can't take time off. I have to protect the clan. I would do anything to get him back, but since I can't, then I will just keep working and working." He gulped. "I've never said that out loud before."

This was what went on inside that gorgeous head of his. Something settled between them.

"Rationally, I know that's not true. So why am I doing it?"

"For love," she whispered.

They looked at each other, not speaking. Then Charles reached a hand to her cheek. "Your granny would not want you to put yourself in danger." He wiped a tear away with his thumb. "Just think of it as a little holiday in the mountains. Then you can go back to your granny's cottage."

She could do that. She leaned her cheek against his palm, rubbing slowly back and forth.

"But your granny wouldn't want you hiding away from life either. She'd want you to live it."

Yikes. Too serious. "It's all changing so fast," she said.

He dropped his hand and stood up. "How about while you're here, we get to know each other better? No pressure, just spend some time together."

"That's a good start," she said.

"Will you come for tea and dessert at my place tomorrow night? I can't get away until then."

"Yes." She wasn't going anywhere.

"In the morning, Dominick and Derrick will take you to an apartment in the main lodge. You'll stay there until the doctor says it's safe for you to go home and the security upgrades are complete."

"Okay." She knew it made sense, but she wasn't happy about it.

* * * *

She was asleep again when there was a knock on the door. A middle-aged man with light brown skin and short black hair entered her room.

"Ms. Mizuki? My name is Waleed."

"Chantelle, please."

"I've got some results for you."

Chantelle sat up as he took the chair near her.

"I work in the Mage Division of the company. We practise a combination of modern science and ancient magicks to support the health and welfare of the clan. We tested your DNA and you have Fae genes."

"What does that mean?"

"Some of your ancestors had magical abilities. You show the potential to wield magic, but it hasn't been developed. According to the reports, you have some healing and possibly some defence skills. We'll need to get you to our testing rooms to confirm."

"Testing rooms?"

"Don't worry. They're more like yoga rooms than scientific labs. We get you to work one-on-one with a mage trainer. They explore the different facets to see what you can do and what you can't."

"What if I can't do anything?"

"You've already shown you can. If you haven't been trained and were unfamiliar with how to summon and project, then you might not know that you have these abilities."

"I'm not planning to stay here long."

"Will you be visiting the compound? If not, someone can come to your home to work with you. It's important that you learn to use your talents. This will prevent accidents and it will help you to defend yourself."

"Like when I'm attacked by wolves?" She tried not to raise her voice. "I think if I stay away from here and the Ducharme family then I'll be fine."

"That may not be true. You may be a target for other reasons. We should try and identify the link between the wolves and you."

"There are no links! The first time I was lost in the woods, and the second time I stopped on the road. It was just coincidence."

"We want to help you." Waleed was talking to her like she was a child. But maybe she was acting like one? She thought she was being reasonable. But maybe she should accept the possibility that he was right.

"Okay," she said.

"There's another matter," he said. "We've identified one or more psychic blocks in your system. They may be related to your memory issues."

"Is this why I can't remember having these abilities?"

"It's possible."

"Did I do this to myself for some reason?"

"Uncertain. Sometimes, after trauma, a mage will introduce blocks—consciously or unconsciously—to help the subject cope or to avoid having to deal with the events. That can be helpful in stressful situations or if having knowledge will put them in danger. Or another mage can place the blocks, often in children, as a form of protection."

"To save them from themselves?"

"Or from others."

Chantelle's heart pounded. "It sounds like I don't want to remember something. Or someone doesn't want me to know what happened." Could something terrible be buried in her mind?

"Maybe it's time for you to know. Especially if the Trois-Rivières pack is after you."

"Do I have to decide now?" There was so much to think about. It was overwhelming.

"No, but think about it. We'll need to review your medications as well."

"I have Concerta for my ADHD and birth control pills. My granny also designed an herbal supplement I take to help with my focus."

"We'll look them over. Derrick and Dominick contacted your friends and picked up some things from your house. Your medications and supplements will be in there."

"Thank you," Chantelle said, yawning. She was getting tired.

"That's enough for now. Get some rest and I'll assign someone to meet with you tomorrow." Waleed left the room.

It was like she had fallen down the rabbit hole. There were so many things to worry about, but she could barely keep her eyes open. She'd deal with them later.

Chapter Ten

Charles sat in the large boardroom with his pack. "Give me an update on René and the Trois-Rivières pack. Why are they after Chantelle?"

"We don't know yet," said Michel. "Chantelle's grandmother lived in their territory for a number of years when Chantelle was growing up. There could have been some incident or a feud."

"Why now?" asked Henri.

"Maybe Trois-Rivières sensed the connection between Chantelle and Charles — they're trying to stop the Fated Mates," said Clem.

Charles went to speak and Henri held up his hand. "There is something between you two. Everyone can sense it."

Charles felt his stomach tie in knots. *What is going on? I like her, that's all.*

"René has always been jealous of you, Charles," Thomas said. "Remember when we used to the play with him when we were kids? He always tried to beat you in any game we played."

"It must have been humiliating for him. I bet his father, Roland, told him it was a reflection on his family," Clem said.

"Do you remember that time René showed up with a black eye at one of the martial arts tournaments? There were rumours that his father hit him when he lost a match," Henri said.

"But how is it connected to the attacks on women in our territory?" Charles asked. "Is it to get us back for offering refuge to families when they leave his clan?"

"We won't let them terrorise defenceless and vulnerable clan members," Thomas said.

"I know. But we have to stop them from committing violence on our territory."

"We have to catch them in the act. We could use Chantelle as bait," Henri said.

Charles growled low. "No." That was a bad idea.

"Sorry, but we should keep it on the table. The pack would protect her. She wouldn't be in danger. We would just dangle her on a line."

Charles growled again. They were not going to do anything to his mate — to Chantelle, whatever she was. He had to keep her safe, above all else.

"All right, let's put a pin in that idea," Thomas said, looking around the table. "You have your action items. Get on them."

Everyone left the room except Henri. He sat down beside Charles and asked, "How are things going with Chantelle? Have you made a move yet?"

"We're getting together tomorrow."

"Don't scare her off, dude," Henri said. "You need to use a little finesse. Tell her you like her and want to get to know her."

"I did." Charles raked a hand through his hair. "But we've already had sex and she's seen me naked."

"That's awkward, I agree. But she's still here so it couldn't have been that traumatic. Besides, the ladies say you are very attractive naked." Henri grinned.

Charles crossed his arms. "She's strong and independent. I love that about her. But my wolf wants me to bend her to my will, claim her."

"Mom was not a submissive Omega. She was a co-partner and equal to Dad. Her strength made the Alpha better and the pack better, too."

"With Alice, we tried to control each other. It was unhealthy. Obsessive. What if that happens again?" Charles scowled.

"Things are different between you and Chantelle."

"I think I should hold back on the physical stuff so we can get to know each other better first." He wanted to take it slow. *That's always better, isn't it?*

"Or you could have more sex and then get to know each other." Henri rubbed his hands together with glee.

Charles shook his head. "She drives me crazy—her body, her scent, everything."

"If you don't take my advice, then you're going to need a lot of cold showers."

"Thanks, bro. You're a big help." Charles had to admit he did feel a little better. But he'd never tell it to Henri.

"Take your time, then. Get to know her better. Chicks love that stuff."

"That's how you form a relationship, dickhead."

"Not my style, but I know it works for you. And if it isn't working, then seduce her with your powerful sex machine." Henri winked and left the boardroom.

* * * *

Chantelle was dressed and ready in the morning when Dominick and Derrick arrived to move her into an apartment in the main lodge. As they took her from the medical building on the clan compound to the large resort building, they explained that many of the clan members worked for the family's company.

"The Ducharmes developed a live-and-work community here. Between the resort and the ski village, we have all the amenities — recreational facilities, medical care and a small childcare and school centre. We also have a weekly shuttle to Montreal for visiting and shopping," said Derrick.

"It's like a dream," she said. The buildings were rustic, reminiscent of old-fashioned log cabins, but with all the latest conveniences. She thought it was an ideal environment to raise a family. And why was she thinking about that? She shook her head.

Her escorts introduced her to reception at the lodge, where Sunita and Marjit were working that morning. They greeted her with genuine warmth. Everyone seemed so happy. But maybe it was like one of those dystopian movies where it turned out they were all on drugs or the government was watching them.

Dominick and Derrick took her through the wing that contained the business offices and central meeting rooms. Then they showed her the dining hall, workout centre, and indoor pool and spa.

"We also have a couple of large seminar rooms where families can gather as well. Behind the main lodge are the chalets for clan families who prefer to live on-site instead of in the village," Dominick said.

They went up an elevator to a long hallway, where tasteful wallpaper and sconces were placed on the walls between the hotel room doors. At the end, the hallway opened into a larger square with four doors, two set on each side of the hall, with a stairwell on the end.

"We use these apartments for longer-term business clients and family guests," Derrick said, opening one of the doors.

The apartment looked like it had come out of a condo brochure. Elegant lines with lots of grey and taupe colours. The open-area main space included a kitchenette, dining area, and seating space with a stone fireplace. The kitchen area's granite countertops and steel appliances complemented the dark wood in the living room, making a quiet, stylish space. Dominick showed her the two bedrooms and bathroom, which carried the same aesthetic throughout.

"This is too big for me." She didn't need all this space. She was one tiny person.

"Clementine picked out the room personally," said Dominick. "It's near her apartment."

"You've all gone to so much trouble," Chantelle protested.

"It's the off-season so most of the resort is empty. We just want to make sure you're comfortable and safe."

"I don't have a choice, do I?"

Derrick smiled at her and she couldn't be angry.

"It's only for a couple days anyway." Chantelle shrugged. She could live with it.

"The kitchen has been stocked with some necessities but you can come to the dining hall for meals. We'll take you there in about an hour for lunch."

"What's going to happen?" She looked at the two men.

"Excuse me, ma'am?" Derrick asked.

"Don't ma'am me! Call me Chantelle. What am I supposed to be doing here?"

The two men exchanged a glance. Dominick led her to a black bar stool at the counter separating the kitchen from the living room. Derrick went to the kitchen and picked up the kettle. He filled it with water, placed it on the stove and turned it on. Then he looked through the cupboard for mugs and tea.

"The group that attacked you are known to us. The Trois-Rivières pack's Alpha, Roland Reynard, is a cruel man who's trying to take over the Ducharme clan."

"Do you think they're behind the attacks?"

"We think so. But we don't know why they were in Marie's village and why they are interested in you. The Ducharme family is very worried for you, for their grand-maman, and for the whole village."

"I didn't know it was that serious." She loved her little community. She didn't want anything to happen to them.

"Our Tech and Security division is upgrading the protection for your house and Marie's. We're posting surveillance teams to keep the village safe. Meanwhile, we are investigating what the connections might be."

"I don't understand any of this!"

"Yes, ma'am—I mean Chantelle. It's a lot to take in," said Dominick.

Derrick brought her a cup of herbal tea. "It's my boyfriend's favourite chamomile blend to help calm your nerves. You've been through a lot."

Chantelle blew on the tea and took a sip.

"We picked up some of your things. After you've looked through them, please let us know what else we can bring from your home," Dominick said.

"Oh, my art supplies! I didn't even think—"

"Give us a list and we'll have someone pick them up this afternoon," Derrick said.

"Thank you. Everyone has been so great. I don't deserve it," she said.

Dominick smiled. "There's a studio in the village community centre that anyone is free to use. We can take you there after your art supplies arrive. The studio should have anything you might not have or you've forgotten. If not, we can order it for you too."

"Is this what it's like to live here? It sounds like utopia."

Derrick beamed. "We came here ten years ago for a consulting gig and never left. We grew up in Louisiana. The clans there are tough. Lots of racist attacks."

"Worse than here in Quebec? It's not the most tolerant of places."

"In the Trois-Rivières clan, there are frequent assaults on immigrant families. We take in a lot of women and children who flee from the Reynards. But in the Laurentian Mountain Clan, it's different. Charles' father had a strong inclusivity policy and created a safe space for all members of the clan."

"Sounds too good to be true."

"We think it is the garden of Eden."

They gave her time to get settled. Chantelle found the master bedroom. It was beautiful—elegant floral drapes and duvet, light beige furniture and another fireplace, this time with light beige curlicue moulding on the mantel. She looked in the dresser and found some of her clothes—jeans, tees and sweaters. In another drawer she saw her socks, camis, bras and panties. After she dressed, washed her face and brushed her teeth, she returned to the main area of the apartment. Dominick and Derrick were reading the newspaper near the fireplace.

"Don't you guys have anything better to do?"

"You are it." Derrick grinned. "The boss asked us to bring you to the dining hall for lunch. He's got a full day of meetings, though, so his brother will meet you."

They made their way down the long hallway, to the elevator and down to the lobby. Following the smells of cooked vegetables and baking bread, they came to a large room with several long wooden tables and benches. At small tables on the side, people talked and ate.

"There is a more formal dining room that we open during the ski season," said Dominick.

It was a relaxed space, the diners speaking quietly and laughing together. They went through the cafeteria line and found a table. Derrick and Dominick sat with her while she ate some soup and pulled apart a sandwich.

Henri appeared in cycle shorts and a workout shirt, carrying a mountain bike on his shoulder. He nodded at the two men and greeted Chantelle. When he sat down, Derrick and Dominick excused themselves and said they would see Chantelle later.

"Do I need to have a security detail?" she asked Henri after they left.

"Things are busy for the family right now. Charles wanted to make sure you were being taken care of."

"He's a little bossy, isn't he?"

Henri laughed. "That's what makes him a good leader."

"What's this whole Alpha thing about anyway?"

"Charles never expected to become Alpha. Our dad and oldest brother Robert died in a car accident."

"I'm sorry. When did that happen?" *How awful for him.*

"Three years ago now. It was sudden and nobody was prepared. When Charles became the head of our family, he was nominated for Alpha, but he didn't want it."

"What changed his mind?"

"Our Uncle Jean."

"Clem and Bertrand's dad?"

"No, another brother. He arrived out of nowhere and tried to take over the clan."

"Charles was forced to become leader? Did he have to fight?"

"He's always been a good fighter. Athletic. Competitive. And Jean was not as young as he used to be."

Chantelle looked at him. "Did Charles have to…"

"No," said Henri. "Jean left after he was defeated. Went out west."

"I don't know what to think about everything." Chantelle fidgeted with her coffee cup.

"You seem to be coping better than I expected."

"It makes sense, somehow. Like I've always known." She shook her head. "I don't know if I can explain it."

"Try me."

"My grandmother used to tell me folk tales and legends when I was little. She made them sound real, like she believed them, so I believed them too. Even when I grew up, I still wanted to believe in Granny Ceci's stories."

"Did she write about loups-garous?"

"Yes, I loved her French-Canadian werewolf stories, even though most of the ones I read later were more moralistic. Her tales didn't punish the loups-garous for not following Catholic beliefs. They were just part of the many creatures of the Laurentians, along with faerie creatures, queens and princesses, magical Canada geese and caribou."

"I'd love to see them."

"I'm going to ask to have her notebook brought here. You're welcome any time." It was nice to make a friend. Henri was better with social niceties, more in touch with his feelings than Charles. But there was something about Charles—he was very attractive. All those muscles and hard lines.

A young person with pink hair and green eyes skipped over to them. "Hello, my queen."

"Chantelle, this is Peaseblossom. They use they/them pronouns. They're an air sprite," said Henri.

"Pleased to meet you, Peaseblossom," Chantelle said.

"Call me Pea," they chirped. They were small, as tall as Chantelle's shoulder. Chantelle leaned forward to take their hand.

When Chantelle touched Pea, a jolt went through her arm.

She saw white mist around the two of them. *Not again! What is it this time?*

Chantelle was seated beside Pea on a fallen log in the woods. It looked like they were in the forest near the compound, but there wasn't a building in sight. "Is this a dream?" she asked.

Pea shook their head. "It's more like a memory. Or maybe a story from the past? I'm not sure yet."

Chantelle looked around and saw three stooping figures dressed in grey robes. They were trudging through the trees by a creek. Chantelle shivered. Something wasn't right about them.

A large man followed the robed people, carrying a child who wasn't moving.

"Is the child asleep or hurt?" whispered Chantelle.

"I don't know," said Pea. "This is coming from you, not me."

Chantelle turned and looked at them. "Really?"

Then the mist carried the scene away, leaving them standing in the dining hall.

Chantelle looked at the sprite. "What happened?"

Henri blinked. "You two have been standing there not moving for an entire minute. I was getting worried."

"We saw something," said Chantelle.

"Our real foes," said Pea. "There is much that you won't understand yet. But you will, when it's time." Pea started to skip away and turned back. "Please stay. Charles needs you." Then they left.

Chantelle looked at Henri. "I don't know what to think about that."

"Pea sees the world differently than most creatures. They don't always make sense but it's never nonsense.

We just can't understand it." Henri took another sip of coffee.

Chantelle tried to remember but the scene was already fading. "I saw some people—at least I think they were people—in robes, walking through the woods. I think it happened in the past."

"Pea will help you make sense of it when the time comes." Henri smiled reassuringly.

Chantelle nodded and changed the subject. "So what's with your older brother?"

"What do you want to know?"

"He's scowling at me one minute and the next he's sticking his tongue down my throat."

Henri spit a mouthful of coffee across the table.

"Is that what shifters are like?" Chantelle continued after he had recovered.

"Not all shifters. But when our wolf likes someone, it can be pretty aggressive. Our human side can't always control it."

"He has this intensity I'm drawn to. But I'm never sure where I stand with him."

"He's always been serious."

"I think I like him, but it's a lot for a girl to handle."

"You're no girl. You're a warrior princess!" He looked like Charles when he smiled.

"That's what my Granny Ceci called me."

He furrowed his brow. "You're dealing with a lot right now. I'm sure it doesn't help that he's coming on so strong."

"I know I'm being stupid. Who wouldn't want to get to know this gorgeous, sexy man?" *What is wrong with me?*

"He likes you. But he needs to figure out what he wants."

"Me too." Chantelle sighed.

"When his girlfriend Alice left him last year, he shut down. He threw himself into work. I think Pea is right. He needs you."

"I'll try, but it's a lot to handle," Chantelle said. "Do you have time to show me around some more?"

"Sure. We can walk around the property but then back to your apartment for a rest. Alpha's orders. I'll send over something to eat later and Dominick and Derrick will take you to Charles' chalet around eight."

Chapter Eleven

Dominick and Derrick guided Chantelle from her apartment across the complex. Derrick explained that Charles had moved into the Alpha's residence after his father and older brother Robert died.

"He resisted at first," Dominick said. "But he knew the pack needed him in the Alpha's chalet. We needed a sense of normalcy again."

That must have been devastating for Charles. Thrust into a position he'd never thought he'd have. Showing leadership when he was grieving.

They reached a large chalet in the middle of the resort, set in the centre of a semi-circle of chalets, townhouse-style residences spread out behind them. She didn't know how, but it seemed both imposing and cosy at the same time. A long porch strung with white fairy lights anchored the log A-frame across the front. The anterior windows stretched up the two full stories in the centre. It looked like her childhood dream of Christmas in the woods.

She looked up at the stars twinkling in the sky. Even the heavens conspired to make this the most romantic place in the world.

Charles opened the door. He greeted Dominick and Derrick and the two men went back to the lodge. He took her hand and kissed it, then led her inside.

He was dressed in a blue button-up, navy cardigan, and brown trousers. He looked casual, groomed and sexy — like he had just stepped out of a Ralph Lauren ad. Everything fit him perfectly. The shirt hugged his chest and abs snugly, showing off his muscled frame. He'd pulled up the sleeves of the sweater, revealing strong forearms and hands. Her heart skipped a beat.

"I like your place." She looked around, trying to act casual. The chalet's spacious entrance revealed a split-level open area on the right. On the left side, a staircase led up to several rooms on a second-floor hallway. On the right, she could see a sunken living room at the back of the chalet, with kitchen and dining areas near the front. At the back of the home, there was a row of picture windows and French doors leading to a large deck. The colour scheme was masculine and muted, greys, dark browns and blacks. It was understated, but classy.

"My surroundings influence my mood." He led her to the living room, in front of a rustic fieldstone fireplace area with a comfortable leather sofa and chairs. Soft throws and cushions the colours of mountains and forest were scattered thoughtfully upon them.

"It suits your personality," she said, caressing a faux-fur throw on the back of the dark-brown leather couch. It was such a tactile space she wanted to touch and feel everything. *I should have guessed he would have a place like this.*

"How are you adjusting?" He looked at her like she was the only thing in the world that mattered.

They settled on the sofa across from the rustic fieldstone fireplace. "It's overwhelming," she said. "There are such things as werewolves. I can do magic. Someone might be chasing me and I don't know why." Those eyes, dark and shining. *Take a deep breath.*

"I'm here. I can help."

"Maybe I'm holding on to you because you're the anchor in the storm. Or maybe you're the storm."

"Chantelle." He breathed her name and the hairs on her arms stood on end. He leaned in and brushed his lips gently against hers, slowly. He knew what to do, grazing against her mouth with the lightest of touches.

There was a whistling in the kitchen.

"The kettle is boiling. I'll be right back." He roused himself and moved to the kitchen area. There was a handknit throw on the back of the chair, a couple of jazz books on the coffee table. She leafed through one while she waited. He returned with the tea tray and sat on the sofa. When he turned towards her, grazing his knee against her leg, she almost jumped out of her skin.

Relax, girl!

"I've got regular and herbal varieties. Cream, milk and sugar. And some of chef's famous sugar pie."

He held up the two teapots and when she gestured at the herbal tea, he poured then passed her the cup.

"Honey?" He passed her a honey pot with a wooden dipper.

"I haven't seen a dipper like this since I was a kid!"

His fingers lightly caressed hers as she took the honey pot and electric tingles went up her arm.

"Sometimes I just use my fingers," said Charles. "Here, let me…"

He dipped his finger in and brought it up to her mouth, cupping his other hand to catch any drips. Surprised, she held out her tongue and slowly brought his finger into her mouth. She swirled it around, getting every last taste of syrupy liquid. *What am I doing?*

His face was right in front of hers. He looked at her lips. "You missed a drop." He opened his mouth and licked along her lower lip. He was wicked. And tasty. Latching his lips onto hers, he tipped her head back with his hands. Exploring her mouth with his tongue, he found every crevice, their tongues dancing together. He tasted like honey and tea, smoke and cream.

When they broke off, she sighed. "You are very good at that."

"I'm good at a lot of things. But we might have to try it a few times to get it right."

"Do you think so?" She chuckled.

"But first, I want you to taste something." He got up and walked to the kitchen, returning with a fancy box. "I've got a box of Clem's favourite chocolates — they make them by hand in Paris." He opened the box, knelt in front of her and held one up.

"Okay, one bite," she said.

He brought the delicate treat to her mouth and teased it along her bottom lip. She caught a whiff of dark chocolate and caramel. Opening her mouth and closing her eyes, she waited. She felt the hard shell of chocolate and the liquid gush of caramel on her tongue — sharp and luscious. She caught his long finger between her lips and sucked as he gasped. So delicious. The chocolate and the man. She moaned. "Better than sex."

"That's what Clem says. Watching you eat it is also pretty sexy." He snared her again with his smouldering eyes. Her breasts started aching. He was leaning towards her, his free hand running along her outer thigh.

Câlice, the man has skills!

"It's my turn to feed you one," she said. *If I can stand it.*

He leaned back to grab the box and offer it to her. Then he put the box on the floor and opened his mouth obediently. After she dropped the chocolate on his tongue, he grabbed her fingers and licked them slowly, sensuously. She moaned and squirmed as her core heated up. His eyes grew dark as he reached for her other hand and licked each digit. Slow and long, like he had all the time in the world. Her pussy grew damp as she squirmed in her seat. The marble-hard peaks of her nipples rubbed against the lace of her bra.

"You taste like chocolate," he said.

"I think the chocolate tastes like chocolate."

"You taste like honey, actually. Sweet and rich, with a hint of earthiness." He wrapped his strong arms around her waist then skimmed his hands along her back. A flood of heat rushed through her body. She could stay like this all night.

"Where did you come from? Oh right, the middle of the forest in the mountains." She took a big breath and leaned back on the couch, resting her hands on his chest. Her thighs fell open as he brought his torso closer to hers. *That chest. Solid and smooth and waiting to be explored.*

She shook her head. "Umm, I think I need to cool off a bit."

He sat back on his heels.

"Everyone tells me you're too good for me," he said, sweeping her hair over her shoulder.

"What? Says the man who dates supermodels!"

"I haven't dated for a while."

"Oh. That's not what your lips said." Maybe he was ready to kiss her again.

He ducked his head. "There's something about you. I can't explain it."

"I feel it too." She reached for his broad and powerful chest and held him. When she opened her eyes and looked over his shoulder, she saw some small figurines on the fireplace mantel. "That's weird," she said.

He looked behind him. "What is it?"

"On your mantel." There were figures of caribou and wolves on the shelf. In the middle was a small statue—a religious icon. Catholic, judging by the mitre and crozier. How did she know that? She pointed up at the statuette. "Where did you get this?" she asked.

Charles looked over. "My father left it for me. It's been in the family for generations."

It clicked. "He's in my granny's notebook."

He stood up, grabbed the figurine and brought it down to show her. "It's Saint Patrick."

When her fingers touched his, something sparked, electricity jolting up her arm. She couldn't pull her hand back—it was stuck. The statuette held them together, pulsing energy between the two of them, her sitting on the couch, him standing and reaching out to her. They were caught in an arc and couldn't move. They both stood still, transfixed, their feet glued to the floor.

Her arms were tingling, but it didn't hurt. As the energy pulsed between them, all barriers fell down.

Chantelle was laid bare. No hiding, no secrets, no excuses. Just the two of them, facing each other and knowing they were connected. Physically, emotionally, psychically connected.

She couldn't think. She couldn't speak. But she wasn't afraid. She dropped the figurine and reached for him. His strong hands slid up her body. When she tilted her head up, he knelt down. Their mouths met, demanding and insistent. Molten and languid. All things and no things. She was filled with a need to be with this man, to touch and taste him.

Their hands moved frantically, undoing the buttons on his shirt and pulling off her sweater at the same time, needing to be skin-to-skin. Firm chest and swollen breasts pressed against each other. Her sensitive nipples rubbed against the hairs of his chest. She shivered as he brushed his rough hands down her arms, making goosebumps erupt. It was inexplicable, but it felt right.

He claimed her lips, probing her willing mouth with his insistent tongue. *My, he's good. Too good.* She sighed and skimmed her hands down the sculpted muscles of his back. The feel of his soft skin underneath her hands was heaven. She wanted all of it. Chantelle couldn't think anymore. Just feel. *Just let go, soak up the sensations, revel in them.*

She needed him. Charles pushed the coffee table out of the way so they could lie on the soft rug in front of the fireplace. *This is perfect.*

Chantelle took his shoulders and pushed him down on his back. Then she straddled his waist, feeling his solid body underneath her. He was so big—everywhere. Just what she wanted—to feel his hardness under her. He moaned and reached his hands around to her back, running his fingers gently up and down, brushing along her bare skin. He reached for her heavy breasts and her nerve endings tingled exquisitely. She couldn't stop now and she didn't want to. It was meant to be.

Charles groaned as Chantelle climbed on top of him. He was glad he still had his pants on. They were keeping his rigid, aching cock from exploding.

She sighed and leaned down. "Every time I touch you, I just want to strip you down and lick you all over."

He moaned at her words, feeling his erection stiffen even more. Pulling her into his arms, he breathed her in. Fragrant flowers and rain. Her special scent—nobody else was like her. Kissing the top of her head, he ran his hands along her curtain of black glossy hair. So sleek and beautiful…he could tangle his hands in it for hours.

He pulled down her face and kissed her, teasing her lips open. Exploring her mouth with his tongue, he relished all the nooks and crannies of its warm depths. When she moaned into his ready mouth, he fought the urge to scoop her up and carry her to his bed. Instead, he ran his hands along the top of her jeans. He trailed kisses down her chin to the curve of her neck, then nuzzled and licked his way between the exposed mounds of her breasts. Her scent and taste overwhelmed him. Her mouth-watering peaks were perfect in his hands, like they were meant only for him.

"You deserve so much. You should have happiness and love and tenderness—" His wolf reached out as he kissed her full lips again.

Mine, the beast said.

No.

Keep her, the wolf pushed.

Give me time, let me —

Chantelle hissed in pleasure as she planted her hands on his chest. She pushed him backwards so that his head was on the floor. Her gaze fierce, she leaned down to kiss him, swirling her wet tongue inside his mouth. "Mmm. Don't stop." She bent down again and settled herself on top of him.

When her glistening lips met his, he felt himself falling away, spiralling down. What would it be like to make love to this vibrant, sexy woman? To lay her bare and give her all of himself? To bring her to climax over and over again until they were completely spent? He reached for her slender hips again, running his hands along the curves of her torso, up then down to her pliant buttocks. She squirmed against him, panting lightly in his mouth. He liked everything about her. How she smelled, how she felt in his arms, how her hair begged to be touched.

Skimming his hands along her flat stomach, he grasped her hips and pulled her close against him. She moaned as he squeezed her supple cheeks, luxuriating in her pliable flesh in his hands. When he pressed his eager length against her jeans-clad centre, a little thrill of pleasure shuddered down his spine.

"*Chère,* you are magnificent. This feels so good," he growled low. She gasped as he ground his bulging erection against her. How could he be so aroused when they were only half naked? He kneaded her firm buttocks, making small circles with the tips of his fingers. The sensations were overwhelming. Watching her lost in pleasure on top of him was the icing on the cake. She was panting and leaning her head back, gyrating in his lap.

"Just keep rocking like that." He groaned, feeling her quiver on top of him. He was aching so much he thought he would burst apart. He increased the friction, bringing a hand between them to help stimulate her sensitive bundle of nerves. Moaning, she increased her movement, leaning into him. Soon she exploded in convulsive gasps, clutching his arms and shoulders. He gripped her hips, keeping up the pressure for a few more strokes until he reached his own climax. It pulsed through him as he grunted and held her tight.

He was spent. Sated. Hard to believe he could feel so naked with layers of clothing still between them. Pulling her down, he enveloped her lithe form in his arms, bringing her dreamy face to his and showering it with kisses. "You are so beautiful. You deserve it all, not just sex."

"No, I don't—"

"What are you talking about?"

"I just…I don't know why you would want me." When she looked at him shyly, it almost broke him.

"You are passionate, sexy and fiery. Of course I want you." He pulled her close and rolled so that she was lying beside him, brushing her hair away, as though he had done it a million times before. They had been together—were meant to be together—for all time.

What did that mean? He sat up on one elbow. It was fuzzy, but he felt like they had been talking about something important. Then they were ripping each other's clothes off.

"Chantelle—"

She looked at him, uncertainty flitting across her perfect face.

"What happened? Before we —"

"What do you mean?"

"I don't know. Something on the mantel, maybe?"

She sat up and looked over. "I was holding a rock. No, a statue?"

"We were looking somewhere. Then we were kissing."

She stood up and walked one step to the couch, looking around. When she bent down and picked up his little Saint Patrick statue, she crumpled to the floor and didn't get up.

He rushed over, his heart pounding. Was she okay?

She was white as a sheet, and her pulse flickered. He wanted to get his comms, but remembered she was still half naked. *I should fix that first. But she needs help.*

He grabbed his phone and dialled while he knelt beside Chantelle. He gently eased her sweater over her head and pulled it down. Then he brought her to the couch. *Werewolves are really bad for her. This poor woman spends too much time unconscious and resting. Maybe I just need to leave her alone.*

He held her close, remembering her episode in the SUV. She had made it that time, and she would make it this time, too. He counted the minutes, praying someone would come soon.

When the medic arrived, Dominick and Derrick were already there. They had rushed over when the call came through. The medic asked Charles questions as she took Chantelle's vitals. He couldn't remember a lot of details. Why was it so fuzzy?

It only took a few minutes to rouse Chantelle again, but they felt like an eternity.

"Are you okay?" he asked.

"Yeah, I think I am. I forgot to eat dinner." She smiled wanly.

The medic shrugged. "It would explain the dive in her blood sugar and low blood pressure. Everything seems normal now but I want her to check in with the doctor in the morning."

"You are staying here tonight. I'll keep an eye on you," Charles said.

"Don't be ridiculous! I'm fine." She looked pale.

"This isn't a debate." He turned to Dominick. "I have to be up early for a meeting. Come back at eight. And bring breakfast for her."

The man nodded and passed him a protein bar and juice. "Take these," Charles said to Chantelle.

"You're being silly!"

"No arguments." He smoothed her hair and watched her finish the snack before he picked her up and carried her upstairs. Her eyes closed a couple times and she groaned. "Too fast?" he asked.

"I'm fine. I just—"

"Close your eyes. I'll get you tucked in and you can rest." He brought her to the room next to his, opening the door and bringing her to the bed. This was not the way he'd imagined getting her upstairs, but he needed to show her that he would protect her. He pulled down the covers on one side of the bed, set her between the sheets, and tucked the blankets around her. Kneeling beside the bed, he contemplated just sitting and watching her sleep, making sure she was all right.

No, too much like a stalker. Bertrand had complained about romance movies idealising the overprotective boyfriend who watched his girlfriend at night. Charles would only stay until he was sure she was asleep. Sighing, he brushed her cheek with the back of his hand. She stirred, then settled into the pillow. He would give anything to lie next to her.

He sat beside the bed, near her, watching her breathe. What had happened tonight? The images and feelings were confused in his mind. They had made out, that he remembered. It was seared onto his brain. Her sweet softness, her little moans, the taste of her delicious mouth.

But why had she passed out? It was probably just fatigue and a missed meal. She needed to get checked out more thoroughly tomorrow. For now, she should rest. Her breathing slowed, nice and steady now. He smoothed her forehead and left the room.

Chapter Twelve

Charles was on a morning call to Germany when Thomas barged into his office.

"Mr. Ducharme has a family emergency. He'll call back later." Thomas clicked the button to end the call.

"Emergency — is Grand-maman all right?" Charles asked.

"Your insensitive behaviour is the emergency."

"What are you talking about?"

"She's packing right now. Dominick and Derrick are driving her home in an hour." Thomas stared at him, eyebrow raised.

"No, she's not. The doctor said she was fine. She just forgot to eat dinner." Charles stood up. This couldn't be happening.

Thomas put an arm out to stop him. "What did you do?"

"I didn't do anything — oh. I cancelled our date tomorrow night." Charles knew he had made a mistake.

"What? Are you out of your mind?"

"Clem needs to go over some figures — *ostie!*" He'd made a big mistake.

"And tell me you didn't sleep with her last night." Thomas looked right through him.

Charles' face went hot. "Well, not exactly...then she passed out and I was worried about her." Things were so complicated with her. Why couldn't they be simple?

"You win the prize for most thoughtless man ever. You know she has trust issues, right?" Thomas' nostrils flared.

"It's not like that..." *Yeah, I blew it.*

"I can't believe you're my brother."

"It's just — " Charles started.

"Don't even try. Go and stop her."

"Wait a minute — " What was he going to say? That he wanted her to stay? That he had feelings for her? He didn't, he couldn't. Could he?

"Go!" said Thomas. "Tell her why you're screwing up the first good thing you've had in a year. Maybe ever!"

"But — "

"Tell her that because you're too afraid to open up, you're just going to sabotage yourself before you even try. That you don't think this beautiful, smart, sexy woman — who likes you, God knows why — is worth taking a risk for. That you don't think she could be the one, if only you took the time to find out. That you'd rather spend your life alone and unfulfilled."

Charles looked at him. *Ostie.* His brother was right. He was an idiot.

"I'm done with you. *Decrisse!* Get out! Go find her!" Thomas shooed Charles out of his office, stopping to talk to Kenneth on his way out.

Charles hurried down the hallway, wondering what he should say or do. He knew Thomas was right. But what if he wasn't ready for a relationship? If he was honest with himself, he knew that wasn't true. He could be ready if he dealt with his issues from his last relationship. Instead of meeting them head-on, he had told himself he wasn't ready.

He took the stairs two at a time until he reached her floor. How was he going to fix this mess? He couldn't keep avoiding his problems by staying away. Thomas was right.

He nodded at Dominick and Derrick and knocked on the door. No answer. This was bad.

He pounded loudly. "Chantelle, let me in."

She opened it and he pushed past her, closing the door behind him. Raising an eyebrow, she crossed her arms. He closed in on her, putting his hands on her shoulders. "You aren't leaving." She wasn't going to run away from him.

She broke away and glared at him. "Were you just using me?" she said.

"No." This wasn't going to be easy to fix.

"That's what it feels like. I thought we were actually making a connection. Then you blew me off."

"I can't—" he started. He tried to touch her again and she backed away. He stepped back and gestured to the living room. "Sit down. Please." He needed to explain things.

She hesitated then walked quickly ahead of him to sit on a chair. He sat on the couch. When he tried to put his knee near her leg, she brought her legs up to her chest and put her arms around them.

"You're better off without me. And the pack," he said.

"You're kidding me. Is this because of the orgasms or because I passed out?"

He didn't know how to explain. And was he just avoiding things? "It's too dangerous for you to be here."

"What's the problem?" Tears fell down her face.

He had made her cry. He knelt in front of her and put his arms around her. "I have a strong physical reaction to you." He rubbed his hands along her arm, up and down slowly. "But it's confusing."

"I feel it too."

"I've never felt like this about anyone before. It's like I'm out of control." He breathed her in and immediately he was calmer.

"Maybe we should just get it out of the way. The sex."

"Do you really want to?" He looked at her lips. They were just begging to be kissed. Should he? Suddenly, she leaned towards him. Her mouth came down on his, soft and wet. His centre ached for her as he swept his tongue inside her mouth. He kissed her, full of fire and passion, pulling her into his lap on the floor.

"Henri says we need to just sleep together." He kissed her again.

"He does?" She kissed him back, running her hands along his shoulders. He shivered under her touch.

"I really want to strip you naked so we can have sexy time. I just—" He paused and looked at her. He ran his hands along her back. What did he want? Why did she mess with him so much?

"Just stay." He kissed her cheek and nibbled his way to her neck. "Please." He inhaled her scent, so perfect for him.

"Ummm." She gasped for breath. "It's hard to think like this." Her hands grabbed fistfuls of his hair and his scalp tingled.

"That was my plan." He chuckled into her hair. He nuzzled her and said in a low voice against her neck, "If I fucked you, would you stay? Or would you go?"

"I want you to be honest with me."

He raised his head and looked in her eyes, searching. "Will you stay if I try?"

She hesitated, then nodded.

"Please stay." He gathered her up and sat them both on the couch. He kissed the top of her head. Lilies and honeysuckle.

"What about this?" He kissed her again. His hands traced circles on her back.

"I don't know."

"Okay." He pulled her off his lap and stood up, holding out his hand to her. "I'm taking you for lunch. Then I've got some work to do this afternoon. But I'll drop by tonight just to talk."

"Yes," she said, taking his hand and smiling.

"Tomorrow night you're getting the full works for our date." He pulled her up and put his arm around her. He was still going to have to show her he cared. Convince her that she belonged with him, here.

When they left her apartment, Dominick asked, "Should I cancel the limo, Ms. Mizuki?"

"Yes, please," she said. She held Charles' hand as they walked to the dining hall and his heart soared.

* * * *

Chantelle entered the Mage offices and was greeted by Gwen and a tall, handsome man with red hair.

124

"Welcome, Chantelle," said Gwen. "This is Edwin, one of our Fae teachers. You'll have some one-on-one lessons with him and you might work with his partner, Erik, too. They are our best mages."

Edwin laughed, "Except for you, Gwen, of course."

Gwen smiled at him.

Chantelle looked more closely at Edwin. Something wasn't normal. As she looked at him, she began to see a purple streak of light emanating from his chest.

"Wow!" said Chantelle. "I can see the magic shimmering out of you."

"It takes many years of practice," said Gwen.

"Someday you could do it," offered Edwin.

"I doubt it. I've always been flaky."

"What some people call flaky, others see as creative and rejuvenating. You are special, never doubt it," Edwin said.

Chantelle beamed at the man. She wasn't used to being valued for her talents.

Gwen picked up a file from her desk. "I reviewed your test results. You definitely have Fae blood in your family."

"I don't know much about my birth parents. Granny Ceci took me in when I was little. My mom was her daughter."

Gwen smiled. "Your Fae background is similar to the European descendants of this area. Many of the early Fae settlers came from Brittany and Spain, escaping from the witch trials and the Inquisition. They settled together in New France north of Montreal. There are also pockets in the eastern townships."

"So my powers probably come from my mother's side. My father's side is from out west. I have relatives in Vancouver. They're Japanese-Canadian."

"Was your father's family here in Canada during World War Two? Or did they emigrate after?"

"My great-uncle survived the Japanese-Canadian internment camps from that time."

"So both sides of your family faced persecution for their ethnic backgrounds." Gwen shook her head. "Humans invariably fear what they don't understand."

"Granny Ceci always told me to embrace the unknown, to learn and grow by staying curious. She would talk to anybody. She said deep down we were all the same."

"She sounds like an amazing woman," said Gwen.

Chantelle nodded. After a pause, she asked, "Do most people with Fae abilities know about it? Am I unusual?"

Edwin answered her. "Things have changed since the days when Fae families and communities were close and traditions were handed down. It is not unusual for people who were raised as human to find out later that they have latent abilities, or for lines to get blurred because of deaths and adoptions, for example. Also, prejudice has led many Fae to hide their abilities."

"Can I do anything with my skills?"

"Yes," said Edwin. "I will be able to train you so that you can use your magicks intentionally and direct them to certain purposes." He stood and excused himself. "I have another meeting now, but I'll be in touch soon to set up an appointment. It was a pleasure meeting you, Chantelle."

Chantelle nodded as the man left the room.

Gwen gestured for her to sit down and asked, "Do you have psychic dreams often?"

"That's what my emo friend in college called them, psychic flashes. I thought she was exaggerating.

Sometimes I would just get a feeling or an image. Nothing big."

"Was your mother the same way?"

"I don't know. My granny did, though. We have a few family stories about that."

"What about recently?"

Chantelle shifted in her chair. "These things seem to happen when I'm with Charles." It was a little embarrassing to discuss with a relative stranger.

"How do you mean?"

"Well…" Her face got hot. "The first time we met, he bumped into me and I had these flashes. Sort of like a dream but I was awake."

"Fascinating," said Gwen. "Have there been any other occurrences?"

"After we were at his grandmother's house, we got into a fight and the same kind of thing happened. And then one other time."

"Were the images all very similar or different each time?"

"I think so. I can't remember them very well. But he and I were in all of them."

"And physical contact appears to precipitate these psychic events?" Gwen said, leaning forward.

"I guess so." Was that a clue?

"Tell me what happened at the Alpha's residence."

"I touched this little statue of Saint Patrick."

"He's the patron saint of shifters."

"Really?" Chantelle asked. That was interesting. "Then I was kissing Charles and seeing images of me with him. But we were different. Younger, and then older. It didn't make a lot of sense." It was still jumbled up in her head.

"That is common in were-mage pairings. Physical intimacy can produce certain images or provoke memories. It's the magic combining with the wolf genetics. It makes both stronger."

"I'm not a mage." Why did these people keep thinking she could do things that she couldn't? She wasn't special. She couldn't do magic. She wasn't the Alpha's mate.

"Not yet, but you have great potential to become one. We'll explore this further over the next days."

Chantelle sighed and closed her eyes.

"I think that's enough for one day," Gwen said. She walked Chantelle back to her apartment.

Chantelle lingered in the hallway. "Are you married to a werewolf?"

"His name is Ralph. He's from Alberta."

"What is it like? Are all were-males the same?"

"Stubborn and annoying, you mean?" Gwen laughed. "Yeah. Werewolf culture is different from humans. Mating practices can be unusual if you aren't familiar with them."

"Charles is very protective. He's acting like we're married or something."

"I remember when Ralph and I started dating. He's an articulate man—he's got a PhD in geology—but it was like he'd lost his ability to reason and became a Neanderthal."

"Why do they act like this?"

"Well, the stronger and smarter weres seem to suffer the most—the more alpha they are, the more potent their mating instincts are. It can be related to personality or to background, but it is overwhelming for many partners. Mages can find it especially challenging because a lot of our practices foster independence and autonomy."

"Can you stop them from acting like idiots?"

"Doesn't everybody act like an idiot when they're in love?"

"We're not in love. We practically just met!"

"Sometimes they don't know the difference. That's a cultural thing. They love and feel passionately. Some shifters are players. They sleep around a lot and don't form attachments. Others—like Charles and Ralph—they wear their hearts on their sleeves. And when they fall, they fall fast and hard."

"It's overwhelming."

"I wouldn't have my Ralph any other way, but yes, it can be overwhelming. He is loyal, true and would sacrifice everything for my happiness."

"He sounds really great."

"He is. Give your man a chance, too. Charles is passionate, generous and caring."

"He's also bossy, opinionated and controlling."

"That's what makes him a good *Marc'heg*," said Gwen.

"Excuse me?"

"*Marc'heg.* A knight, a warrior. He holds power, he keeps control, and he keeps his pack safe and protected. The pack has to obey so that he can fulfil his responsibilities to them."

"Obey?"

"It's an important phase for a werewolf. He is their leader, becoming independent and learning how to use his powers for the good of others. But as clan Alpha, Charles has to lead more than his pack, he has to grow into *Lozac'h-Prins*, the head of the family. In this role, he tempers his power and responsibilities with his obligations to his mate. He learns how to share authority and collaborate in an equal pairing that benefits the whole clan. His fire and passion find their match in his mate and together they find the wisdom and balance for the good of the clan."

"Sounds like Granny Ceci's tales of the Wolf Prince and Fae Queen."

"The stories about the Wolf Prince and Fae Queen are allegories about the roles of the Alpha and his mate. That these figures unite and protect their people is a powerful story and helps cement clan loyalty. But many people believe they also tell the history and foretell the future of our leaders."

"I guess it helps them to believe in their Alpha."

"Charles has done a great job stepping into his father's role. He is transitioning from his youthful phase — for weres this can go on into what humans call midlife — and he needs to learn how to temper his hormones and instincts with the maturity that comes from age, experience and a stable relationship."

"I've only known him for a few weeks."

"You don't have to decide to spend the rest of your life with him right now. There is context and culture, and the community has expectations, but if it's not right for you, then you aren't stuck here. Just give it a try and see what happens."

They had reached Chantelle's apartment. Chantelle said goodbye to Gwen. She had a lot to think about. She liked Charles and she liked this community. But was there a place for her here? She didn't know yet. But she thought she might like if there were.

Chapter Thirteen

Charles walked down the hall towards Chantelle's apartment a few minutes before eight o'clock. He wanted to make a good impression tonight, so he'd had a cold shower to help tamp down his fire. It hadn't done much good, though. He was still half-hard at the thought of seeing her in the dress he'd chosen.

His family had given him all kinds of advice today. Henri's suggestions were not what he needed—act cool, dazzle her with money, don't go too slow. Clem and Thomas knew she wouldn't be impressed by wealth and told him to follow her lead tonight. When Thomas was dating the Montreal socialite Amie last year, he became an expert on dating "in the modern world," as he called it. Thomas liked to learn all the rules of the game so he could win. And he could have won with Amie, except she had found someone even wealthier to run after. She'd broken Thomas' heart, but Charles hoped he would find the love of his life soon.

In the meantime, Charles had to survive this date. He reached her door, smoothed back his hair, and checked his buttons. He knocked.

When she opened the door, he whistled. "*T'es ben chix!* You are so beautiful," he said.

She wore the dark red maxi dress he had chosen for her. The V-necked bodice was tight-fitting and sleeveless, with thin spaghetti straps that he knew criss-crossed behind and laced up at the small of her back. He followed the slit in the fuller skirt from her ankle to the middle of her left thigh. She looked so sexy from the front that he couldn't wait to see how she looked from behind. Her hair was gathered to one side.

"You look handsome," she said. He had opted for a dark blue suit and tie. One of his favourites. The comfortable outfit hugged his form and was tailored from impeccable material.

"I prefer my sexy lumberjack look, as you call it. But tonight's special."

"It's a nice change. I haven't worn much besides sweatpants and jeans for the last two years."

"You should dress up like this all the time." He took her hand and led her down to the dining hall. His stomach fluttered — why was he so nervous? He'd always been confident in the dating world. Women flocked to him and he knew how to make them feel special. But tonight was different. "We're in the private dining room."

"You've gone to a lot of trouble."

"Henri and Thomas insisted. They told me to splurge a little. Make it a fun evening."

"You'll have to thank them for me." She smiled. It felt like they were just two regular people out for an evening. Except that his brothers believed she was his mate. And so did his wolf.

Where the dining hall was large and bright, this space was cosy and quiet. A little oasis. The lights were turned down and soft music played in the background.

He put a hand on the small of her back, grazing his fingers over the criss-cross straps. He led her to a table where candlelight glinted off crystal goblets. A single-stemmed light pink rose gleamed in a crystal vase. Charles held the chair for her. When she was seated, he adjusted her hair to the side again and skimmed his fingers lightly across her shoulders. Her silky skin was cool under his touch.

He opened the wine and served them. "I ordered a cold menu so we could be alone, no one waiting on us." And nobody to tell him to stop staring at her décolleté. He had her all to himself tonight.

"Everyone has been so kind. I'm not used to being waited on though." Her cheeks coloured slightly.

"Has it been intrusive?" He had ensured everyone treated her well. She was his personal guest.

"Not really, it's just that people know that I know you. They look at me differently."

"I don't always like that part of being Alpha, but that's the way it is." In return, he looked after them. All of them.

"Everyone speaks so highly of you. They want you to be happy."

"Yeah, I've been a miserable SOB for a while. They want you to stay around so I'll be less cranky." And it was true — she had made him happier. He liked being with her.

She shifted in her chair and the dress fell open at the slit, revealing her crossed legs. His cock stood at attention when he saw her creamy skin. He moved a hand to gently trace a line from her calf to her outer thigh. So soft, just a whisper of a touch. It made her shiver. She licked her lips and he caressed her knee for a moment before letting go. *Not too fast. But show her I'm interested.*

She cleared her throat and changed the subject. "So, what is under those silver cloches on the buffet table?"

Charles went over and made up two plates. "We've got smoked salmon and capers, cold lobster rolls, caviar and salads and fruit." He brought them back and placed them on the table. He loved how happy she looked.

"This looks delicious!"

"Chef likes to cook with seafood but doesn't often get the chance. They flew the lobsters in from the coast." Charles had asked him for the favour. He knew Chantelle liked lobster but had rarely eaten it.

"You'll have to thank them for me. This is amazing." She took her fork and started in on the plate.

He looked at her sampling the food. He could watch her eat—stare at her mouth—for hours. He imagined her lips all over him.

"What do you do for fun?" Chantelle asked. "I know you play the fiddle. What else?"

"I like old movies."

"Black and white movies?"

"Yes. Screwball comedies. The ones with the fast-talking repartee. Cary Grant was so smooth back in the day. And Katharine Hepburn."

"I think I've only seen one Cary Grant movie."

"Really? We're going to have to fix that."

"I'd like that," she said.

Charles poured more wine. He didn't want to use alcohol as a crutch, but he thought a second glass might make him more relaxed. More like his usual, confident self.

"Do you usually bring your dates here for dinner?" She looked at the floor. Was she uncomfortable thinking about other women?

"No. I only dated in the city or in New York. Except for Alice. She joined the clan after being tortured by Trois-Rivières pack."

"Oh, I'm sorry." She took a sip of wine. "Why didn't you bring your other girlfriends here?"

"Just didn't feel right. Too many complications." He put down his fork and wiped his mouth with the cloth napkin.

"Yeah, it is complicated here," she said.

He took her hand and brought it to his mouth. "Too complicated?" He nibbled her knuckles.

"Mmm," she said. "No."

"It's different with you. I want you to know everything." He pulled her towards him, reaching for her cheek to guide her warm mouth to his. Another light caress, smooth feathering of lips on lips. His other hand reached towards her thigh, feeling the soft, creamy skin beneath his rough fingers. He couldn't explain it. But it felt right to have her here with his clan.

He insisted she try all the dishes, watching her enjoy the rich food, that tongue darting out and licking her lips. He wanted it on his skin and pictured her licking her way down his torso, from his nipples to his navel. His cock grew thick and swollen as they sat there.

Soon Chantelle patted her stomach. "I'm stuffed!"

"What about dessert?" Charles had ideas for what that might be.

"Can we take something back for later? Maybe I'll be able to eat a mouthful or two in a few hours."

Charles put some choice morsels on a plate to take with them. She could always enjoy them tomorrow if they didn't have time for them.

They popped into the kitchen to say thanks to the staff and chef. "I think you're the only person who works longer hours than I do," said Charles to the chef. Then they left the dining room.

* * * *

Chantelle walked with Charles hand in hand back to her apartment. This had been a magical night so far. The food was amazing, the dining room beautiful and the company superb.

"Would you like another drink?" Chantelle asked. She didn't want the night to end yet.

Charles nodded and they entered her apartment. She poured them a glass of wine in the kitchen and they perched on stools at the kitchen island. He put an elbow on the counter, turning sideways to look at her.

When he took a sip of his wine, she was mesmerised by his beautiful mouth. *He can do wicked things with that mouth, I bet.*

She leaned towards him and put her hand over his glass. His eyes were flinty. She had to kiss him. She applied gentle pressure, tasting him, feeling him beside her.

He licked along the seam of her mouth and then probed inside her lips. She opened to him, taking him in and luxuriating in the way he possessed her mouth. It lit a fire inside her. She gasped when he grabbed her by the shoulders and stood up, pulling her body tight against his. Running his hands down her back to her buttocks he hoisted her onto the island, spilling their wine.

I should clean that up. Mmm, maybe later. Much later.

As she held on to his shoulders, he kissed his way up her jawline to nibble on her ear. His hot breath tickled her neck and she ran her hands through his hair, tugging gently. She moaned and returned his kiss, their tongues entwined and searching. She had never felt like this before. So full of desire. Breasts throbbing, nipples pulsing, pussy aching.

God, she wanted him right there, in the kitchen. Groaning in his mouth, she ran her hands along his shoulders and down his arms. So muscular, so sexy. *He should come with a warning label.*

He rumbled in his chest, the vibrations going right through her. Her pussy tingled in response, liquid trickling into her panties. *Mmm, so good.* When his broad hands roamed along her back, coming to rest on her hips, she snaked her legs around his firm waist, enjoying the sensation of his large hips on her thighs. This was better than anything she'd ever felt.

"Charles," she said.

"Mmm?" He kissed down her neck to the valley between her aroused breasts.

"Why don't I go change into something else?"

He looked up at her. "No. You're not taking off this dress while I'm here unless I'm watching or helping." His eyes glowed with yellow flecks and he nipped his way back to her waiting mouth. She mewed, cream soaking her panties.

His head travelled down her chest again and stopped at her navel. He wrapped his arms around her trembling thighs. "Did you know," he started in a deep voice that rumbled right through her, "that I can smell your honey?" His head moved down another excruciating inch. "It blends with your flowery scent so well." He continued his downward trajectory. "I just want to lick you from the bottom to the top."

"Ooooh, that would make me all wet." She squirmed beneath him.

He chuckled, sending another rumble through her core. Quivering, she thought she might come just from the vibrations. Suddenly he stood up. He hooked her legs around his waist and picked her up. Locking his firm lips on hers, he carried her into the living area, heading for the couch. Her heart raced as she held on tight.

His legs bumped against the arm of the couch. He ground his stiff cock against her core before laying her down and impatiently running his hands along her thighs to her knees. Breathless, she imagined all the things he was going to do to her. Rip off her dress. Bury his face in her sex. Drive into her, over and over again, until they both came.

He looked down at his prize. Licking his lips, he raked his hungry gaze over her. Taking off his jacket and tie, he leaned over to lay them on a nearby chair.

"Hurry," she whispered. "I need you."

She barely registered it when he knocked some papers off the coffee table. But he froze. Turning to the table, he picked up the sheets.

She looked up.

"What is this?" he asked, looking over the papers.

"What is what? Why are you over there and not here?" She was ready for him to come back and help her out of her dress.

"This." He held out a sketch to her.

Lying across the couch, her legs hanging over the arm, she suddenly felt exposed. "It's my sketches for the folk tale I'm working on. The Fae Princess and her Wolf Lord."

He waved the paper in her face. "Why does he look like me?" His face grew dark.

"What?" There was his scowl.

"And you. It's us together." His eyes were smouldering, but not in the way she liked.

"I didn't—" She struggled and sat up to think. "I saw it in a dream. It's what the characters looked like when they came into my mind."

"Before we met?"

"I don't remember. I think I started working on these after I met you the first time."

He moved to the kitchen area and took out his cell. "Gwen? Come to Chantelle's apartment. Right away." He returned and rifled through the pile of sketches.

"I don't understand the problem," Chantelle said. She tried to fix her dress and hair. Something had changed pretty quickly. She felt lost.

He jabbed a finger at the papers. "*This* is what I saw when I kissed you the first time."

"You saw?" She gasped as the details came back to her. Flooding her with images of their kisses—at her house, at his chalet. How could he see the same scenes as she did? That was impossible. What was going on? Could it be that Fated Mates thing people were talking about? *It's not real, though, is it?*

They heard a loud popping noise and a small person, half the size of Charles, stood with them. It was Peaseblossom. They reached for her hand and held it. "Be calm," they whispered, and the adrenaline leaked out of Chantelle, leaving her light and peaceful.

"Pea, what are you doing?" Charles asked.

"*Marc'heg*, she doesn't know. Tread lightly. Touch softly. This moment could change everything."

Pea led Chantelle to the couch and sat her down. "Be still, my queen. Everything's fine." They held her hand and beckoned Charles. "I've been waiting for you to see." When Charles came close, they took his hand as well.

"See what?" Charles asked, his face relaxing. Pea manoeuvred him so that he sat beside Chantelle.

"The tale. The connection. You are the Wolf Lord and she the Fae Queen. You didn't know that?" Pea giggled.

"You're talking about the story?" Chantelle asked. "My granny made that up."

"No, silly. She wrote it down. Two different things."

"But we can't be…those people!" said Chantelle. She was uncertain, but part of her knew it could be true.

Pea nodded. "Yes, you can. You two will unite and protect the kingdom."

"You mean the clan?" asked Charles.

Pea nodded again.

Chantelle knew this couldn't be true. She protested, "That's absurd."

"Ridiculous humans!" said Pea. "You're so stuck on free will. Shifters know there's more to it than that."

"I don't believe in Fated Mates," Charles said. He looked confused but not angry. She felt the same way. Pea's influence was helping them deal with the revelation.

Peaseblossom sighed. "It's happened before and it will happen again. Your foremothers hid the truth from you. But now you're together. And together you must rise up and defeat our foes."

"That's dramatic," said Chantelle.

"And dramatic it will be, m'Lady. Just you wait and see." Pea disappeared in another pop of air. Chantelle stared at Charles, who looked as bewildered as she felt.

Dominick and Derrick let Gwen into the apartment. Chantelle spent the next hour arguing with Gwen and Charles. Why didn't they believe her? She didn't know why she'd made the drawings like that. Maybe her subconscious had conjured it up. But when Gwen probed her and Charles' memories, she confirmed they both had these identical images in their minds. How could that have happened?

She thought back to things that had happened in her childhood. Sometimes she drew events that took place later or she had a flash that she sketched out. Granny Ceci had told her she had a bit of the Fae about her, but she had always thought it was a joke. But Granny had always hugged her when she said it and told her it was their little secret. This must be why.

"Does Pea really know things?" she finally asked.

"They function differently than most of us. Time is different. They can see things not all of us do, but they can't manipulate reality."

"But they can teleport, like in *Star Trek*?"

"Yes," said Gwen. "A rare gift among their species."

Chantelle was more confused after the discussion than before. There were too many unanswered questions. She and Charles weren't destined to be together. Sure, she was drawn to Charles, but that was just physical attraction. And he was generous and kind. But it wasn't more than that.

She needed to get home as soon as possible. Tomorrow morning. She had to get back to her nice, boring life in the village. Leave all the werewolves in the woods.

Chapter Fourteen

Thomas was in his office going through his morning email when he got a call.

"It's Dominick. Can you find Charles? He needs you."

"What did he do this time?" Getting up from his desk he rushed out the door, seeking his link to the Alpha. *In his chalet? No, outside the chalet.* He hurried out of the main lodge towards the central A-frame.

Rounding the side of the Alpha's residence, he found Charles sitting on his back deck looking towards the mountains. Thomas slowed down and walked up to his brother. *Stay cool.*

"Hey, bro. What's up?"

Charles didn't move, just stared into the horizon. "She's going home."

"Okay." Thomas blew out a breath. "What do you need me to do?"

"It's too late. She won't talk to me."

"Are you giving up that easily?"

"She's right. This is too hard. I should just let her go back to her normal life."

"Grand-maman always said that normal is just a setting on a washing machine."

Charles looked up. "Jokes won't help."

Oh, this is bad.

"I don't deserve her. Not after everything I've done," Charles said.

"You've done what you had to do for the pack."

"No, I haven't. I wasn't there for Dad. For Robert." He put his head in his hands.

Thomas sat down. "You couldn't have known. You can't hold yourself responsible for everyone's safety."

"But I —" Charles broke off. "I never told you. Alice made me stay. I was supposed to go with them, but instead I stayed to have sex. Instead of doing my duty, I let my dick make the decisions."

"You've been carrying this burden alone the whole time?" Thomas knew this must have weighed his brother down, stopped him from moving on from his father's death and his break-up with Alice.

Charles didn't answer.

"So now you think you can never love again? Or have sex again?"

"When you put it that way it sounds stupid," Charles raked a hand through his hair. "It's just that everything I touch gets ruined. I can't do that to her too."

"Oh, bro," Thomas said. Charles always had a flair for the dramatic, but he would usually listen to reason. "Will you go and talk to her before she leaves?"

"She's better off without me."

"You're making a big mistake. You know that?"

He put his head in his hands again. "Probably. But what can I do?"

Thomas stood up. "I'll leave you to your wallowing. When you're ready to be a man, let me know." He turned on his heel and walked back towards the main building. *I have to find out how Chantelle is doing.* Could he salvage this for them? Or was it too late?

Thomas walked through the apartment wing. Greeting Derrick and Dominick, he knocked on her door. "Chantelle? It's Thomas. Please let me in." He waited. The door opened just as he was going to knock again. Chantelle looked down the hallway, eyes flashing.

"It's just me," Thomas said, his arms open, palms up. "Can I come in?" She moved aside silently and he entered. "Do you have a minute?"

"I'm packing," she said, moving back towards the bedroom.

"Can we sit down for a minute? Have you had breakfast yet?"

Chantelle turned around. "No, I haven't."

"Let me make you tea, then. Come sit for a minute."

She looked at him, sighed and came over to the kitchen island. He gestured to a stool and she sat down. He tried to keep things bright. "Anything I can I help with?"

Her eyes filled with tears as she bit her lip. *Oh, this is a mess.* Then she started talking. About prophecies and destiny and getting too far over her head. By the time the tea was ready and poured, she had let it all out and the tears had stopped.

He put a cup in front of her. "Drink. Milk and sugar?"

She nodded, watched him fix the cup and then took a sip.

"So," he started, putting some bread in the toaster and finding a jar of peanut butter. "I can understand why you're feeling overwhelmed. This is a lot to take in."

Her shoulders slumped. "I can't be this thing they think I am. I'm just a little nobody."

"*Chère*, you are far from a little nobody. Everyone can see that. Except for you."

She looked in his eyes, searching for something.

"You know, Charles went through something similar when our dad and brother died. Being thrust into a leadership role isn't easy. He could help you understand."

"That was different! He didn't have a choice."

"We all have roles to play. Some we choose and others we don't."

"I don't know what to do," she whispered, tears running down her face again.

He sat down beside her. "What do you usually do? What did Granny Ceci do when something bad happened?"

"We ran and hid. She didn't want the bad guys to find me."

If only these two could see they are both running away from the past, then maybe they could walk together into the future.

"Are you planning to run and hide again?"

She put her head in her hands, elbows on the counter. "Yes. Back to the village. Away from all of you. From him."

"*Chère*, you know that won't solve anything, don't you?"

"What do I do then?"

He could hardly hear her words. He put his arm around her shoulders. "Go home and be with your friends. But don't shut him out. He needs you. Not because you're destined to be soulmates or rule over a magical kingdom. Because he wants to be with you."

She took in a big breath and let it out slowly. "Can I think about it?"

Well, this is some progress. "Will you come back next weekend for the Harvest Moon Fête? As my guest?"

She swallowed. "Okay."

"It's always a lot of fun. Now let's get you packed." He stood up. Crisis averted? Or at least delayed?

"No, you have more important things to do."

"Nonsense! Family is the most important thing." *And helping our Alpha keep his mate is part of that.* He looked over the small suitcase and her art supplies. "Do you have anything else?"

"Clem lent me some clothes. And I don't want the food in the fridge to go bad."

"I can take care of those things." He'd have to get Clem to speak to Chantelle at the Harvest Moon party. See if she could talk some sense into her. He'd work on Charles.

"Oh," she said and her face fell. "The dress Charles gave me for last night."

"He'd want you to keep that. Here, bring it to me and I'll have it put in a proper garment bag and delivered to your house." He smoothed it out.

She rushed back to the bedroom and returned with the dress on the hanger.

When they were ready, they opened the apartment door. Thomas turned to Dominick. "Can you please let Charles know Chantelle is leaving now?" Dominick gave a curt nod and stayed for a moment on his comms while Derrick and Chantelle followed Thomas down the hallway.

"Dominick and Derrick will be staying with you at your house." He looked at Chantelle. "We still haven't stopped the attacks and our pack feels responsible for your safety. Do you understand?"

"Okay, I can live with that." She sighed. "I'll actually sleep better with them there. I'd forgotten what happened with the Trois-Rivières pack while I've been here in the compound."

They walked through the front entrance to the waiting limo. Derrick put the bags in the trunk and opened the car door for Chantelle. "I'll come pick you up for the party, okay?" said Thomas. "You can dance with Clem and Bertrand."

Chantelle looked up at him. "I would like that." She took his arm and patted it before she got into the car.

He tried to keep the smile on his face as she drove away. She waved. He watched her sad, pale face in the window until the car pulled out of sight. He turned back to the lodge and saw Charles behind the doors of the entrance — another sad, pale face caught in glass. Charles had watched her leave. He had let her go.

Chu dans marde. This family has more than its fair share of troubles.

* * * *

Chantelle watched the brightly coloured trees zip past as the limo drove her back to her home. She held back the tears.

So that was it. A week in Wonderland and now it was back to normal life. She was better off without the complications. She knew that, but there was still a part of her that felt like it was a mistake. She tried to shake it off.

She would miss them. Him. His smouldering eyes. His hard muscles. Even his scowl. But most of all she would miss those bright moments when he smiled and lit her up like a Christmas tree. She sighed and turned back to the scenery.

When they arrived at her house, Dominick and Derrick inspected her small property before allowing Chantelle to enter. They showed her how the alarms worked and where they had installed the security cameras. She said it was too much, but Dominick insisted that it would increase her resale value. Any buyer would appreciate being able to keep their summer cabin safe while they were in the city or elsewhere.

"Now, what is this about having the security tied in to the resort? Can you watch me get changed and go to the bathroom and everything?" she asked.

"No." Derrick chuckled. "We have cameras on the entrances as well as all main floor windows. There are perimeter alarms and motion detectors you can turn on and off. And we installed phones with direct lines to security in the bedroom and bathrooms, so you can call and speak to someone twenty-four-seven. But no hidden cameras in bedrooms or bathrooms."

"Okay, that sounds all right."

"We'll be here too. We'll make sure you're safe."

"Will you two play cards with me tonight? I play a mean gin rummy, you know."

"Absolutely." Derrick smiled.

"And I'm having my friends over for our regular Friday pizza and movie date."

Dominick chimed in, "We like pizza and movies!"

"Of course, you can join us. I think you'll like them. Kat is a gorgeous trans woman and Yvette has the cutest daughter. By the way, Kat is single."

"So is Dominick," said Derrick.

"No set-ups, you two," Dominick replied.

Maybe everything would be okay. It would be good to see the youth at the After-School Club again. Her life was busy. She was happy with the way things were.

* * * *

Chantelle had made it to Friday night. Yvette and Nadiya set up the movie and got out the pizza boxes. Dominick was talking with Kat, comparing notes on sourdough bread traditions. Derrick had just got off the phone with his partner.

Her friends had been her rock this week. They had cried and laughed with her. Kept her busy and sane while she mourned for what could have been.

Nadiya whispered something to Yvette and giggled. Yvette looked over, shushing her.

"What are you two conspiring about?" Chantelle asked.

"Nothing!" said Nadiya, a little too loudly.

Chantelle went into the kitchen to grab the bottle of wine for refills. There was a shriek. She came running. "What is it?"

Covering her mouth, Nadiya pointed outside. Her heart racing, she looked in the driveway. There was a large white van pulling in. Kidnappers?

Derrick looked out the window. "It's all right. Just a delivery from the resort. Come with me, Chantelle." She took a big breath and tried to slow her heart. They left the house. Derrick walked to the back of the van, opened the doors and started picking up boxes.

"What are all these things?" she asked.

Someone came around from the side of the van. "They're from me."

She turned. Charles. Looking hot as hell. He was playing the sexy lumberjack card tonight—beanie casually pulled on over his shaggy hair, two-day growth on his chin, and a soft plaid jacket that begged to be touched.

"What are you doing here?" She backed up.

"I came to apologise. Beg, if I have to." He slowly advanced but stopped out of arm's reach. Derrick disappeared inside the house, closing the door behind him. Only she and Charles remained.

"There's nothing to apologise for. It just didn't work out." She stood her ground.

"I should have fought for you. Not retreated into my shell."

"Stop shooting those smouldering rays from your eyes. I don't want them anymore," she said. If only she could convince her body that was true.

"Will you give me another chance?" He took a step forward. She didn't back away, but she didn't close the distance between them. *Câlice, he looks good enough to eat.*

"What's the point? All those things Pea and Gwen said. Those things we saw." She looked at the ground. "I can't be that person for you. For your clan."

"I don't need her. I want *you*." He stepped towards her, reaching up to touch her face. Calloused fingers brushed against her cheek. Sweet friction. He tilted her face up, looking into her eyes. *Damn those smoulder rays.*

She opened her mouth, but nothing came out. He brought her face close to his, breathing in and out. His scent — pine, moss and all male — was intoxicating. She took it in, closing her eyes. Sighed as he brushed his lips so gently against hers. Not closing into a kiss yet. Instead, his tongue licked at her bottom lip. She opened it wider. *More.*

As he pulled her close, she felt a rumble low in his chest, bubbling up to his throat and mouth. It vibrated right through her. How could it feel so good if it was wrong? His lips met hers, crushing and searching, saying all the things he didn't put in words. She melted into him, feeling his warmth course through her. Her breasts ached as she arched into him, his hard chest rubbing against the tips of her nipples. *So tingly! I could get used to feeling this way.*

He broke off and looked at her again. "Will you let me back in? Do you forgive me?"

"I want to try. I won't run away this time."

He slid his arms around her.

When she brought her hand up to cradle his cheek, noises erupted behind her. She looked and saw her friends — Kat and Yvette and Nadiya, Derrick and Dominick — cheering from the picture window. She laughed. "I should be embarrassed. But I'm not." She rested her head on his chest.

"I owe your friends a big thank you. They drove out to the resort this week to give me hell. Told me I was ruining the best thing I'd ever have and I'd better fix it before it was too late."

"They're very protective."

"You deserve it." He kissed her lightly on the top of her head. "Now, I have some presents to deliver." He looked at the crowd in the window and signalled them to come out.

Nadiya came running and arrived first. "Are you Charles? You sure are tall."

Charles bowed low. "It is a pleasure to meet you, Miss Nadiya. I've heard a lot about you."

Nadiya smiled at him and curtsied. She looked shyly back at her mom and giggled as the others reached their place and greeted Charles.

"I've got some things for you here, Nadiya. Give me a minute," he said. He walked back to the van and returned with two large, brightly coloured gift bags. "For you, mademoiselle."

Nadiya thanked him and took the bags. She ripped out the tissue. In one were three giant bags of fancy popcorn and a large assortment of chocolate and candy. In the other were several DVDs.

Charles bent down so he was at eye-level with the girl. "These movies are just being released so I think you won't have seen them yet."

Nadiya's eyes goggled. "How did you get these? They're not out on any streaming services yet."

"Someone who used to work for me. They're a producer now in Toronto."

"Thank you!" Nadiya tried to open the plastic on a DVD with her fingernail, but it snagged. "Ow!" she cried.

"Let me look at it," said Chantelle. Nadiya obediently put out her hand and Chantelle saw blood trickling from a small cut. "It's not too bad. Here." She felt the urge to wrap her hands around Nadiya's finger, pressing on the wound. Warmth surged from her chest and through her arms. Her hands prickled and she felt an overwhelming feeling of love for the little girl. After a minute, she lifted Nadiya's hand up and looked at it. "Your cut is gone." *Did I do that?*

"What?" asked Nadiya. "How did you do that?"

Charles came to look. "Chantelle has some talents that she's just discovering. Does that make you afraid?"

Nadiya looked up at them. "Afraid? No way. This is cool! Look, Mom!" Nadiya showed off her hand. She chattered away to Yvette and Kat as they walked back into the house.

Chantelle looked at him. "That was really nice, what you did for Nadiya."

"You, too." He smiled, the lights in his eyes doing funny things to her stomach.

She helped him bring in the rest of the bags and boxes. Charles tallied up the packages. "We've got more pizza. Plus flowers, chocolate, ice cream and wine. Croissants and bagels for you in the morning. And I brought some bags of books and crafts for the library. Tori thought it looked a little spare in the main room."

She was sure her eyes looked just like Nadiya's had. "You're full of surprises, aren't you?" He smiled like the Cheshire cat. *More tingles.* "What are these other baskets?" she asked.

"Oh, those are for Kat and Yvette." He gave them to the women who oohed and aahed over the luxury spa items he had chosen for them. *More points for the sexy lumberjack.*

"You didn't have to do this, Charles," Chantelle said. Her heart was so full. When had this happened?

"You are generous with your time and your passions. And you have friends who love you. I admire that."

She squeezed his hand. Then they handed out more food and started the film Nadiya chose. Chantelle revelled in sharing the evening with all her favourite people. She didn't know what would happen in the future. But she could enjoy the present now. She would worry about the future later.

* * * *

Charles stood up and stretched when the movie ended. He went to the kitchen, put the dishes in the sink and started the hot water. Light footsteps pattered behind him while he filled up the sink. He caught the scent of lilies and honeysuckle behind him. Chantelle cuddled her front against his back, so yielding and warm. Her hands reached around his waist and then plunged into the soapy water beside him. He ducked when she splashed him.

"Just washing my hands!" She rubbed herself against him. *Little vixen.*

He turned around and put his wet hands on her face, drawing her up for a kiss. He lingered, running his tongue over her lips, then going in to explore every crevice of her mouth. She tasted good — wine, tomato sauce, basil. He could eat her right up.

When he came up for air, he saw Yvette enter the kitchen. She brought herself up short, saying, "Sorry!" Then she put a hand on her cheek. "Oh, I just remembered I have to get Nadiya home now. We have to be up early tomorrow," she said.

Chantelle turned her head, leaning against his chest. She belonged right there. "You don't have to go!" she protested.

"Kat said she had to get to the café early in the morning." Yvette turned around, called for her daughter, then stepped into the living room.

Charles cradled Chantelle for a millisecond, then let her go so they could follow Yvette.

Nadiya packed up her gift bags and looked up at Charles. "Thanks for the movies, Charles."

That was the best part of the night—so far. Pleasing her friends. But maybe there would be better parts with her soon.

Everyone tidied up the living room. Dominick was talking to Kat. Derrick reported that he was heading back to the resort for the night and Dominick would stay at Marie's. "If you need him to come back here, just text. We're not presuming anything but we want to give you your privacy." Charles watched Chantelle blush—she was so adorable when she did that. So many of the women he had dated didn't want privacy. They wanted the whole world to know they were going out with a billionaire. Chantelle was different.

After a flurry of farewells, he was suddenly alone with Chantelle at the door. He wrapped her in his arms. "I thought they'd never leave!"

"I feel bad," Chantelle said. "They practically ran away when we started kissing."

"They looked happy. Besides Kat and Yvette gave me their blessing this week. But if I hurt you, they said they'll show no mercy."

"Kat is scary when she's angry. And Yvette is a typical mama bear. So you'd better be careful."

He gave her a hug, tucking her head under his chin. Just the way he liked to hold her. "I had a great night. I love having a full house. Reminds me of holidays at Grand-maman's." She put her arms around him and it felt like he was home. "When I was a kid, I told Grand-maman that I was going to have ten kids and thirty grandkids."

"Those are some big numbers!" She pulled away, took his hand and led him back to the kitchen.

"I've scaled it back with age. Only seven kids and fifteen grandkids."

"Where are you going to find someone who will give birth to seven of your children? They will be gigantic." She snuggled into him as stood by the sink. He laughed and tickled her, then picked her up.

"Where are you taking me?"

"I think I'll finish the dishes later. Right now, it's time for dessert." He carried her over his shoulder into the living room. She squealed as he deposited her on the couch, then sat beside her.

Chapter Fifteen

Chantelle laughed as Charles deposited her on the couch. "Are we having actual dessert? Or something else?"

"Both," he said. "Stay here." When he went to the kitchen, she sat up. What was he doing? He returned carrying a plate of strawberries and a bowl of whipped cream. *Holy moly!* He made quite a picture as he licked his lips and put the dishes on the coffee table. She squirmed in her seat, her core tingling.

"Was this what you meant the other night when you were talking about licking me all over?"

"Mmm, yes. What do you think?"

"I think you'd better get started." But then she sat up and looked at the floor, her stomach churning.

"Something wrong?" He knelt in front of her and waited.

"It's kind of embarrassing," she said, her face heating up. He reached out, tipped up her chin with a finger and kissed her. *Just get it over with. Deep breath.* "I haven't had a lot of orgasms with someone else for a while."

"Well, you have been single." He kissed her again, short and sweet, and looked at her expectantly.

"It was before that, actually..." She didn't know how to say this.

"You mean—" A look of understanding came over his face.

Before she could change her mind, she said, "My boyfriend, I didn't—"

"Wait, what? Never or not always?"

"Almost never."

"Not even from oral sex?"

She blurted it out. "He said he didn't like going down on me."

Charles cupped her face with his hands and looked deep in her eyes. "*Ca s'peut pas!* What a selfish bastard. A woman's vagina is the most sacred and beautiful thing in the world. It should be worshipped."

Chantelle squirmed, her most sacred thing tingling.

"Since the moment we first touched, I've been dreaming about feasting on your beautiful pussy. Licking and sucking you all night long. Bringing you to multiple orgasms in as many ways as I can think of."

Chantelle's centre pulsated, her panties damp already. *Wo pa laille! This man isn't real, is he?*

He kissed her. "We've got to make up for lost time. Can I kiss you everywhere?" He pinned her with his gaze.

She gulped and stared.

"I think you'll like it. My mouth and tongue have great Yelp ratings."

She giggled. "Yes. You can show me the reviews later."

"Much, much later." He picked her up, as if she were light as a feather, and carried her to the bedroom. "I'll be keeping my pants on. This is all about you."

Oh God! My dreams have come true!

He laid her on the bed and looked her over with hungry eyes. Then he started to peel off her clothes, one piece at a time. Sweater and cami first, so he could run his calloused hands along her smooth torso, sampling her breasts, her shoulders, her arms. She was already humming with pleasure at the attention.

He snapped the button on her jeans. "Lift," he said hoarsely, tugging her jeans down and sliding his deft fingers along her exposed thighs and calves. She gasped as he brought the tip of his nose and his hot mouth along the sensitive inside of her legs. He alternated between feather-light brushes of wet lips over skin and playful nips and licks concentrated on one spot at a time. She thought she might explode. *I can't take much more of this.*

Charles gave a throaty chuckle. "*Chère*, we're just getting started."

How did he know what she was thinking? Maybe she'd said it out loud?

Her legs weakened as he feathered kisses on her knees before moving on to gentle licks and stronger, wetter kisses on her creamy thighs. She shivered with need. He certainly was treating her body like a temple.

Her centre ached. He nipped her outer thigh, now slick and wet, and worked his way quickly from the curve of her hip to the swell of her breasts. She squirmed on the bed, sighing. "You skipped some parts," she said.

"Don't worry, they'll get the attention they deserve. Soon." He laved her right areola, tracing the outline of her engorged breast with his hand. Her firm nipples hardened further under his ministrations. He kissed and tugged until her aroused peak was taut and aching. Every suck jolted like a thunderbolt to her wet pussy. He made his way to her left mound and set about kneading and licking the creamy flesh. She moaned as he settled on the sensitive tip and suckled on it.

He pulled his face up to hers. "Your body is perfect. I could do this all day and night." He kissed her hungrily and disappeared.

"Oh," she sighed, as he kissed her quivering navel and ran a finger underneath the string of her sodden bikini panties. He put a finger from his other hand on the other string and shimmied her panties slowly down her hips and thighs, skimming his hot hands over her waiting curves. He quickly drew the material down her calves then threw them off the bed. He returned and continued to kiss and lick his way down to the downy thatch of hair between her thighs. She trembled as his fingers played with the curls, so lightly it was like a whisper of a touch.

He looked up at her and she hitched in a breath. He smiled wickedly. "Spread your legs for me, beautiful. I want to see it all before I devour you."

"God, yes," she moaned. Shivering, she planted her knees and opened her thighs wide. He brought his face close to the apex of her legs and breathed in. "Mmm, you smell like honey. So luscious. I just want to lap it all up." She moved her hips to bring him closer but he held her tight. "Hold still for me, *chère*. Just like that."

She tried to relax but she was coiled tight in anticipation. She whimpered as he drew a finger along her slickness of her lips, top to bottom and back up to the top. He set to work, first licking her aching clit with his tongue then circling around her lips. She fell down into the sensations as he drew his tongue down her dripping folds to her entrance. She moaned as his fingers moved up to play gently with her swollen clit. The sensitive cluster of nerves throbbed while his tongue lashed around and inside her.

"Feels so good," she sighed, writhing against his mouth.

"You are so wet for me." He moved his tongue to her engorged nub again, using his finger to trace the outside of her entrance. "Do you like this?" he asked, pausing. She nodded, grabbing his hair and running her fingers through it. He devoured her, inserting his tongue in her pussy and licking up all the cream he could take. She started to whimper, pulling him closer. He teased her hard button as he parted her folds with his fingers. When he breathed on her labia, she shuddered again.

"You are so beautiful when I'm pleasuring you," he growled, the vibrations causing her walls to pulse.

"This feels so good," she moaned, writhing against his hand and mouth. Nobody had made her feel like this before. It was like paradise. Her breath started to hitch as he increased the pressure on her clit and picked up the rhythm of his licking and sucking. She thrust against him, groaning.

His tongue speared her, in and out, as he held and massaged her folds with his fingers. Her pussy walls started to clench, a pulsing from deep within her. The tension inside her erupted. She cried out and bucked, shuddering and moaning against his tongue and lips and hands. It was strong and fierce and beautiful. She thought it would go on forever. As she crested the waves, he eased off slowly, following her lead down to stillness. "Oh my God," she said, heart pounding. She was completely and thoroughly sated.

He flopped on the bed beside her. "I could lap you up all day long." He pulled her to him and rested his mouth on top of her head, kissing her hair.

"I didn't know it could be like this," she whispered. Her body felt like jelly.

"It can be really great. When both of you want the same thing and take your time. Women take longer to become aroused and climax, but that just makes it more fun."

"Thank you," she said.

"No need to thank me. It's my job, ma'am." He chuckled.

After a few minutes he sat up. "Can I leave you here for a few minutes while I clean up?"

"Are you sure you don't want—"

"No, that was perfect."

"What about you?"

"I can take care of myself later," he said. "I'm a big boy."

"Yes, you are a big boy. I've seen you naked. Why don't you do it now." She sat up and stroked the bulge in his pants. "I could watch you." She licked her lips suggestively. She wanted to do this for him, to let him know how much she appreciated his gift.

"God, I want to," he growled. "You are so sexy."

"I have another idea." She sat up on her knees and took hold of his hands.

"I want you to think about me while you stroke yourself in the bathroom right now." She took his hand and put it between her legs, rubbing his fingers against her slippery folds. When he wiggled his hand against her swollen lips, she gasped.

He caught her mouth in a deep kiss. "You're still sensitive. I can take you over the edge again."

"Oooohhh." She rubbed his fingers along her damp cleft, back and forth. He increased the pressure, nipping at her mouth at the same time.

"I don't think I can—"

"Yes, you can," Charles said. "You are passionate and full of fire. Let yourself feel it."

"Oh, it feels glorious." She kissed him, rocking back and forth against his hand.

He reached his other hand to grab the curve of her buttocks. "Do you know how much I love seeing and touching your ass? I just want to squeeze it all night long." She breathed into his mouth, bouncing up and down against his hand. "Fingers. In me now," she whimpered, burning with need.

He moved his free hand from her cheeks down the crevice towards her pussy. She couldn't wait much longer. She was on the edge, her pussy walls starting to clench, as he reached in and thrust two fingers in her channel. *Yes.* She rubbed her tender breasts against his chest, moaning.

"Fuck," he said. "Come for me now, *chère.*"

She cried out and grabbed his shoulders as her pussy convulsed around his fingers. Cream gushed as she moaned in his arms. She had never climaxed twice in a row. This was the best she had ever felt in her life.

Still shuddering from the aftershocks, she reached over and undid his pants, pulling them down to his thighs. "Now take my cum and spread it on your big cock. I want you to feel me all around you, smell my scent while you stroke yourself until you come."

He growled, kissed her roughly and practically ran to the bathroom. She collapsed on the bed, all her bones turned to liquid.

Charles thought he'd died and gone to heaven as he went to Chantelle's bathroom and closed the door. That gorgeous woman was doing things to him that nobody else had ever done — touched parts of him that had been locked up for so long. It wasn't just the sex, even though that was scorching hot. She had a body to die for. She was so responsive — she showed him what she liked and loved what he did to her.

It had taken a lot of willpower not to take his raging erection and thrust it deep inside her beautiful pussy. He liked giving her pleasure. It was so sexy. His father had told him that the key to a successful relationship was to put your partner's needs first. Then, after she had had an explosive orgasm, she wanted to make sure he was satisfied too. That was so special. He had practically climaxed in his pants when she rubbed his fingers all over her soaking pussy.

He had left his pants in the bedroom. He pulled himself free from his boxers in the bathroom. Fisting his swollen and throbbing cock, he stroked it, slicking her sweet juices all over. His member grew larger and more rigid as he remembered how she had taken command then. It would only take a few strokes to reach his climax. He rubbed his cock, jerking and moaning as he remembered her shining eyes and parted lips when she came. He squeezed and thrust his hips back and forth, moaning. With one long exhale, he shot ropes of thick, white cum all over the mirror and sink, groaning with release.

God, I needed that. It was such a turn-on the way she wanted to be included in the act. She was so generous and sexy. Screw it, he should just go back to her bed and spend all night fucking her, listening to her sexy moans and feeling her enticing pussy clench around his cock. He was starting to get aroused again just thinking about it.

No, he had to get his head on straight. That was how he had ruined his last relationship. He should take it slow, give themselves time for an emotional connection to develop. He splashed his face with cold water and quickly cleaned himself up. He put his boxers back on and wiped up the bathroom. He was going to need a cold shower when he got to Grand-maman's.

He brought Chantelle a warm, wet washcloth and wiped her folds and thighs before settling in beside her. He put his arms around her and she snuggled in, looking sleepy.

"Do you want me to stay?" he asked.

"I'm not sure I'm ready for that."

"I'll just cuddle you for a while before I go. You are so sexy." He held her close.

"My last boyfriend said I was cold."

"He was a coward. He should have stood up like a man and taken responsibility for cheating on you."

"Rationally, I know you're right, but emotionally…."

He tipped her head up and kissed her. "Every time I look at you, I just want to eat you up, crush your body against mine and suck all the sexy I can get from you."

"You make me want to do all kinds of naughty things, too."

He rested his head on hers, gathered her up even closer in his arms and leaned back on the pillows.

She cuddled up, sighing. "Stay for a little longer, just like this."

After a few minutes, she was asleep. He looked at the trusting, vibrant creature in his arms. His wolf was right—she was the one. Every fibre of his being told him that.

But could he hang on to her? Could he get her to see that they belonged together? They were meant to be mates, he knew it. He'd just have to keep her satisfied and coming back for more. Romance her, sate her delectable body and stay by her side until she was ready for a commitment.

She stirred a little in his arms and he hugged her gently. Nuzzling his nose in her hair, he breathed in her perfect scent. He'd stay here for a few more minutes. Then he'd go to his cold and lonely bed at Grand-maman's.

He closed his eyes. Just a few more minutes in paradise.

* * * *

Chantelle woke up to the smell of coffee. She hadn't slept that well in a long time.

She could hardly hear Dominick and Derrick in the kitchen—just a murmur of voices. Usually, they were arguing about world affairs by now. Maybe they thought she wanted to sleep in. She pulled on a T-shirt and boy shorts and padded down the hallway.

Charles was at the stove. He looked put together already, in a new button-down with the sleeves rolled up and tailored to hug his muscular frame. His form-fitting khakis also enhanced the view as he made breakfast for the two large men – her men – sitting at the tiny kitchen table.

"Hi," she said.

Charles turned around. "Good morning!" He walked towards her, swooped her up off her feet and kissed her. Hard.

"You look great. All dishevelled and sexy. I want to carry you off to your room and spend the whole day there." He nuzzled her ear for a moment, hot breath blowing on her neck, then set her down on one of the kitchen chairs.

Dominick had already taken over at the stove. Derrick moved over so Charles could sit beside her. Chantelle reddened, thinking that they probably knew what had happened between her and Charles. But when she looked at Derrick, she saw no judgement, no disappointment, only happiness for her. Her heart glowed.

"Grand-maman sent over some loaves of bread," Charles said.

"That's so nice of her." Just as generous as her grandson – but in different departments.

"After breakfast, I have to head back to the resort. Dominick and Derrick are staying with you," Charles said.

"They must have better things to do. Nothing's happened all week!"

Derrick turned around from the stove and gave her a stern look. "No arguments!"

She lifted up her hands in surrender.

"I'm going to be busy today. Thomas said he's picking you up for the Harvest Moon Party tonight, right?"

"Yes," she said.

He beamed, lighting her all the way from the top of her head to the tip of her toes. Derrick served up the plates of food. They ate and chatted until Charles had to leave. He kissed her, picked her up from her seat, and carried her to the door with him. Putting her down, he folded her in his arms and kissed the top of her head.

"See you tonight," he said.

She closed the door behind him and went to get dressed. Today was going to be a great day.

* * * *

Charles pulled out of Chantelle's driveway and thought about this amazing woman. How could she be so perfect? He counted his lucky stars to be this blessed. Now if he could find a way not to blow it and get her to open up to him completely.

She was still shy about making a commitment, Lord knew, but when she opened up, she was crazy sexy and totally worth waiting for. And he had to work on his control issues too.

He turned onto the highway back to the resort. Tonight would be important. How could he make her know how much he cared? How much he wanted her? She didn't care about material wealth. She cared about the little things — meeting her friends, remembering things she told him, bringing her little treats to say he was thinking of her. He'd have to step this up if he wanted to impress her tonight.

When he got to his office, Henri was waiting for him. "Did you do it last night?"

"You are obsessed with my sex life."

"Well, you need to take it to the next level ASAP. Lock her down before you lose her."

"What are you talking about?"

"You think she's the one? Fuck her brains out and make her stay." Henri crossed his arms.

Charles stepped in closer. *I'm going to punch that smug smile right off his face. He can't talk about fucking and my Chantelle in the same sentence.*

Henri backed up. "Whoa, bro. I'm just sayin' you got to use your moves."

"Believe me, I am. But she's still skittish so I have to give her some space."

"She's coming to the Harvest Moon Fête tonight?"

"Yes."

"Okay, that's your chance to 'woo her'." Henri used air quotes. "You're not getting any younger. We're all counting on you."

"Don't tell me that! It's like I'm an old widower that everyone pities."

Henri patted him on the back. "Yep, in a couple of years that'll be you. So show her what you've got at the Fête."

"I'll think of something," he said. Maybe Clem or Thomas could help.

Chapter Sixteen

Chantelle waited for Thomas to arrive. Her friends had come by to help her get ready. Nadiya took a dozen photos, making her twirl and pose. She felt silly, but it was fun.

"It's just a regular outfit," Chantelle said.

"But it's a big date with Charles!" Nadiya replied.

"We want to hear all about it when you get home," Kat said. "Well, tomorrow. Not tonight." She waggled her eyebrows.

"All right." Chantelle looked for her coat. "I feel like a puffball. I have to put on some heavy layers since the party's outdoors." But she had her prettiest and laciest balconette bra and matching thong underneath her off-the-shoulder silk tee and best jeans. She wanted to be prepared for whatever might come later.

When the doorbell rang, she opened the door.

"M'Lady, your escort has arrived," Thomas said. He made an elaborate bow and offered her his hand. He was dressed in muted flannels and denim.

"I've only seen you in a suit," she said. "This is a nice change."

"For me, too. I'm just as much a workaholic as Charles is."

"Thanks so much for coming to get me."

"Charles was sorry he couldn't do it. He has to get ready for the performance — he goes on at the start."

Chantelle said goodbye to her friends and closed the door. They were going to lock up for her after she left. "I can't wait to hear Charles play."

"It's one of the few times he lets loose."

It would be nice to see him having fun. Thomas opened her car door and she got into the stretch limo. He went around and got into the other side. "Do you want a drink? Champagne? Beer?"

"A soft drink would be nice."

He poured them each a soda and studied her. "You look happy."

"I think I am."

"Is he behaving?"

"Yeah, it's still confusing — too little and too much all at once."

"That's Charles. He's a special person, but he's afraid to open himself up."

Chantelle bit her bottom lip. "My last boyfriend really screwed me up. I don't want to fall into something like that again."

"The whole community puts their trust in him every day. He doesn't disappoint them."

"I'm afraid I'll get hurt."

"Aren't we all?" He squinted his eyes. "Believe me, if Charles did that to you, then I would murder him. You are a treasure — you deserve all the beauty and happiness in the world."

"You look just like Charles when you say that."

"Did I mention you have great taste?"

The time passed quickly while they chatted. When the car stopped inside the resort, Thomas came around and helped her out of the limo. Laughter and song wafted up from behind the lodge.

They followed the sounds of music and talking behind the main lodge and towards the woods. At the back of the complex, there was a large open area illuminated by dozens of strings of twinkly lights. Chantelle breathed in the crisp air, a tinge of acrid smoke carrying across it. A perfect night. A stage was set up at the far end and on the right were tables laden with food and drink. Smoke wafted from the large bonfire, fenced in to keep anyone from falling into it.

It reminded Chantelle of one of the scenes in her granny's stories, when the loups-garous and seigneurs gathered to celebrate the Harvest Moon in New France, before the English invaded. Her heart sped up. This must be the same party—later generations had continued the festive tradition. In the tale, the seigneurs waged battle against a group of corrupt friars who had turned the town against them. She wondered why loups-garous in the early stories were persecuted by religious men, accused of hurting townspeople and performing the work of the devil. Was it scapegoating, cutting down those who opposed the Catholic Church? Priests were rich and powerful in the early settler days.

She followed Thomas over to his family, waiting near the stage for Charles to play. Bertrand brought her a plate and Clem poured her a cider from the keg. She nibbled and made small talk until somebody turned on a microphone.

One of the Elders — a Joshua somebody — introduced the first act. Charles strode on stage carrying his fiddle, followed by several other musicians. Chantelle saw an accordion, guitar, mandolin and some singers. Everyone clapped and whistled. Charles counted them in and they started playing traditional Quebec jigs, then a call and response number. He was fantastic — so animated, so engaged with his band, so energised by the crowd. Her heart raced.

Chantelle turned to Clem. "He's really good!"

"I wish he took more time to play. He's been working so hard since my uncle passed."

"Grief is strange — it can hit you at weird times. It makes you act in unusual ways."

Clem gave her a hug. "I'm glad you're here. I think it's good for both of you."

Chantelle hugged her back, saying, "Me too." She hoped things worked out with Charles. She was starting to fall in love with his family too.

Thomas asked her to dance. Clem held her drink and he whisked her away, the music swirling around them.

Charles fiddled and watched Chantelle dancing with his family. His heart warmed as he saw her laughing. She had been through so much — his tender, tough flower.

After the set was done, he rushed to pack away his fiddle and thank his musicians. He found Chantelle talking with Henri. His wolf huffed happily. *Packmates care for mate, too.* Yes, that was true.

"You were amazing!" Chantelle hugged him.

"I had a great time. I'm going to try and relax for the rest of the night." She felt so right in his arms. He could hold on to her forever.

"I will too — not think, just have fun."

He pulled her onto the dance floor and they joined the contradance, laughing and twirling together. When a slow song started, he pulled her in close. Burying his face in her hair, he breathed in her scent, saying, "You always smell so good." She was strength and beauty in one amazing package. When he ran a hand down her side, she tucked her head into his chest so he could rest his chin on her crown. It was like she belonged there. It felt so right.

When the song ended, she looked up at him. "Do you have to stay for the whole party? Or can you leave early?"

He grabbed her hips and pressed her against him. His cock was already hard. He moved his hands up to her face and kissed her. "We can go any time you want." *Say now.* She stepped back and put out her hand. He took it and led her away from the dancers, past the tables and twinkly lights, and towards the semicircle of chalets. He thought his heart would burst.

When they were in sight of his chalet, he stopped and pulled her in for a kiss. She tasted like honey and flowers. He scooped her up in his arms, kissed her again, and carried her to his door. He couldn't wait to get her in his bed — it had been a long time coming and he was going to make sure it was perfect for both of them.

I'll make this the best night of her life. Then she'll fall for me the way I've fallen for her.

Chantelle held on tight as Charles carried her into the chalet. She felt light as a feather in his arms. They pulled off their toques and jackets and threw them by the door. They kissed again and started fumbling with their tops. Chantelle unbuttoned his shirt and Charles pulled off her tee, revealing a satin cami underneath. She shivered as he slid his capable hands down her bare arms.

"You play that fiddle like the devil. Those fingers…so talented." She giggled. "I think I had a little too much cider."

"Do you want to sober up? I could put the kettle on." He started to pull her towards the kitchen, still kissing her.

"No, no," she said. "It was only two glasses. It's helping me to not overthink things and just enjoy myself." She waggled a finger. "You don't let go enough."

"You don't either," he said, then his mouth claimed hers, greedy, demanding. He tasted like whisky and smoke. Sweet and tart at the same time.

"I haven't been with anyone else for months," Charles said, breaking off their kiss.

"It's been longer for me. I'm on the pill so we don't have to worry about getting pregnant."

"Do you want me to use a condom?" Charles asked.

"No. I want it to be just you and me, nothing between us." This was a big step, but she was ready. She wanted to have all of him, body and soul.

Charles lifted her up in his strong arms and sped them into his bedroom. She looked around and her heart fluttered. There were flameless candles all around the room, twinkly lights on the four-poster bed and rose petals on the bed covers. Champagne was chilling in a bucket with glasses on the bench at the end of the bed. A fire roared in the fireplace. Anita Baker sang on the stereo.

"This is so beautiful! You didn't have to."

"I wanted to." He placed her gently on the bed. She revelled in the feel of the silky rose petals, satin coverlets, and a faux-fur throw. He lay down beside her, those amazing eyes shining in the lights. She kissed him again, running her tongue along his open lips. Then she pushed him back and climbed on top to straddle his muscular form.

"Charles?"

"*Oui, chére?*"

"I want you to lie back and give you a gift." She shifted position, feeling her core heating up from his warmth beneath her.

"No," he said, pushing up on his elbows.

"Just let go. Give in to me." She ran her hands along the hard ridges of his chest.

He half sat up as his smoky eyes pierced into her soul. "I'll make you a deal. I'll lie back if you'll stay the night."

She paused for a moment. Was she ready? "Okay." It felt right. *I can do this.*

"*Chère.*" When he raised his head, she pushed him down by the shoulders. She felt sexy and powerful as she lowered the straps of her satin cami. He licked his sinful lips and she shivered, thinking of what he could do with that mouth. She let the satiny material fall down to her waist as he gyrated underneath her, moaning with pleasure. Crossing her arms, she pulled down her lacy bra straps and eased her arms out, letting her bared breasts fall forward. He looked at her with heavy-lidded desire. She leaned down and held his arms down beside his torso, brushing her tight nipples against his muscular chest. He groaned and wriggled but didn't push her way.

I think he likes this.

She slowly lowered first one plump mound then the other to his eager mouth, drawing away before he could take a deep taste. When she leaned over again, he took a nipple between his wet lips. She gasped as he circled her areola and lapped at the stiff peak.

"You know I like that, don't you?" she asked huskily as he continued his attention. Her breasts ached, their throbbing nubs responding to his lips and tongue. Arching into him, she felt the sensations reach all the way down her core. The moistness between her legs trickled into her panties. She wanted more. She wanted all of him. She stopped, climbed off and shimmied down her jeans.

His eyes smouldered as he looked at her in only the lacy thong. "I'm going to make sure you have several orgasms tonight."

"Oh." She froze in place. Her thoughts wandered, then she shook her head. "No distracting me. And take off your pants." After he had followed her commands, she resumed her position on top of him. The little scrap of thong fabric was so thin between his chiselled abs and her most tender flesh. When she caressed his smooth chest, he closed his eyes and pumped his hips up and down.

"It's my turn to pleasure you." She sighed. "I'm going to take you in my mouth and suck you until you come. Then I'll swallow you all down."

"Wait," he said.

"No, I'm in charge."

He groaned. "Ah, *cherie*, I can't stand it." He gripped her hips, moved her down and gyrated his pelvis against her. *Boy, that feels good. Too good. Wait, is there such a thing as too good with this man?* She scooted down and pulled down his boxers. His large, erect penis sprang out, surrounded by dark, curly hair. He was bigger than she remembered from the wolfhandling incident. Or maybe it was warmer in here?

She wondered if she could take him all. She wanted to find out. Pulling his boxers all the way off, she looked up at him. He moaned, his eyes lidded with desire.

"Mmm, that looks tasty," she said, licking her lips. She got close and breathed in his earthy scent.

"*Chère*, give me a minute. I'm going to come as soon as you touch me."

She flipped her hair so it brushed his cock. "No. You just wait." She reached out to the heavy purple tip of his cock and touched the slit with her finger, taking the droplets of precum and rubbing them around the head. He groaned again.

"You make the sweetest sounds," she breathed as she leaned down to lick his entire length.

"*Ostie!*" he swore.

"Such language." She grinned as she bent close and breathed in his salty scent. She reached one hand around him and his shaft grew as he moaned. Gripping the base, she opened her mouth wide and took in his engorged head. He was big and firm, smooth and velvety. Just perfect. She slid her hand up and down while she sucked on his fullness. As she tasted his throbbing erection, she didn't think she could get even more aroused, but his rigid flesh and salty taste made her slick pussy quiver.

"Oh, *chérie*, I can't wait!" He groaned. Pulling him further in, she licked and sucked at his length. He thrust his shaft in and out, losing himself and groaning with desire. "I'm going to come—" He thrust two more times as she fondled his taut ball sac. His cock was as hard as steel and she knew it was time. When his body bucked and he exploded in her mouth, she swallowed him down. Her channel clenched as she kept up the suction with her lips and tongue. It felt so right to do this for him. He was a beautiful man inside and out.

When he was spent, he looked down at her, chest heaving and eyes wide. "*Chère*, that was the best thing in the world. I loved seeing you loving me like that."

She smiled, climbed up and flopped down beside him. "That's what happens when you don't try to control everything."

He kissed her like his life depended on it. After his breathing had settled, he growled, "Come here, you sexy minx." She loved his silly pet names. He sat up and pulled her into his bulging arms. Then he gently flipped her over and moved her further up the bed, facing the upholstered headboard. He arranged her hands on top of the panel. After running his rough, greedy hands over the swell of her breasts and the curves of her hips, he positioned her in a kneeling position and traced along her sensitive buttocks with his fingers, making her throb with anticipation. Her breath hitched as she imagined what might come next.

He crouched behind her and ran a long finger down the lacy string of the thong, from the curve of her waist down her backside to her aching pussy. His fingers pushed the material to the side then slid into her waiting folds. He slowly probed her slippery channel. Her tight passage pulsed around him. She whimpered when he withdrew his deft fingers, feeling so empty, needing more.

"So wet," he breathed. "I'm going to lick off all of your cream." She gasped as she heard him sucking and humming behind her. She was going to come before he even fucked her. He moved, taking her knees and spreading them wider. The bed jostled then he was lying down on the bed, his head between her trembling thighs.

"Oh God," she said.

He reached up and parted her wet folds as he positioned her sex over top of his mouth. "You are so sweet. I can't get enough." He lapped at her slick, wet heat and she shuddered.

"You make me so hot," she sighed.

When he made long strokes with his tongue, she bounced a little, whimpering. Reaching one hand up to fondle a swollen breast, he used the other hand to play with her throbbing clit. She gasped as he teased her sensitive nipple. *So good.* How did he know what she wanted?

She gripped the headboard and started to gyrate on top of him as his tongue tantalised her. Losing herself in a rhythm of thrusts, she started to spiral upward. He moved his hand from her breast to grip her fleshy buttocks, squeezing a cheek while continuing to lick and suck her pussy. She had never felt this good before. She moaned and panted as he continued to lash her with his tongue. When he worked his fingers into her, she started climaxing, throwing back her head and gripping the headboard like a life raft. Her pussy walls clenched, her muscles convulsing as her cum flowed down her thighs. He lapped her up, stroking and sucking until she started coming down. When the waves subsided, she reached down to touch his cheeks, breathing out a big breath.

Then she scooted down and laid her body along his, her head on his chest. They lay like this for precious minutes, just the two of them in the whole world. Then she pulled herself up and kissed him. "More," she said.

He laid her on her back and straddled her on his knees. Charles brought her aching nipples to attention, the buds snapping up — one in his mouth, the other in his hand — and bringing aftershocks to her pussy. Then he was kissing her. She tasted herself on his tongue and lips. It made her even hotter to know he had brought her to ecstasy so easily. When she felt his rigid shaft against her thigh, she moved to open her legs and hooked them around his waist. He moaned and brought his hips down, rubbing the tip of his cock on her sensitive clit, all around the hood. She gyrated and he rumbled his approval.

She moved her centre up and forward so that his cock was positioned at the entrance to her pussy. She sighed as he held still. "More," she moaned.

"Yes." He thrust in — slowly — inch by delicious inch. He was big. She was glad he had brought her to climax already. Her pussy was relaxed and wet, adjusting to take his large size. He took his time, thrusting in a little at a time until she had enclosed him to his hilt. "Oh, so perfect. You fit me like a glove." He moaned. It was glorious having him fill her up like that. His eyes were half-closed with desire, his teeth biting his lower lip as he kept himself in control inside of her. She put a finger to his mouth. He opened and sucked on it greedily, making her liquid flow all around his cock.

They began moving together, starting with slow thrusts, but soon neither could hold back as they bucked and gyrated together. Panting, he grabbed onto her hips and thrust deep inside her. She climbed higher, over top of the last orgasm, so that when this one came it was earth-shattering. Her pussy clenched and throbbed around him. She grabbed his shoulders and her legs clung to his hips and buttocks. Her walls kept pulsing, as she floated away in waves of ecstasy.

When she looked up in his smoky eyes — glinted with a bit of yellow — he whispered, "*Caradec.*" Then he was spurting into her, filling her up with hot jets of seed. She held on to him, revelling in the intense, delicious sensations. She thought it might never end. She didn't want it to.

He turned them so they were on their sides, cradling her in his arms. Snuggling up, she sighed. She had put her fears aside for the night and enjoyed herself. Not worrying about the past or the future, she had just focused on her needs and her pleasures. Something inside her eased and she fell gently to sleep.

An hour later, she roused to kisses down her chest as he woke her to do it all again, delivering on his promise of multiple orgasms. Afterwards they lay spooning, skin-to-skin. This was everything she had ever wanted. What she had been waiting for all her life. As Charles nuzzled behind her ear, they fell asleep again, exhausted.

Chapter Seventeen

Charles had been asleep for a couple of hours when she stirred. He snapped awake when she sat up.

"Something's wrong," she said.

As soon as the words were out of her mouth, Thomas opened the door to his bedroom. Charles jumped up. His phone and comms were downstairs. *Tabernak.* He rushed to the door.

"Code Forty-Two," Thomas said. "We've got teams out but objective still unclear."

"Chantelle is in my bed. I can't leave her alone." He felt his heart pounding. He had the urge to go to Chantelle and take her somewhere far away.

Thomas spoke on the comms. He turned back. "Derrick and Dominick are on their way. When they arrive, rendezvous at Head Security and we'll update you then." He slipped away.

Charles returned to the bed and kissed Chantelle. She looked so beautiful and pure that he wished he could just stay there forever.

"*Chérie*, I need you to get up. You have to go to the basement." He started to get dressed.

"I don't know where I put my clothes." She was only half awake.

"Here, take my T-shirt."

She put it on and it went down to her knees. *She looks adorable. Can't I just pull her back into bed?* She looked around, found her panties and put them on. "What kind of danger is it?" His cock grew hard at the memory of her little lace thong. *I don't have time to think about that.*

"An attack. I don't have details yet. Once you're safe, I'll find out more." He drew her close for one last kiss.

When Derrick and Dominick entered, he looked at them.

"We'll keep her safe," said Derrick.

Turning back to his beautiful woman, he squared his shoulders. "Chantelle, they're going to take you to the basement." *Please, don't let anything happen to her.*

"Don't you think they would be better used elsewhere? I'm not that important."

Derrick and Dominick looked at him. Dominick said slowly, "It's protocol. You can't be on your own during a Code Forty-Two."

Chantelle bobbed her head, her face turning pale.

He plastered a smile on his face. "Everything'll be fine. Just stay with them."

Derrick and Dominick put her between the two of them, pulled out their guns and took her out of the bedroom. Charles said a prayer, finished getting dressed and slipped out to the main lodge.

Chantelle followed Dominic and Derrick down the stairs. She kept a hand on Dominick's back as he walked ahead of her down the stairs.

When they paused on the main floor, Derrick touched her shoulder, speaking quietly. "We've got security coming. They're our team. I'd put my life in any of their hands." He tried to smile at her. She smiled back but she was sure it looked like she was grimacing. She'd had a bad feeling when she woke up. Was it a dream? A flash? There wasn't time to think about it now.

"Thanks, guys," she said. "We can keep moving."

They progressed to the back of the chalet and down the stairs to the basement. It looked like any old cellar space — musty concrete, wispy cobwebs and rickety wooden stairs. Dominick took Chantelle to the back of the space, farthest away from the stairs. Derrick moved under the stairs and opened up a weapons locker. When Chantelle was seated behind a workbench Dominick turned and flipped open a panel on the wall behind her. Behind the panel was a bank of monitors and a shelf with communication devices. Dominick flicked on the monitors and they could see the front and back entrances as well as individual rooms in the chalet. Dominick pulled out a headset from the shelf and got on the comms to update Head Security.

When he finished his update, he turned to Chantelle. "So? You were sleeping over?"

Chantelle's face got hot and she looked down at the ground.

"Don't be embarrassed. The boss man is a good guy. You two look really cute together."

This was weird. But she was glad her men approved. That was weird, too. When had she become so involved with everyone here?

"I know I can't protect your heart, but I'll always have your back." He turned back to the monitors and adjusted the earpiece for his comms.

Chantelle blinked, trying to stop the tears from falling. She had never felt this way before. To know that she had people who would protect her, who would care for her, who might love her.

* * * *

Charles made his way across the compound and opened the door to the Head Security Office. Thomas and Michel were looking at the monitors. On the screens he could pick out Juana, Clem and Henri leading their teams. Two other teams were heading out of the main lodge.

Michel filled him in. The wires had been tripped a mile out. There were at least two groups of attackers, one coming from the woods behind the complex and another heading for the fence by the Harvest Fête area. Shifters. Their goal wasn't clear yet.

Charles paid attention to the briefing but his mind was racing. He kept thinking about Chantelle and how frightened she must be. She looked pale but alert on the security feed from his chalet. He knew she was strong. But he couldn't stop himself—he wanted her here with him.

"Michel, I should be with Chantelle." He paced the small room.

"The emergency protocol we developed includes arrangements for significant others for clan leaders. You know this."

"I still don't like it," he growled.

"You have to live with it. A full team is with her at your chalet. They're in position now."

"I know, I just can't help it. I need to be there with her." Why didn't they understand?

Michel and Thomas exchanged looks. Thomas started speaking but then they heard something over the comms.

"They've turned off power to the residences," Thomas reported.

Charles focused on the monitors. "They cut the lines to the perimeter alarms and made their way to the boundary check-in points. They must have our security codes." This was bad news.

"They have help from the inside," Thomas said. "Otherwise, how could they—"

"More news." Michel held up a hand and listened to his headset. "Team Delta has identified the attackers as members of the Trois-Rivières pack."

"Do we know what they're after yet?" Charles said looking at the screens. "Wait, what's going on at my place?"

Several dark shapes gathered in front of the Alpha's chalet. One shifted to human form and gained entry to the back door. The intruders made their way quickly and quietly into the residence where his mate waited.

* * * *

Chantelle was crouched in the basement watching Dominick and Derrick talk in low voices with the other members of their team. Dominick identified them in a low voice as they took positions. Two pairs stayed upstairs—Jade and Alfonso by the front door and Nasir and Jean at the back. Monique and Jordan flanked the stairs in the cellar.

Dominick reported from the comms that the attackers had entered the other side of the compound. The power went off and the auxiliary generator kicked in. Dominick told Chantelle to relax, but said they still had to be prepared for anything.

"We'll be fine, see?" Derrick called from his location by the stairs.

Dominick whistled low and Derrick sprinted over. A small group of wolves had made their way towards Charles' chalet. The guards in the basement went quiet and took up their positions. Derrick came back. He and Dominick flanked Chantelle while the other guards spread out by the stairs. Chantelle couldn't breathe. She huddled over, covered her face and gasped for air.

"Six wolves at the front door." Dominick's mouth was set in a grim line. The invaders were silent and fast. Derrick and Dominick moved in front of Chantelle and their team checked their weapons.

"What do I do?" asked Chantelle.

"You stay behind us, no heroics," Derrick said firmly. "I'm putting a gun beside you. Don't touch it unless you need it."

"Granny Ceci taught me to use a rifle when I was growing up."

"Of course she did. Don't forget the safety."

Chantelle nodded. She had never shot a creature, just old cans and homemade targets. But this could be life or death.

"Don't worry," Dominick said. "We'll take care of these attackers. You won't have to do anything."

Chantelle crouched on the floor, her heart racing. She had confidence in her men. It was hard to wait, not knowing what would happen. On the monitor, the scene played out upstairs. A human forced open the door and led six wolves into the chalet. Jade and Alfonso took out two of them, but when the others entered, they moved to hand-to-hand combat. When the claws dug in, they had to shift in the middle of the battle. They were beautiful in their ferocity.

After the struggle, there were three attackers left and more had arrived. Jade was down and Alfonso was doing first aid as the wolves pushed past them. Another half-dozen wolves gained entry to the chalet. She felt anger bubbling up inside her again, like when the wolves had attacked her in Marie's meadow. Fear held her tight at the same time. Gwen had been working with her on focusing, so she took some cleansing breaths and tried to concentrate. It wouldn't help if she lost control and let her emotions take over.

Dominick turned and squeezed her hand before he moved silently to the stairs. Derrick stayed in front her, holding her behind him. The first two wolves came down and were quickly dispatched. Dominick nodded. Monique and Jordan shifted into wolf form. He remained in position with firearms in both hands.

When the other wolves came down together, Dominick and Derrick's team was outnumbered. The noise and motion were unbearable — fur flying, snarls and snaps as wolves rolled together, shots firing in the enclosed space. She felt the tide turning and her team losing ground. There were too many attackers and not enough of the good guys.

Chantelle felt the prickles building up. The familiar warmth spread through her centre. It felt different this time as it moved through her body to her hands. Bigger. Scarier. Better.

The buzzing roared in her ears and the energy built up in her chest. She tried to control her heart, tamp down her emotions. But the energy wouldn't stay put. It flowed down her arms to her hands. She could feel it moving, coursing through her. It made her feel strong, powerful.

When the energy started pulsing, she raised her hands and pointed them at the attackers. The energy surged out from her centre. She closed her eyes to focus, keeping the scene in her mind's eye. She imagined red lights pushing out from her hands, wrapping around the attackers, knocking them down.

When she pushed out, the force of the energy knocked her back against the wall. Dizzy, she opened her eyes and took in the room. Her ears still buzzed so the sounds around her were muted. But her team was bustling around the basement. What had happened?

She looked around the cellar. Derrick was okay. The wolves—the attackers—were down, knocked out. Were they alive? Dead? It was hard to tell. Monique and Jordan, still in wolf form, snarled around the bodies. Thank God they were okay, just a little blood.

Where was Dominick? Her heart pounding, she saw him on the ground, his leg torn up. He had to be okay. Was he still breathing? How much blood had he lost? When Derrick went to check on him, all she could do was watch, unmoving and panicky. She could hear again, but her team was quiet, like the silence after a storm.

"He's got a deep leg wound but he's going to be okay." Derrick opened his mouth again, looked back at her then closed it.

Chantelle let out a big whoosh of air. She could breathe again. Putting her face in her hands, she crouched against the wall. She would never have forgiven herself if he hadn't made it.

Derrick tapped his comms. "We're safe. But when the resort is secured, the Alpha needs to come back to his residence. Chantelle is fine. But we need to talk."

Derrick touched Chantelle's arm and she looked up. "I don't feel so good," she said. She blinked a few times and slid into unconsciousness.

* * * *

Charles watched the monitors in the Security Office. When the wolves slunk down the stairs in his chalet, he roared and Michel and Thomas held him back. His chest tightened up and he clenched his fists.

"You have to stay here," Thomas snarled, pushing his shoulder against Charles.

Charles gasped. "I can't." His wolf growled and tried to get loose.

Thomas and Michel held him tight. "Derrick will look after her. Michel just sent another team over and they'll secure the area," said Thomas.

Charles still fought them. "My wolf won't let me calm down. He needs to see her."

Thomas looked at Michel, then back to Charles. "We'll get you to her as soon as we can. We have to secure the compound first."

Charles slumped against them and let go, unable to fight anymore. There wasn't anything else he could do right now. He had to trust his people to protect her.

Derrick's voice crackled on the comms. "We're safe. But when the resort is secured, the Alpha needs to come back to his residence. Chantelle is fine. But we need to talk."

"Explain," ordered Michel, peering at the monitors.

"Not over comms. We'll need the Alpha's brothers and cousins to come here as soon as possible. And Gwen and Edwin too."

Charles still held on to Thomas and Michel and wiped his face. "I'm sorry I was such an ass."

Michel said, "We'll have to keep you and Chantelle together in the next emergency. Thomas and I will stay in the Security Office. We'll set up a direct comm line to you in some kind of safe room at your chalet."

"I can't hide! I'm the Alpha."

"That's what your Lieutenant will do now. We're going to adapt."

Charles felt all the emotions swirling around inside him. He paused and looked at his brother. "I love her."

Thomas put a hand on his shoulder. "I know. I'm happy for you."

Henri's voice came over the comms. "I'm with Chantelle now. She's fine. Just a little tired from the excitement."

Charles heart stopped thudding. "Was she injured?"

"Not a scratch," said Henri. "Dominick took a hit and we lost Jade. Everyone else is good, just minor injuries."

"What the hell happened?" Charles asked. They couldn't know about her, could they? That they were Fated Mates? Something bigger was going on but he couldn't make sense of it.

"It's safe for you to go home now," Michel said.

"I'll come with you," said Thomas. "Michel, meet us there when you can."

It took all of his willpower not to sprint to the chalet. Thomas kept up with him, both of them using shifter power to increase their speed. Derrick and Henri met them at the door and started to debrief them.

Chapter Eighteen

Chantelle opened her eyes. She was still in the basement. But the fight was over. Gwen and Edwin looked her over.

"M'Lady, how are you feeling?" asked Edwin.

"What?" She put a hand to her head. "I feel a little dizzy."

"You expended a lot of energy. We'd like to move you. Can you walk?"

She tried to gather her strength but her arms were too weak. Gwen and Edwin helped her into a sitting position. After they got her on her feet, they supported her to the cellar stairs. It was crowded. Too many people in the small basement space — medics and more security bustled around. They spoke in hushed tones.

"What's going on?" Her head hurt.

Gwen and Edwin exchanged a look. Gwen said, "We're taking care of our people and sorting out some things." The two mages cleared a path and took her up the stairs. It seemed like the workers just parted around them, moving silently and purposefully out of the way.

"Dominick and Derrick?" She suddenly remembered. Were they okay?

Derrick appeared at her elbow. "Right here, m'Lady. Dominick is going to be fine. He just needs some stitches."

Chantelle took his hand and squeezed it. "Thank you." She owed them both so much.

"Thank you, m'Lady." His eyes shone. He had never looked at her like that before. What had happened?

The mages took her upstairs, away from the noise and people. She breathed a sigh of relief. They kept going past the main floor and up the stairs to Charles' bedroom, where they sat her on the bed.

"How do you feel?" Edwin asked.

"Not bad. I can't remember much though."

"Charles will be here soon. Before you talk to him, there's something you should know."

Chantelle blinked. Everything was still a little fuzzy. Charles was okay, though. That was a relief.

"Charles' ex-girlfriend Alice was one of the shifters who infiltrated the chalet. She is one of the wolves you...stopped in the basement."

"What?" It all came flooding back. Gwen held her shoulders, sitting beside her on the bed. "What did I do?" Chantelle cried. A lump caught in her throat as she fought back tears.

Gwen answered, "You did what you were born to do. What you had to do to protect your — Charles' — pack."

"What do you mean?" None of that made any sense.

"You saved all our people in the basement," Edwin said. "But we have to talk about Charles' ex. We don't know yet how she's involved."

"She really hurt Charles. He's going to need you," Gwen said.

"I'll do everything I can," Chantelle said, wiping her face.

Charles burst in the bedroom and ran to her side. Henri and Thomas were right behind him. "Are you all right? Did they hurt you?" Charles hugged her tight then looked her over.

"I'm fine. Don't worry about me." She held him, knowing everything was going to be all right.

When Charles looked at Gwen and Edwin, they nodded. He exhaled loudly and pushed the hair from his forehead. "Okay, what else?" Edwin took Chantelle's hand and squeezed it before turning to Charles. Gwen led Edwin, Thomas and Charles out of the room.

Henri stepped in to sit beside Chantelle. He gave her a big hug. "How's my Fae Queen?"

Chantelle started to shake. "What did I do?"

"You must be pretty overwhelmed. You'll get through this." Henri held her and she started to calm down.

"I'm supposed to be there for Charles, too. How can I do that when I don't even know who I am and what I'm doing?"

"Just keep being you — nothing different. You are a bad-ass warrior princess."

She tried to hide inside his arms, so much like Charles'.

"Just rest for the moment. Thomas and I will shift with him and we'll go for a run," Henri said. "Shifting can help heal emotional and physical wounds, but he'll need you when he comes back. We'll bring him back here when we're done."

"Is he going to be okay?"

"Yes. We all will make sure of that. Family is the most important thing."

She rested her head against him. He moved and pulled back the covers on the bed. Rose petals fluttered to the ground, but she was too tired to cry. Henri helped her lie down and tucked the blankets around her.

Kissing the top of her head, he said, "Get some rest now." Overcome with exhaustion, she fell asleep.

Charles went with the group down the stairs and into the basement, where Derrick was waiting. There was still a lot to discuss. Gwen looked at Derrick. "What are we going to deal with first?"

Derrick said, "Chantelle."

"Tell us what you saw," Gwen said.

"It was like what you did that one time, Gwen. When we had the training exercise in the spring. Do you remember you dropped something like a magical EMP and it levelled a dozen shifters around you?"

"What?" Gwen's eyes widened. "That's not possible for an untrained Fae."

"I've only seen that much magical force from you. That one time," Derrick said. "Chantelle cut down all six of the wolves here. And she could direct it. It only affected the intruders. None of our people was hit."

Charles didn't know what they were talking about. He hadn't seen this on the monitor. Everything had happened so quickly.

Henri joined them. "What's the situation?"

"The Alpha's mate just took out half a dozen wolves who were threatening our clan. With her bare hands. And a whole lot of untamed magic," Gwen said.

"She can't do that, can she?" Charles asked. His head was spinning.

"She knew she was directing a working but I don't think she knew what was going to happen," replied Derrick.

Henri looked at Edwin. "The stories?"

"The *Rouanez* — the Fae Queen — will cut down her Lord's enemies," Edwin replied.

Charles snorted. "You don't believe those old tales, do you? It must be something else." Every time he thought his clan got over the Fated Mates thing, it came back.

"There's more, though," said Derrick, leading them to one of the fallen figures.

Charles looked down at the body of his ex-girlfriend, crumpled and lifeless on the cellar floor. "That's Alice." He swayed. Henri put his arm around him and held him up. "Chantelle did this?" Charles managed. Alice was involved. It was all his fault then.

Derrick nodded.

"But why is she in the chalet?"

Henri said, "She was part of the infiltration team here. We don't know have other answers yet."

"This is how they got through their defences. I made this happen." His knees buckled and Henri helped him sit down while the others continued talking.

"The *Rouanez* will destroy the one who betrayed her Lord," said Edwin.

"Do you think she's the one?" asked Derrick.

"She's definitely Charles' mate," said Edwin. "Pea predicted she would be powerful and would help protect the clan. But is she the one from the ancient stories?"

Charles was at the breaking point. He couldn't put it all together. His beautiful mate could destroy others. And his ex had betrayed him. A rival pack had attacked their compound, come into his home, and targeted Chantelle again. How did it all fit together?

He couldn't think anymore. His wolf took over, padding to the front and pushing through. He shifted, fast and painfully. Calling on his brothers, he watched them shift. They nosed him and he whined. Then they herded him upstairs. His clan members made way and opened the back door. Charles led the way out onto the patio and howled, the pain pouring out of him. Thomas and Henri joined him. They knew, they felt his pain. And they shared it. Together they ran into the forest.

* * * *

Chantelle woke from a dream of blood and vengeance. Something wet and hairy touched her hand, licking her. She pulled her hand back under the covers. The wet, hairy thing found her again.

"Nice doggy," she mumbled.

A heavy mass jumped onto the bed. Something furry nosed into her face. Rolling over, she waved her hand to get the fur out of her face. But it came back, snorting and huffing.

She opened an eye and saw the most beautiful wolf looking at her. She had seen him once before, on the road, when he had rescued her. Golden eyes with specks of steel grey. The shiny charcoal coat of fur looked soft enough to run her fingers through it. She did. It was muddy in places, wet. The muzzle too. But she could see Charles' spirit, his intelligence and his vulnerability in his eyes.

"Okay, okay." She sat up. "Let's get you a bath." There were two other wolves in the room, but when she got out of bed, they disappeared.

She drew water into the double-sized bathtub. Looking through the luxury brands of bubble baths she picked something rose-scented — her favourite — and sudsy. Her wolf had followed her, whining and sitting on the tile floor.

While the tub filled, the wolf bounced in the bathroom. Chantelle petted him and spoke in soothing tones. When she bent close, he covered her face with doggy kisses, wagging his tail.

Clem poked her head in to see if everything was all right.

"How do I get him in the tub? Do I need someone else to help?" Chantelle asked.

"Shifters only trust their mates with this intimacy. And believe me, you can handle him just fine." She closed the door.

When the water was ready, Chantelle placed the wolf's paws on the slippery edge of the tub and he jumped in. He fit nicely. Chantelle wondered if all the tubs in the compound were designed with large wolves in mind. Certainly the bath in the Alpha's residence would have been. As her wolf settled in, water splashed over the sides. He woofed and rumbled as she caressed him, washing and brushing his coat. She was completely soaked by the time it was done, but she was smiling from ear to ear.

"How do you feel now?" she asked him. He wagged his tail at her and rumbled. She got a couple of giant bath sheets from the cupboard, helped him hop out of the tub and dried him off. His fur shone and he licked her face.

"You're all done. I'm just going to jump in the shower and clean off, too. I'm a mess, you know!" She ruffled the fur on his head and he barked playfully. She opened the bathroom door so he could go into the rest of the chalet.

She opened the large glass door of the shower stall and turned on the faucet. When the water warmed up, she stripped off and climbed in the shower. This space was also double-size and Chantelle thought it would be a good place for enjoying some time with Charles. The stress started to wash away with the water. The bath-time fun had helped too. She could see some of that friskiness and playfulness when he was in his human form too, but it was such a different thing in his wolf form. He was beautiful, a wild and graceful creature.

When she was washing her hair, the shower door opened. She jumped. It was Charles, back in his human form. He stood there in all his naked glory. His majestic cock stood at attention, his sculpted muscles gleaming. There were tears in his eyes. She reached to wipe the tears away but instead grabbed his arms and pulled him into the shower stall.

He took the soap from the holder, washing her gently from top to bottom. Slow, smooth strokes, his hands heating up her skin. He knelt to wash her calves and feet and she felt herself relax. Soaping up his hands again, he reached around to her buttocks, circling and rubbing them with his strong hands. The heat of his hands and the water soaked into her core. He placed his cheek against her navel and sighed. She could stay here forever. Just the two of them. No attacks, no powers, no interruptions.

"*Caradec*," he whispered, and the sound went straight to her centre. He kissed her belly and stroked her hips. Her pussy tingled in anticipation.

His cock brushed against her legs, hard and insistent. She moaned, raising a leg and leaning against the shower wall. He grabbed her buttocks and sucked at her inner thigh, kissing and nipping his way to her sex. She pulsed with need, threading her fingers through his wet hair. *Yes. More.*

When he reached her mound, he flicked his tongue on her sensitive bud. She gasped. He spread her delicate folds with his fingers and rumbled in his chest. The vibrations were made just for her — deep and strong, quivering through her core. He drew his tongue along the labia, making long licks up and down. She moaned, holding his head against her. Moving to short lapping strokes, he took the tip of a finger and circled her clit. Her pussy throbbed so much she couldn't think.

He settled his tongue at her entrance. Moving it in and out, he stroked a finger over her swollen clit until she was moaning in ecstasy. Then he moved his mouth up to her button and sucked until she panted and grabbed his hair. She wanted him inside her. She wanted to feel him thrusting and sighing with her until they both exploded, water showering all around.

He brought her right to the precipice then stood up and lifted her legs around his hips. Her breath hitched as he held her in his dark eyes. "*Chère*," he breathed, bringing his swollen cock to her trembling centre. She squirmed in his arms. As he thrust home, they groaned together. He moved back and forth inside her, slowly, languidly. This coupling was slower than earlier that night. Tender, a different kind of lovemaking. Sweet and sad and beautiful. Like they were speaking to each other.

She held him tight as she went over the edge in wave after wave of pleasure. As her cream gushed, she felt his climax deep inside her, filling her up, sending her spiralling even higher into another orgasm. This one was a joining unlike anything she had ever experienced. They were truly one, experiencing the other's pleasure in a feedback loop that spun them higher and higher until they could go no further and fell back to earth.

She didn't want to hold back anymore. She had spent too long hiding and putting up walls. She just wanted to feel and to love. She held him as he cried, the two of them in a tangle on the shower floor, water pooling around them. She shed tears of her own, for those she had lost in the past and those who had died that day. Her life had changed. But she could face it if she stayed with this beautiful man. They were both wounded, but together they were stronger.

Chapter Nineteen

Chantelle sat on the floor of the shower, Charles holding her tight, his head on her shoulder. The water fell around them as she soothed this big man. Running her hand down his head and neck, smoothing his wet hair, she hummed a lullaby Granny Ceci used to sing to her. She kissed him on the top of his head and his wracked sobs gave way to sighs.

When he began snoring lightly, she chuckled. He'd been through a lot, God knew. The sleep would do him good. When she moved, he stirred and whimpered. She stopped and he settled back to sleep. She was stuck.

"Psssst! Hey!" She aimed for a stage whisper. "Is anybody out there?" People had to be close by their Alpha, given everything that had happened.

"Derrick?" she guessed. Her two men were always there when she needed them. But now Dominick was injured. He had been hurt trying to protect her. More to worry about.

The door opened just enough to let a pair of eyes peek through. Eyebrows raised but the voice was steady. "Yes, my Lady?" It was Derrick.

"Stop calling me that and help me move Charles. The big lug fell asleep on me."

His eyes twinkled. "Hold on." The door closed. A minute later it opened again and different hands carried bath sheets and robes. It was Henri. He looked at her and smiled sadly — so many words carried in just one look. "Hey, *chère*." That was what Charles called her. Her heart stuttered.

"I'm kind of stuck —"

Sharp eyes assessed the situation. He came forward and turned off the shower faucet. Throwing a bath sheet over her torso, he explained that shifters were comfortable with nudity but he would try his best to respect her privacy. He disentangled Charles then hoisted his brother up. He slung him over his shoulder and threw a towel over him.

"Wait here," he said. When he returned in a minute, he grinned. "Your turn." He helped her to stand and put on her robe.

"Not over your shoulder, I hope?"

He chuckled and scooped her up to carry her in his arms. "I can walk. I'm not a baby!" She didn't actually mind, though. It was comforting.

He kissed her chastely on the top of her head as he continued walking. "You certainly are not a baby, my Lady. You are every bit my Alpha's mate, his *Caradec*." He deposited her gently on her bed, beside the sleeping giant of her man. Her man — when had that happened? Her eyes started to leak tears as Henri sat beside her, scooching her over so she touched Charles on the other side.

He turned to look behind him, speaking a few words in a low voice. Then he swivelled back and started arranging pillows. "Let's get you tucked in again." Pulling the blankets up, he put his arm around her, easing them back onto a pile of pillows. They sat together in silence while she wept. Big sniffling sobs, not delicate lady-tears. She felt like a wrung-out rag.

A mug appeared and Henri took it. He handed her one of Charles' T-shirts. "Put this on first." She did as she was told, slipping out of the robe. He gave her the cup, saying "A hot toddy for my Lady. Grand-maman's recipe. And Gwen added a little extra something to help you sleep. No bad dreams."

She took the mug in her hands and leaned against this man. Family.

"Drink," he ordered. "I have strict instructions to make sure you take the whole thing."

She looked up at him through her tears and drank half the mug right away. "I killed people." She blew out a big sigh.

"I know."

"Not just people — someone. Is Charles going to hate me?" She was afraid to look in his eyes.

"No. He's upset and angry that you had to be the one to do it. And he was afraid he was going to lose you. He's got it bad for you."

"I like him a lot, too."

She touched Henri's chest. "You are still hurting. I can feel it."

His Adam's apple bobbed. "My father," he whispered.

"I still miss my grandmother so much," she continued. "She told me before she died that all the love you feel for someone and all the love they have for you fills your heart when they die. It makes your heart stronger, even when you think it will break."

She passed her hand over his heart. He breathed out like she had knocked the wind out of him. The drink was starting to numb her senses and she thought maybe she had imagined it. Then he grasped her hands, holding them tightly against his chest. "I feel lighter than I have in years. Since Father died. How did you do that?"

"Hmm." She squeezed his hands. "I don't know. I'm feeling sleepy."

"If my brother hadn't met you first, I would have asked you out myself. But you are so good for him, I wouldn't want it any other way."

"Family," she mumbled drowsily.

He tucked her back in against him. "He needs you, even if he can't always say it. And after tonight he's going to need you even more."

"What if I can't do it?"

Henri chuckled, deep and low like Charles did. "You can. You are his *Caradec*. You are strong and smart and beautiful and full of power."

"*Caradec*. What does that even mean?" she asked, her eyelids drooping.

As she faded off to sleep, she heard him answer, "His everything."

Henri tucked Chantelle in beside Charles, putting his brother's arm around her. Charles would sleep better—and heal better—if he could feel his mate beside him. He looked at the sleeping pair and sent a prayer that his brother wouldn't screw this up. She was so different from Alice, so giving, so loving. And she didn't let him get away with anything. Henri used to think having to answer to someone like that was a prison, but watching these two made him realise that this kind of a relationship brought out the best in both people. He envied that.

He shook his head. Maybe someday. He was still too young and there was fun to be had. But still, after today – seeing friends and clan mates wounded in their own home – he was starting to think about the big picture. Maybe he needed more in his life. A steady person who held his heart. Someone to share his bed on a regular basis. His thoughts drifted to Juana.

Henri left the bedroom and closed the door. Derrick was stationed outside the room, cleaning his gun. He had circles under his eyes.

"Let us know the moment they wake up," Henri said. "Unless, you know…"

Derrick nodded.

Nobody else was going to get any sleep tonight. At least his brother and his mate could heal and rest. The clan was going to need their strength soon enough. And Charles needed to learn that the whole place wouldn't shut down if he had to step away and care for himself or his mate. That was just the way it was going to be now that he was stepping into his role as Wolf Lord with his mate as his Queen.

He went down to the main floor. Clem waited at the bottom of the stairs and asked how they were.

"Sleeping like babies," he said.

Clem filled Henri in on the status of the compound. They went to the living room area to talk with the rest of the family, who had gathered in Charles' chalet. Thomas wanted them close to their Alpha, so they set up a temporary command station in the open area space. Cleaning crews were removing bodies and cleaning up the mess in the basement.

Charles was going to have to change now that Chantelle was in his life. It would be good for him and the pack. But that meant Henri was going to have to step up soon. He thought he might be ready. Especially after tonight. He had to help fight for their clan and be ready to defend their community. Protect his people and defend them. Become a leader. Settle down.

It was a lot to think about. But for now, he just had to worry about supporting Charles and stopping any further threats to the clan.

* * * *

Charles started, his heart racing. He was in his bed. It was dark. Chantelle's soft form was pressed up against him. His world was falling apart but he was in bed with the most beautiful woman in the world. She stirred and he kissed her.

"Charles?" she asked sleepily.

"Yes, *chère*,"

"What time is it?"

"The middle of the night. Go back to sleep."

She cuddled in closer and sighed.

"*Chère*?" he asked.

"Mmm."

"If you could have anything in the world, what would it be?"

"My teddy bear from first grade. Maybe world peace."

"How about an electric car instead?" He grinned, running his hand in circles on her back.

"I'll think about it. Leave you a list on the kitchen island." She sighed once more and fell back to sleep.

That sounded so normal. How could he be this lucky? He didn't deserve it. All the suffering and all the pain in his life. But he would cherish her forever if he got the chance.

Chapter Twenty

Charles woke up in his bed with Chantelle folded up in his arms. It had been three days since the attack and they still didn't have all the answers. She was sleeping so peacefully that he didn't want to wake her. Breathing in the scent of her hair, he kissed the top of her head. He knew he should get up. He just wanted another minute of peace and quiet before he had to get back to the real world.

Charles slipped out of the bed, dressed quickly and went downstairs. They knew the Trois-Rivières pack was trying to undermine them, but it felt like there was something more going on. He couldn't puzzle it out. His pack had set up his living room as a temporary war room. For the past few days, his advisors had argued and planned their next steps while Chantelle sat beside him, in front of him or behind him. He couldn't let go of her. His fingers entwined in her hair, his hand lightly touching her back or waist, their thighs rubbing against each other as they sat holding hands.

It wasn't just him. Chantelle was the same, staying by his side as much as she could. When she grew tired during meetings, which happened often as she recuperated from the attack, she fell asleep curled around him or with her head in his lap.

Everyone simply worked around them, content for their Alpha to have his mate with him. He was surprised how quickly everyone had adjusted. Better than he and Chantelle had. Things had changed between them. For the better, mostly. Deeper. More serious. But everything seemed to have more meaning. Sometimes he feared their individual losses and suffering hung heavily between them.

He went to the kitchen and poured a cup of coffee, adding cream and sugar. Time to face the day. The pack was dealing with new information. Uncle Jean had disappeared again, right after the attack. Michel concluded Jean was involved and likely was planning to take over the clan if Charles was taken out. When the invasion had failed, he fled.

Charles turned on the kettle and took out tea for Chantelle. They had made some progress on Alice's involvement. She had been seen with the René Reynard, son of the Trois-Rivières pack's Alpha, in the last few months. It looked like René was using Alice to get back at Laurentian pack. Did that mean Alice had been lying about everything? She hadn't been abused by the Reynards. She hadn't loved him. He shuddered when he thought of it. He had made so many mistakes, not protected his father and brother, not seen the traitor in their midst. How could he trust himself again?

Derrick carried several small shipping boxes into the kitchen. "Morning, boss. Chantelle awake? Your purchases arrived."

Charles grabbed a tea bag and poured hot water into a mug. He followed Derrick upstairs.

Going into the bedroom, he saw Chantelle in the bed. *My bed,* he thought, standing up straighter. He kissed her on the cheek. *She's so sexy when she just wakes up.* "I have some things for you," he whispered. He passed her the cup of tea while Derrick put the boxes on the bureau and left the room.

Chantelle sat up. "What is it?" she asked.

Charles put a red duffel bag on the bureau where she had stashed a couple pairs of sweatpants and underthings Clem had loaned her. She crossed to the bureau and opened the boxes, pulling out the new clothes he had bought for her. Cashmere sweaters that felt like butter. Camisoles that were silky and stylish. Designer jeans that looked like they were already broken in.

"These are beautiful! They must be expensive." She pressed a hand to her chest.

"I asked Clem for suggestions of eco-conscious, equity and diversity-conscious retailers—I thought you'd approve."

"Jardigans! I've always wanted one—and now I have two!" She pulled out the colourful, stretchy pieces and grinned, eyes glowing. Then she frowned. "But these clothes are very form-fitting. I'm used to wearing baggy sweats and sweaters."

"You have a gorgeous, sexy body. You shouldn't be hiding it in shapeless clothes." He gathered her up in an embrace. "I promise they'll be comfortable. I know what you like."

"How could you know?" she huffed, struggling in his arms.

He put her down and stared right into those brown eyes. "You like elegant yet comfortable looks. You favour neutral greys and blues but you glow in the colours of the autumn forest — golden yellow, rich red, harvest orange. They bring out your gorgeous brown eyes and your creamy, beige skin. Cosy textures and warm fabrics for winter are your pick."

Running her hands over the luxurious fabrics, she replied, "You wear blues, greens and browns — they look beautiful against your olive skin and dark hair. You'd rather be out hiking so when you're working you leave a button or two open at your collar or roll up your sleeves when you can. Your casual clothes are like your work clothes. Like it's hard for you to relax. But the button-ups, khakis and loafers make it look like it's effortless. Rugged and handsome and outdoorsy and sexy." She beamed.

"I wasn't sure about loungewear but I assumed you preferred simple nightshirts and pyjamas."

She nodded.

"I noticed you've been wearing my T-shirt since the night of the...since that night."

Chantelle looked down. "I don't think I've changed in a couple days."

"It's okay. We haven't left the chalet." She didn't need to worry about silly things like that.

"But you've been holding your war room meetings in the living room. Maybe I need to be more dressed up or should I stay out of the way?"

No way. She was staying right where she was. "Everyone accepts you as you are. You've been through a lot. I almost lost you and..."

"I just wanted to check." She looked down at the large tee hanging to her knees. "I know it's weird but I like to wear your shirt—I need to be able to smell you. Sorry, I probably sound like a stalker."

Charles pulled her against him. "Not at all. Shifters mark their mate with scent and touch. It becomes a symbiotic relationship where your scent and touch are matched with mine. And it's not surprising that you need something reassuring right now."

"You're right, it's soothing," she said, tucking her head on his chest and putting her arms around him. "You're still tense."

"I'm worried about trying to protect you."

"I can take care of myself!" Chantelle protested.

"I know you can, my queen. But I almost lost it thinking of you being in danger during the attack."

"And why does everyone call me things like lady or queen? Are they poking fun at me? Or did I scare them when I hurt the attackers in the chalet?"

"No, it's not anything like that. You know your granny's stories about the fae queen and her wolf prince? Our pack has a legend about the couple going into battle together to protect the community."

"Wait, your clan doesn't think that we're…?"

"I can't stop them from talking about it. Believe me, I tried. I think we just have to put up with it for a while until things quiet down."

"All right, but I don't like it."

"They are really proud of you." He kissed the top of her head.

"The clan really loves you a lot. You are definitely their wolf prince." Chantelle turned back to the packages. "Why don't you help me put my new clothes in the bureau and then I can get some breakfast while you start work?"

"Yes," Charles said. Life was perfect. If only this moment could last forever.

* * * *

The next day Chantelle was working in one of the grey Mage rooms with Edwin and his partner, Erik. There was lots of space and little furniture, good for experimenting. She put her head in her hands. "We've been at this for hours! I can't do it."

"Yes, you can," Erik said, running his fingers through his dark blond hair. "You have to learn to focus your powers. Control your outbursts."

"I'll never get it!" This wasn't working.

Edwin said, "Let's try with Erik and me sitting with you. We'll make a connection with you and lead you through it." They arranged themselves on the floor holding hands. They closed their eyes. Chantelle could feel the energy pulsing from their hands into hers. She saw something.

"There's a loop, an infinity loop? It's made of light and there are lots of threads twirled around together. Different colours. I see some jagged edges and threads of light that go off in other directions."

"Can you see her?" Erik asked. Edwin said yes.

Chantelle gasped. "That's you two, isn't it?" The couple laughed. "Here," she said and opened her eyes. "This one is out of place." She reached up into the loop and grabbed a knotted thread.

Erik whooshed out the air in his lungs. Chantelle examined the knot. "Erik. You can release this. There's no need to fear Edwin. Trust him. Feel his love, his loyalty." She pulled other threads closer to the knot and massaged it, looking for a way to release it. Energy pulsed down the thread. When it reached Erik, he was hit by a spark. Then the whole loop pulsed, releasing the knot. The loop glowed more steadily and hummed happily.

When Chantelle let go of the loop, she opened her eyes and smiled at the couple.

Edwin and Erik looked at each other. Edwin turned to Chantelle. "You shouldn't be able to do that. Only Gwen manipulates pairings like that."

"Oh, I didn't know," Chantelle said, taking a big breath.

"You didn't do anything wrong," Erik reassured her. "You're a lot more powerful than you know."

"It scares me," Chantelle admitted, her heart starting to race.

"Embrace it," said Edwin. "Use your positive feelings and desires to make connections in the clan."

"And use your defensive desires to protect and heal your people," Erik said.

Chantelle nodded. "Do Charles and I have the same kind of a loop as you two do?"

Edwin nodded. "Try it."

Chantelle closed her eyes and the couple took her hands again.

Edwin touched Chantelle's forehead. "Try and reach out to link with Charles. Can you find him in the compound?"

She scanned her body with her eyes closed and looked at the threads of her energy. Some circled inside her, while other tendrils reached beyond her body. She examined them, trying to see if she could find out where they went. She followed a promising one through the room and out into the hall. It made its way to Charles' office. *Bingo!*

Chantelle reached her hand out and imagined placing it on his chest. She took some deep breaths. Then a tingle went from her hand to his chest, where she thought her hand would lie if he were in front of her. It was warm and soothing, this energy she sent into him.

Then she caught sight of their loop, the threads tangling together, just like Edwin and Erik's. But it wasn't as orderly. Maybe theirs was still forming?

"I found it," she said.

"Good," replied Edwin.

The energy continued to circle in the loop and she caressed it. Then she felt a rise of power within her. It reminded her of the night in the basement. *Deep breath, centre yourself.* It kept surging inside, rising higher. "Guys, I don't think I can stop now," she said, growing warmer. Her stomach churned. "The colours —"

Erik grabbed her arms and squeezed, while Edwin put his hands on her temples. Her head spun. They breathed with her, detaching her from the energies around them and bringing her back to the room.

When she was in control again, she opened her eyes. "Thank you."

"Control is key," said Edwin. "We will keep working with you until you can do this yourself."

Chantelle nodded, sighing.

Charles came rushing through the door. "Are you okay? I felt something strange."

Edwin smiled. "She's fine. We were doing —"

All at once, Charles snarled and pounced on Chantelle, pushing her over.

"What?" asked Chantelle. She thought she had déjà-vu. *At least he has clothes on this time.* Energy shimmered around the two of them, pink and green tendrils swirling together.

"I think we set something off," said Erik. He tried to lay his hands on Charles, but Charles turned on all fours and growled at him. Erik exchanged glances with Edwin and backed up.

"Are you all right, Chantelle?" Edwin asked.

"Yeah, I'm not sure what to do." She heard a buzzing in her ears for a moment, then tingles spread through her core.

"I think it might be the Fated Mates claiming," Erik said. "We're going to leave you two alone to work this out."

"Seriously?" Chantelle heard the two men close the door behind them. The magic still shimmered and twisted around her and Charles.

Charles growled again, sniffing along her neck and shoulders.

"Oh, yeah, I think we need to be alone." She could feel his large erection pressing against her and her body responded.

As their energies mingled, Chantelle found herself wrapping her legs around Charles. She wiped the hair from his forehead when he looked at her. There were yellow flecks in his eyes. He rubbed his body along her torso and warmth passed between them. His chest rumbled in that way that struck her right to the core. Her pussy tingled and she gyrated underneath him. Magic shimmered around them.

"Mate. Now," he said.

"Yes," she breathed.

Hoisting her up, Charles claimed her mouth and carried her out of the room. She hardly noticed where he was taking her until they were at her apartment. She hadn't stayed there since before the Harvest Fête but it was closer than his chalet. It would take too long going across the compound.

She was already throbbing with need as the magic still swirled around them. When they got through the apartment door she pulled at his shirt. "I want you in me," she gasped. He carried her to the bedroom and they ripped off their clothes.

"I want to claim you, take you as my mate," he growled.

She felt his words tear through her, mixing with her magic into a heady cocktail of desire and love.

"Yes," she moaned. "I claim you, too."

She climbed onto the bed and positioned herself on her hands and knees. Her pussy was so wet she couldn't wait any longer. He set his thick cock against her entrance, taking only a moment to position himself before thrusting deep inside her. He filled her up, slaking the ache inside. Moaning, they gyrated together, a frantic mating that looped their energy together into their magical claiming. Chantelle could feel that they were joined as mates now. After reaching the peak and climbing down, they fell asleep, exhausted and drained.

Chapter Twenty-One

Charles was in the boardroom with his brothers. They sat at one end of the large, modern table. Chantelle was at his chalet sleeping. It was only yesterday that her powers had erupted violently, so he had given orders she was not to be disturbed today.

Thomas reviewed the changes they were making to the clan structure. "And I will step in as Lieutenant, as you have asked."

"You're not leaving?" Charles said, relief coursing through him.

"You have to make some changes now that you have a mate."

"Chantelle." Charles groaned. "She is a problem."

"What?" Henri stared at him.

"She clouds my thinking," Charles said. "I can't make good decisions when I have to worry about her. During the attack all I could think about was keeping her safe. I couldn't concentrate on anything else."

"You've got it bad, brother," said Henri. "But it's your time to become head of the family and let your warriors look after defending the clan now."

Charles stood up. "I'm not ready."

"I don't think anyone ever is. Do you think Father was ready when it was his time?" asked Thomas.

"Father was a great Alpha." *What is Thomas getting at?*

Thomas replied, "When he became leader of the clan, he tempered his responsibilities with his obligations to his mate, learning to become equal partners as they led the pack."

"Like Grand-maman and Grand-papa," said Henri, urging Charles to sit back down.

"When the Alpha's fire and passion find their match in their mate, then together they make wisdom and balance for the good of the clan," said Thomas.

"Wisdom? That's not me. I screwed everything up. It's my fault that Trois-Rivières pack got through out defences. It's my fault Dad and Robert died."

"You're not to blame," said Henri.

"I'm supposed to be a good judge of character. My clan depends on that."

"She fooled everyone. You can't blame yourself," said Thomas.

"One of your best qualities is that you accept people for who they are and you trust them," Henri said. "Don't change this just because someone took advantage of it. Look at Chantelle — she loves you for your trusting nature, your generosity and kindness. Don't second-guess them now."

Thomas said, "You don't have to make all the changes right this minute. We'll start implementing a transition strategy —"

"You and your implementation strategies."

"I know, but it has to be done. We'll make sure you sit on the Elder Council and the Board, start transitioning you into more of a leadership role for the clan."

"What about you, Henri?" asked Charles.

"I'd like to step up and take a more active role. Maybe try out a few divisions first before I decide."

"All right. If Henri can change, then I can change." Charles sighed.

The three brothers stood up. At the door, Henri turned. "Don't work too late in your office. Go back to Chantelle."

"This is all happening too fast. What if it's not right?"

Henri said, "You know it is. She's everything you need. Everything the clan needs."

Charles walked back to his office, brooding. What if he stepped back and something bad happened? Again. It was when he had concentrated on his relationship with Alice that he had screwed up. Maybe this wasn't such a good idea.

* * * *

Chantelle looked at her watch. It was eight o'clock and Charles was still in his office. He had told his assistant he wanted to be alone, but Chantelle was worried about him. She asked Derrick to take her over. After they walked across the compound and into the office wing, she knocked on his office door. No answer. She knocked again and opened the door. Charles was sitting at his desk, a half-empty bottle of scotch in front of him.

"Hey there, gorgeous!" he slurred.

"What's going on?" Chantelle came to his side. He leaned into her and almost fell off his chair. "This isn't like you, Charles."

"I've screwed up everything! And we still haven't got the bad guys."

"We're getting closer. I'm figuring out how to control my magic and you have some ideas about where to look."

He pulled away and looked at her, swaying slightly. "You shouldn't be involved. You should be living a carefree life filled with jars of jam and baskets of flowers."

"But they attacked my house too. I'm not going to walk away."

"I know, but that was because of me." He buried his face in her middle. "You should have a normal, human boyfriend. He can take you to the café in the village and go for long walks with you in the woods. Not some monster like me who keeps you pent up in his compound."

"You're not a monster! What's going on with you?"

"Everything is a mess. You should go and just forget me." He pushed away from his desk, wobbling a bit. "You are so beautiful and you don't even know it." He stood up and kissed her. Even with whisky on his breath she was swept up with passion, catching his scent of pine and leather. They almost fell over as Chantelle tried to prop him up.

"Let's get you home," she said.

"No, I've made up my mind. You're going back home tomorrow." He pulled away.

"Don't shut me out!"

"I don't deserve your help," he said, but his hands and mouth reached for her. "I brought that traitor into my family and my compound. I put everyone in danger. For what? For sex? For lust?" He buried his face in her hair.

"You cared for her and she betrayed you. It's not your fault."

"Chantelle, I'm broken. I'll destroy you, too."

"Everybody's broken in their own way. That's what makes us capable of great things. Terrible things, but also the best things."

"You should go back to your house."

"I've been hiding. You said it yourself. I need to wake up and be a person again. Help me do this."

"What if I can't?"

"You can." She tried to hold on to him.

He nuzzled the side of her face. "You smell so good. Every time I think I can't handle it, then I breathe you in—your lily and honeysuckle scent surrounds you—its tendrils reach out to me and pull me in."

"You are not sending me away."

"You know I can't. You're in me and I'm in you." He put his arms around her and she almost fell over again.

Chantelle called for Derrick. Together they got Charles back to the chalet. By the time they made it across the compound, he was singing folk songs and inviting everyone in for drinks. His clan members waved him off and wished Chantelle and Derrick luck with him. After pouring coffee into him, they took him upstairs and Derrick wrestled him into bed. Then their guard disappeared, leaving Chantelle to take it from there.

She undressed him to his boxers and put one of his T-shirts on herself. He was humming, eyes closed, when she climbed in and cuddled him. He turned her on her side and spooned her, rubbing her belly gently. It was only a few minutes until he started snoring in her ears. She tucked his arms around her tighter. Her heart was so full. She was both afraid and hopeful in equal measures. How could this be so amazing? And terrifying? Closing her eyes, she took some deep breaths and tried to fall asleep.

Chapter Twenty-Two

Charles and Chantelle entered the Mage rooms two days later. Edwin and Erik were seated on the floor and smiled at them. Chantelle squeezed Charles' hand and they sat down beside them. Charles was still a little unsure about where he was at with Chantelle. They had both taken some steps forward in trusting each other, but they had ghosts they needed to exorcise. His mother and father had made it look so easy, but he knew that relationships were hard work. It was worth it, though, with this woman.

"How are you two doing?" Edwin asked.

Charles put his arm around his mate and smiled. "Really good." He felt better than he had in a long time.

"Thanks to both of you for coming to this session. We want you to work together more and learn how to balance each other's powers more effectively."

Chantelle looked at him, her eyes wide. He squeezed her shoulder reassuringly.

"We want you to try some exercises, but first I have some information for Chantelle," said Erik. "The herbal supplements your granny made seem to be contributing to your memory blocks. We've analysed the ingredients. I've got an antidote, more like a concoction that can counteract the effects of the supplement. Would you like to take it?"

Chantelle said, "Yes. It's worth trying. I know what my granny did she thought was for the best. But I have to face it or I can't move on."

Erik nodded. He held out a bottle of pills. "Take one now and then we'll send the rest to the chalet." Then he stretched and sat on the floor, inviting the others to join him. They arranged themselves in a small circle, facing each other.

Edwin invited Chantelle to connect with Charles.

She put her hand on his chest and breathed in and out. He could feel himself opening up to her and he realised she could see everything. Too much! His heart started racing and his belly fluttered. They were spiralling, they were going to get out of control...

"Slow," she said. His pulse slowed, his heartbeat returning to normal. *Whoa.* No longer afraid, he explored their connection. She traced a path inside him, travelling through his memories and feelings. He followed along, walking beside her, holding her hand. He saw flashes of his past, experiences happy and sad. He shared them with her — she was his heart's ease.

They wandered inside his mind until they came to a wooden gate. It looked like it came out of a fairy tale. Vines clambered around it, brilliant flowers blossomed, and ornate carvings festooned the wood. He didn't recognise it. He didn't want to open it. There was a sour taste in his mouth as he stepped back. But Chantelle grinned at him, held his hand, and his heart sang.

They stepped forward together. The gate swung open.

He saw two figures in front of them. Kids, really. A young man—nineteen? Eighteen? He looked like he had at that age. And there was a young woman, maybe sixteen. She had the same eyes as Chantelle, his Chantelle. He looked at his side. Were they the same person? She seemed to be thinking the same thing. Then she nodded, still holding his hand.

They turned back to the younger versions of themselves. Laughing and shouting, children ran in the trees playing hide-and-seek. It was Grand-maman's summer place, where all the cousins gathered together. Family, clan and friends. The older teens still played with the younger children on these occasions.

Charles watched as his brother Henri—a young teen with sandy brown hair and a wide and ready grin—ran away with Michel. The young Chantelle skipped away following someone else. Who was it? He didn't recognise them, their back to him. The young Charles counted to one hundred, his face pressed into the bark of a tree trunk. He was it.

The scene shifted, fading quickly to white then coming back into focus. Charles and Chantelle exchanged glances, then continued to observe their younger selves.

It was quieter. They were following his younger self as he searched in the woods. They heard a sound and teenaged Charles paused. A cry, a girl's voice. He moved silently forward and looked around a tree. Gasping, he saw the younger Chantelle struggling with someone on the ground. A young man, bigger and older than she was. Tears streaked her face and her shirt was torn. The teenaged boy put a hand over her mouth.

Charles watched as his younger self sprang into action. He could see—almost remember—wanting to shift but hesitating. It was faster to use his human form but could he overpower the other person in it?

He lunged forward and knocked the attacker off the young woman. The man snarled and turned to face Charles. It was René—the son of the Trois-Rivières pack's Alpha. Then Charles remembered that the Alpha and his family had joined their party. Charles' dad had told them it was a chance to get to their neighbours better. But he hadn't meant like this.

"You interrupted," snarled René. "This half-breed is mine." Red-faced, chest heaving, he charged Charles. René pushed Charles back as they fought. They were about the same age and size, but René was meaner. Charles landed some good hits before René kicked out and hit his kneecap. Charles crumbled. Screaming, Chantelle jumped on her attacker. She put her palms on his back and René jerked as if he had been hit with a jolt of high-voltage electricity. He fell to the ground, eyes rolling back in his head.

Young Charles limped to Chantelle and whispered one word, "*Rouanez.*" She reached out to him but he toppled over before she could catch him. She bent down, resting her head on his chest. They curled around each other and Chantelle waved her hand. She made a transparent bubble, a shield, around them. Then she started humming. He didn't know how but the sounds numbed the pain from the cuts and the dislocated knee. She whispered, "Rest," and he grew sleepy, closing his eyes and holding her close.

He woke up with the younger Chantelle still in his arms on the ground. He sat up, blinking. What had happened? Everything was fuzzy and his ears were ringing. He kept the young woman in his arms, holding her close and safe. He didn't know why, but he knew this was important. After a few minutes, the clanging subsided and he could hear his brothers and cousins around him. Grand-maman was there and so was Chantelle's grandmother. What was going on? Everyone looked worried.

The young woman's granny was talking to her, but Chantelle's eyes were closed and she was shaking her head. Was she okay?

He touched her face gently. "*Caradec*," he said. He didn't know what that meant. She opened her eyes and stared at him blankly. He caressed her cheek and whispered, "It's okay now. Come back." Then her eyes looked right at him. She was herself again. He let out a huge breath. "My knee. It feels better. Thank you."

She put her head on his chest, sobbing. He held her until her breath returned to normal.

"Your granny. She's worried about you."

Chantelle looked around them. "How did —"

"I don't know. Do you think we can get up now?"

Chantelle closed her eyes and waved an arm, bringing down the bubble. They held on to each other as they stood.

Chantelle's granny reached out for her girl and Charles ran to Grand-maman. "That boy, René…"

Chantelle's granny stepped forward. "We can't let them know about Chantelle."

"What do we do?" Grand-maman held on to him.

"I can erase everything. Please help me keep her out of danger." Grand-maman supported Ceci as she planted memory spells in all of the children. Thomas was sent to keep Roland and his wife away from the children until they could finish. The scene faded to white again.

Charles and Chantelle watched as her grandmother created a gate and locked it up with their younger selves inside. She added a final spell to hold the gate closed, but added a proviso. "Until the time shall come when they meet again and have need of this knowledge."

Charles looked Chantelle. They were holding hands outside of the closed gate. "Was that real?"

"I think so," Chantelle said breathlessly.

Charles saw her look behind him. "What is it?" he asked.

"I saw someone...or something." She walked past him and into a wall of white mist. He almost lost sight of her before he turned and caught up. "They're just ahead," she said.

They took a few more steps into the fog. There were some grey-robed persons ahead of them.

"I've seen them before," Chantelle said. "I have a really bad feeling about them. It's nothing I can actually see, just an aura or something evil clinging to them."

"What are they doing here?" asked Charles.

"I don't know. I don't think they're really here in your mind. Maybe my magic summoned them?" She peered into the gloom.

Charles' heart raced. "Let's get out of here. This isn't good."

"In a minute. I want to find out who they are." Chantelle advanced as the figures slipped into a cave. She tried to follow but Charles pulled her back.

"Too dangerous."

She closed her eyes. "They're in the mountains somewhere, not too far away. I think they're important."

"You can talk to Gwen about them when we get back. We should go." He stifled a shiver.

She opened her eyes and nodded. Reaching up and placing her palm on his chest, she pushed gently. They swirled back through the path they had travelled before.

Suddenly they were back in the Mage rooms, Edwin and Erik sitting with them in the small circle.

"You're back?" asked Erik.

"Yes," Charles said.

Chantelle sucked in a deep breath beside him. "I'm not going to pass out this time."

"Are you telling me, or telling yourself?" asked Charles.

Edwin and Erik put their hands on her shoulders and closed their eyes. They breathed with her, centring her. When she opened her eyes, she explained what they had seen. "The spells were strong, but they were meant to protect us from the Renard family."

"How did René find out then?" asked Edwin.

"Maybe he broke through the memory spells," said Charles.

"This is why my granny kept moving us around so much. She feared he would remember and come looking for us."

Charles felt the adrenaline course through him as he thought about the two of them alone and afraid. "That could be why he targeted you. He might have found out you were living in Lac St. Patrice."

"Did he assault me when we were teens?" She looked down at the ground.

"I think we stopped him. Can you access your own memories now?"

"Most of them. There's still a block somewhere." Chantelle's eyes filled with tears and she laid her head on his chest. Charles scooped her up in his arms and held her in his lap. He put his face in her hair and held her tight. She was safe. Held. Loved.

She sobbed on his shirt. "It's all my fault. Everything."

"Don't you say that. Nothing is your fault." He felt sick thinking about it.

"But he's after your clan. If we hadn't—"

"No. He has to pay for what he's done."

"Did this start your feud with Trois-Rivières pack?"

Charles shook his head. "I don't think so. Something happened when my mother died years ago. My father was making peace when they came to Grand-maman's cabin."

She went pale. "What about your father's death?"

"Do you think?" Charles frowned. *No, it can't be.*

Edwin said, "We'll get Michel to look into it."

"So what do we do?" She clutched at him.

He kissed the top of her head. "We face it together. You, me and the rest of the pack. Family."

Chapter Twenty-Three

It was the weekend. Charles woke up and stretched. Chantelle was sleeping peacefully beside him. He kissed her and threw on a tee and boxers. It was so nice to share these everyday things with someone he cared for. He hadn't thought he'd find someone again.

Walking downstairs, he relished the quiet. No employees or family members waited for him in the living room. He and Chantelle could have a peaceful morning, then he would go into the office for the afternoon.

When he filled the coffee maker and turned it on, he saw a piece of paper on the kitchen island. He brought the note upstairs. Chantelle was in the bathroom brushing her teeth.

"What's this?" he asked, holding up the paper.

"You know," she said, spitting toothpaste into the sink.

"No."

"My list. I said I'd make you one."

"Your list?"

"Read it," she said.

"There are only two things on it."

"Read it."

"Okay. It says, 'One of Clem's special chocolates and you'."

"You asked me if I could have anything in the world, what would it be? That's my list." She continued brushing her teeth.

"*Chère*." He scooped her up in his arms, heading for his bed.

"Wait! My toothbrush!"

He turned around. "Okay, spit and put down the toothbrush. We have some things to take care of in the bedroom."

"Put me down!" She giggled. When Chantelle leaned over the sink, he took a moment to admire her form. Reaching a hand over he slid it under the bottom of her T-shirt — his T-shirt, his heart swelled — pulling it up to her creamy waist so he could run a finger over the sweet curves of her buttocks. She was wearing a little pink thong underneath, leaving her lush cheeks bare for his approval. His cock stood at attention at the sight.

"You are fine," he said.

She turned her head and smiled, the water still running from the faucet. Reaching closer, he hooked a finger under the string of the barely-there thong. When she turned off the water and reached for a towel, Charles moved behind her, pulling down the small strip of fabric. His hands gripped her slender hips, drawing her close, rubbing his torso and groin along her smooth back and buttocks. His wolf rumbled deep inside him as his cock strained against his boxers. God, he wanted her.

She sighed as he trailed one of his hands from the curve of her hip along her rib cage, brushing his fingers on the swell of her soft breast, lightly touching the roundness. The touch of her skin made his balls ache. He eased the shirt over her shoulders and her head. Tossing it to the side, he pulled her close to rest her bare back against his chest. He rubbed his thick length against her naked skin, just the thin fabric of his shorts separating them.

She sighed and stretched, leaning against his shoulders. Like an angel, she had rescued him. But he was afraid of not being good enough for this shining beauty. *Not the time to think about this.*

"You are magnificent, resplendent, luminous," he whispered on her neck. She shivered and leaned her head back on him. He looked at her in the mirror. *I am the luckiest man in the world.*

"Those are some fine words," she murmured.

"That's some sassy mouth, some perky breasts and a sweet ass," he replied, sliding his hands up and down her front, stopping at her smooth hips. He nibbled on her neck, behind her ear, as he slid their almost-naked bodies over so that they were positioned between the two sinks. She sighed as he leaned her forward, skimming his hands up and down along her curved form, kneading her buttocks. She arched her back and gave a little cry when the peaks of her breasts touched the cold marble counter.

"Mmm," he said. "Did that make your nipples hard?" He touched one and rubbed it between a finger and thumb. "Oh, I can see it did." As she squirmed and wiggled her beautiful buttocks, he pressed his swollen length against her. *She is so hot, I could come already.* He slid his other hand from the front of her hip, grazing it along the arch of her ass cheeks, and gripping her taut flesh. Following the bottom of the curve, he took a long finger and traced towards her centre, brushing his knuckles along her damp curls. She trembled beneath his touch.

"Mmm, not ready for me yet." Kneeling down, he brought his other hand back and spread her cheeks apart. *Her pussy is such a beautiful shade of pink.* As it started to glisten, he breathed on her lips. Taking a small lick, he said, "Your cream is so sweet." He circled his tongue around her swollen nub and she whimpered. His mouth devoured her, his tongue making long strokes up and down her wet centre.

"Charles," she sighed, resting her head on her hands on the counter. His fingers teased and worked the folds of her entrance. She whimpered again, wriggling against his touch.

"Now you are nice and wet. I love to lap you up but I need to be in you soon."

"Yes," was all the reply he got. She closed her eyes and moaned. When he stood up, he gripped her backside and inserted a finger in her pussy. The muscles in her wet sheath clenched around his finger as he moved it slowly in and out. His growing erection became insistent against her smooth thigh.

"Please," she whispered, shivering.

He slipped off his boxers and slid his thick length along her swollen lips. She gasped when he rubbed the tip of his shaft on her drenched bud. Then he moved up and prodded at her slick entrance. He had to be in her soon, but he wanted to prolong the anticipation. After another moment of teasing, he pushed against her opening, then slowly filled her up as she squirmed and moaned. When he was buried as deep as he could get, he groaned and gripped her hips.

"My queen, do you want fast or slow?" He held himself still.

"Yes," she said through clenched teeth.

He moved just a bit. When she tried to wriggle, he held her tight. "Fast or slow? My lady decides." He ran a hand along down her back and she shuddered with pleasure.

"Slow, then fast." She moaned.

"Whatever my queen desires," he said. He moved inside her, slowly.

"Yes, like that," she said.

"Exquisite." He groaned. "I can feel all of you. When I'm sliding in and out, I feel your walls around me like a glove. I push in and my tip goes all the way along your wet channel and up to your cervix, my balls rubbing against your clit. It's perfect. You're perfect for me."

"Mmm," she sighed.

This was all he'd ever wanted in his life. Someone who made him feel this way. He felt something shift in his chest. It was like his heart was opening again. He couldn't imagine being with anyone else again. She was made for him and he for her.

She wriggled and pushed against him when he thrust in deep.

"My queen," he moaned. "Are you ready?"

"Yes. More, harder, faster. Everything."

He picked up the speed as her muscles gripped him tighter. "I need all of you," he said. "I need you all the time. Every moment I see you I get so aroused, like I will explode if I can't have you. Just a faint whiff of your scent can set me off. I can't control it."

"It's not about control," she panted. "It's sharing and giving our passion, feeling our love flow in an endless loop."

She lifted up from the counter with her hands, pushing back against him as he thrust deeply in and out. Shifting his weight back, he pulled her to him, so that she perched on his lap and he gripped the counter. Lilies and honeysuckle wafted around him and he almost came. Cradling her against him, one hand held her waist and the other reached up her torso to palm her soft breast.

"Ohhh," she groaned as they spiralled higher.

He pushed them forward and they leaned against the counter again as he thrust faster and faster. His hand travelled from her breast to her navel, pointing his fingers down, just brushing the top of her mound.

"It's time. Show me how you feel." He moved his hand down, finding her sensitive nub with his middle finger.

She jolted as he rubbed her swollen clit. He grazed her shoulders and neck with his teeth, rumbling in his throat. His wolf was near the surface, coming out to play with her. *Mate good.*

"I'm coming for you," she said. As she started to pulse and shudder around him, he thrust deep, releasing his seed, filling her up. They moved together in perfect unison, full of need, reaching the heights of ecstasy that could only be found together. As her muscles relaxed, he came down, still holding her close, his cock softening inside her.

They leaned against the bathroom counter, panting together. He felt so empty when he pulled out. Kissing the top of her head, he carried her to the bed and laid her down beside him.

"I should take the day off," he said.

"What?" Chantelle half sat up. "Do you ever take a day off?"

"No. But I think I will today." He tickled her side and his heart was full.

"And what do you plan to do with this day off?" she asked, touching his shoulders and arms.

"What do you think?" He grinned. "We could just stay here all day."

She thought for a moment. "How about a hike? I haven't explored the area outside the compound."

"I used to explore the woods when I was younger. I haven't had much time since I became Alpha."

"Then it's a date!"

"Let's go in the afternoon." He pulled her back down and spread her hair out on the pillow. "I think we should spend the morning in bed, relaxing and exploring some other things," he said, nuzzling her shoulder.

"You are insatiable!" Chantelle said, her eyes glossy.

"Only for you." Charles took her in his arms again and didn't let her go for a long time.

* * * *

A few days later, Chantelle looked across the group of people at the memorial in the recreation hall. They came from all walks of life — they were all colours and all sizes. Just what the world should look like. And here they were together, mourning the dead from a brutal attack on their clan and their way of life.

It wasn't fair. They had lost some good men and women that night after the Harvest Fête. These people had put their lives on the line to defend their community and their values. Some of them had lost their lives or been injured because of her. It was a hard pill to swallow.

She saw Dominick, still pale, standing beside Derrick and his boyfriend. It broke her heart to think what had happened to her men that night.

Gwen led the memorial, speaking at the dais about the fallen and their courage.

Everyone here was committed to keeping the clan strong. The trust and loyalty Charles and his family inspired were amazing. Chantelle wanted to be a part of it. This was personal for her now.

When she saw Jade's son and wife, she broke down again. It was her fault this child would grow up without a parent. She wiped at her tears and pushed back her shoulders. Jade's wife was pale. Edwin and Erik flanked her, their arms around her. It wasn't going to be easy. She had gone down the path of grief herself. It was a long and lonely one.

Charles approached the dais. It was his turn to speak. He had to be strong for his people even though he was hurting inside. How did he live this way? So much responsibility and suffering. Then he turned and caught her glance. His eyes were shining. The electricity between them filled them up, kept them going, like an endless loop of love. They would help each other get through this.

At the reception in the recreational centre, Charles brought her a cup of tea. She tried to drink, but it got stuck in her throat.

"Is something wrong?" he asked.

"No, I'm fine."

He raised an eyebrow.

"It's just—this is overwhelming."

"What are you talking about?"

"This whole Wolf Lord thing. It's too much for you to look after your girlfriend when you're supposed to be leading your clan. And running a company."

"What do you mean?"

"I'm not a Fae Queen. I can't help you lead."

"You're kidding." Charles blinked at her. "You *are* a leader. Everyone loves and respects you. And you make me better, stronger."

She walked away from him and headed for the door. Charles followed her outside. "What's going on?"

"I can't do this," she sobbed.

"You can do anything. Just tell me."

She paused, her stomach roiling, heart racing. "Jade's wife wouldn't accept my apology," she said, tears rolling down her face. "She said it was her duty and she was proud of her. But that's wrong! She wouldn't have died if I weren't here. I'm to blame."

"*Chère*, she was a soldier. It's part of the job."

"It's a horrible job!" She put her face in her hands, trying to hide from his scrutiny.

Charles reached his arms around her, pulled her close. "Everything is happening so fast," he said. She struggled against him but he held on and continued, "We've got something here." He kissed her on the top of her head and she settled into his arms, leaning her head against his chest. Her breathing slowed. She sniffled and wiped her eyes.

"I can't be happy," she said. She felt like she was ripping off a scab. It was tender underneath.

"Sure we can."

"*I* can't be happy. I don't deserve it." She tried to push him away. *I don't know how to heal the wounds.*

"Of course you do. Just tell me." He held her shoulders.

She mumbled, "Everybody I love ends up dead. Or they leave me." Tears spilled from her eyes, clouding her vision.

"*Chère*," Charles said, pulling her close and wrapping his arms around her again. She couldn't hold back the sobs and revelled in his warmth as he held her.

When she could talk again, she took a deep breath. "What if I do the same thing to you? What if I make you die too? Your family—" She buried her head in his chest.

"*Chère*, you saved me. If I hadn't found you, I would have been the same as dead. You kissed the sleeping prince and he woke up."

She looked at him, her eyes shining with tears. "There's a part of me that's scared to live." She was finally opening up completely, baring her soul to him. Would it make him run away? Or would she finally find peace?

His grey eyes looked deep inside her. "Do it for me," he said.

She nodded and took a deep breath. It was going to be all right.

"Now can I take you home?" he asked.

She laughed and took his hand. Home, that sounded good.

Chapter Twenty-Four

Saturday morning, bright and early, Chantelle zipped up her duffel bag. Charles hadn't told her their destination, but he brought her a parka, mittens, toque and scarf when he told her they were going away for the weekend. Her palms were sweaty. This was a big step — for both of them. Charles was taking two whole days off from work and she had promised to stop doubting herself.

Charles called up, "Time to go!"

Derrick and Dominick — back to work — picked up their bags downstairs as they left the chalet. Her men were coming too. Chantelle couldn't talk Charles into giving them the time off. He said they might need them and it was non-negotiable. But they agreed that the two guards could have a week off when they got back to the compound. She knew part of her role was to look after them, just as they looked after her.

She walked hand in hand with Charles through the semi-circle of chalets. When she turned towards the parking lot, Charles chuckled and pulled her in the opposite direction.

"We're using the helo today."

Chantelle's stomach got fluttery. "Where are we going, anyway?"

"You won't know until we get there."

"Tell me now!" When she tackled him, he laughed and picked her up in his arms.

"We'll be relaxing at a very exclusive, very small ski resort. We rent it out to our VIP guests. I've booked the whole complex so we won't be disturbed."

"Was that Dominick and Derrick's idea to book the whole place? For security arrangements?"

"They encouraged it. And we have to take a whole team with us too. But you'll be pleased that I convinced them to stay in the chalet closest to ours instead of in the other bedroom of our chalet so we can have some privacy. They will be doing walk-throughs at regular intervals. So be prepared!" He set her down.

They walked to the helicopter where Derrick and Dominick were waiting. Chantelle climbed in and Charles sat beside her. She felt safe and warm with him so near. The two guards climbed in across from them, put on their headsets and communicated with the pilot. When they took off, Chantelle's heart jumped in her throat. It was her first helicopter trip, and her first time leaving the complex since the attack. It was strange. The whole world had been moving on without them all this time.

It was a beautiful morning, quiet and still. The fall weather was holding but turning crisper. Many of the leaves had fallen but there were still golds and oranges to be seen among the bare trees. When they had been in the air for about thirty minutes, they turned towards a lake and sped towards a nearby peak. A small building nestled among the trees halfway up the mountain. When they got closer, Chantelle could make out a cosy timber-log lodge and a few smaller A-line chalets. What a gorgeous view the resort must have, overlooking the mountains and the lake below. They made for a small landing area close to a parking lot beside the chalets. The pilot made arrangements to pick them up Sunday evening.

"Mmm, that's wonderful! Almost two full days here!" said Chantelle. She squeezed Charles' hand.

Dominick and Derrick insisted that they secure the area before she and Charles could enter the grounds.

"I think they're making too much of a fuss," said Chantelle.

"They're just doing their job," said Charles. "Once they've checked in with the security team and everyone is settled into their residences, we can all relax."

They walked to the small main lodge and were greeted by the hotel staff. Chantelle admired the combination of rustic décor and sleek amenities that she had grown accustomed to at the main compound. VIP guests would expect not only ambience but also luxury, and this small resort in the mountains delivered both.

The concierge gave them a walkie-talkie, saying, "We know you value your privacy, so you can reach me any time, day or night, with this. And here are the codes for the other members of staff." They made the other arrangements and chatted for a few minutes before Charles thanked them and they left the building.

Dominick and Derrick walked them to their chalet. They opened the door and stepped into a handsome kitchen. There was a doorway that led upstairs on the left side of the kitchen space. Past the marble counters, stainless-steel appliances and natural wood cupboards were a large, hand-hewn wooden dining table and chairs. Beyond that were floor-to-ceiling windows with a magnificent view.

"I called ahead and your favourite teas are waiting here. I'll make you one while you unpack," Charles said. Chantelle's heart filled, and she thought how grateful she was to have such an attentive mate.

When he had completed one final check, Dominick asked them if they needed anything else. "Just call us on comms and we will take care of it," he said.

"You two should have some time off, too," said Chantelle.

"Don't you worry about us, m'Lady. We're looking forward to the hot tub and some great food," said Dominick.

"We bring in an executive chef for our guests so expect to enjoy your meals," Charles said.

"Once you two are tucked in for the night, we will relax, I promise. We've got eyes on all entrances and exits for your chalet as well as the kitchen and living room, just so you are aware. But the upstairs is camera-free for your personal enjoyment." Derrick's eyes twinkled. Chantelle's face grew warm, but she knew her men were supportive of her relationship with Charles.

"You two need some time to be alone and just relax," said Dominick.

She was so lucky to have them. "Thank you, all of you."

Chantelle looked around the chalet. A huge field stone fireplace was the centrepiece of the open-concept downstairs. She thought she'd fallen into an episode of

Yellowstone, all the wood and colourful, natural fabrics contributing to the room's rustic chic feel. The stairs led up to three bedrooms, the master with a large en-suite that contained a giant soaker tub and a walk-in shower as well as two marble sinks. The basement included an entertainment room, with a fully stocked movie collection, bar and pool table. It was bigger than her cottage. *I could live here happily.*

Chantelle skipped around the space, stopping at the windows. "Can we go for a walk today? I'd love to see more of the area and admire the view."

"There are some great hiking trails. We just have to take your men with us."

"All right. Dominick likes hiking so he'll enjoy it, I'm sure. And Derrick likes to paint so he will appreciate the gorgeous scenery."

When the staff arrived with lunch, the chef appeared to introduce herself. Charles always took the time to thank the people who worked for him, ensuring they knew he valued and appreciated their work. That was one of the many things she admired about him. He was a natural leader. He might not have expected to become Alpha, but he was not only direct and a good decision-maker but also kind and compassionate. It was a heady combination. Chantelle bounced on her toes and prepared for the best weekend of her life.

* * * *

Charles luxuriated in the time away from the business. After lunch and a hike, he asked Chantelle if she wanted to paint. A fire was roaring in the fireplace and he poured them each a glass of wine. As she set up her brushes and paints at the dining table, he took out his fiddle and practised a few tunes.

Chantelle looked over, her eyes bright. "You look so content when you play."

"You're going to think this is silly. But do you know the song *Thank God I'm a Country Boy*? It's by John Denver."

She nodded.

He picked the strings, singing a few lines. "Got me a wife, got me a fiddle. Sun's coming up, I got cakes on the griddle..." She joined him for the chorus.

"That's all I've ever wanted," he said, looking over at his mate. "A little cabin, a family to love and music in my heart."

"That's poetry," she said, putting her hands to her cheeks and getting paint in her hair. His artsy, absentminded mate was so adorable when she was creating.

"How about you?" he asked, picking out another tune.

"I lost my parents when I was young. I've spent a lot of time trying to help improve the lives of children and youth. I can't do much, but I do what I can."

"Now you have a whole clan to look after!"

"Growing up, I always wished I had a big family. But I never thought it would be this big." She gave a sigh of contentment.

He put down his fiddle and came over to kiss her, thinking of her all alone as a child. She looked up at him, her eyes shining. She reached out and he held her close while she rubbed her face on his chest. He thought his heart was breaking but then he realised it was knitting itself together again—not from Chantelle's magic, but her love. She loved him. And he loved her.

After they ate a sumptuous dinner, Chantelle told Charles to relax while she drew them a bath. Charles stole a kiss before she went upstairs, breathing in her floral scent and knowing everything was right with the world.

He sat on the couch and looked at her paintings. She was so talented. Her work as a children's book illustrator was important to her. But he was glad she had time to spend on other paintings. He admired her creative side. It was an integral part of who she was. He had to make sure she got the time to create as they planned their lives together.

When she called him upstairs, he followed the scent of jasmine bubble bath and candles. The lights were dimmed in the master bedroom, flameless candles flickering on the bureaus. Rose petals on the bed—just like their first night at his chalet. His heart sang.

Moving to the en-suite bathroom, he was greeted with a delectable sight. Standing in front of a giant soaker tub, Chantelle wore a rose-coloured satin kimono that reached her mid-thighs. It was tied at her waist. When she leaned over to turn off the faucet, he could see her inner thighs. His cock immediately stood at attention. Rumbling, he looked her over, taking his fill of her shapely legs and buttocks.

Her hair was in a loose bun, wisps falling around her face. She looked up and her smile filled him with contentment. When he came up to fold her in his arms she stopped him, saying, "Let's get you out of those clothes first."

She stood on her tiptoes to give him a kiss then started unbuttoning his shirt. He closed his eyes, luxuriating in the sensations of her fingers whispering along his bare skin. She skimmed her small hands along his chest and shoulders, pulling his shirt back and down his arms until it swished to the floor. The nerve endings in his chest and torso tingled under her sweet touch.

She reached for his waist, then unbuckled his belt. Smoothing her hands along his hips, she moved to his button and zipper. Her fingers lightly brushed along his length and down his thighs as she pulled down his pants. His cock swelled so much he thought it would burst.

Her fingers curled around the waistband of his boxers and pulled them down, allowing his proud, jutting cock to spring free. Kneeling — *her lips are so close!* — she helped him take his feet out and moved the clothing away. His balls ached, growing tight as she slid the robe off her shoulders and let it fall to the floor. She was a thing of beauty, naked and soft and beautiful in front of him. He wanted to treasure her.

She looked at him with hooded eyes. "Not yet," she said, licking her lips. "First I need to get you clean and help you relax."

He helped her stand, brushing his hands along her curves, then he got into the tub. She pushed him forward into the middle of the tub so she could sit behind him. She uncorked a bottle and he breathed in the jasmine scent. A fluffy bath mitt made small, lazy circles on his back. As his shoulders relaxed, he rubbed his fingers along her lithe legs. When she leaned forward to wash his arms, he felt her stiff nipples tickling his back. She moved in front to wash his legs and feet and he couldn't stop himself from touching her bare, soapy skin all over. He wanted all of it. Trying to calm his body down, he reached out and brought her to lie against him, her smooth back against his chest. She sighed as she melted into him.

"Thanks so much for this weekend," she said. "I feel like a pampered celebrity."

"Yes, my Fae Queen."

She chuckled. "My Wolf Prince. It's nice to get away from everything and just be ourselves for a couple of days."

He ran his hands down her beautiful shoulders. "I could stay here forever."

They lay contented until he thought she had fallen asleep and the bath water had turned tepid. But then she stirred, telling him it was time to move to the bedroom. She towelled him off with a nice fluffy bath sheet. He smelled more jasmine as she rubbed lotion all over his skin and he luxuriated in the feel of her hands touching every part of his body. Then he took the bottle and did the same to her. The scent mixed with her natural floral scents into a heady concoction that went straight to his soul.

She led him to the bed and made him lie down on his back. He thought he had died and gone to heaven when she stood astride his waist, then reached up to take his hands and place his arms above his head. As she leaned over on all fours, he caught one of her pert nipples with his mouth. She sighed and his cock swelled even more. When he let go, she sat up and admired him.

"Your arms look so sexy above your head. All muscly and bulging—I could eat them up. Leave them just like that." She moved down his tingling body, reaching down and placing a hand around his throbbing penis, squeezing gently as he thrust up and down. She sat across his legs, thighs open and rubbing against him. Then she trailed her hand up and down his length, crooning, "So thick and stiff." She wrapped her slender fingers around the base and closed them with a firm, teasing grip.

He hissed from pleasure, closing his eyes and swivelling his hips a little. She settled herself by his knees, ass pointed up, leaning forward this time to tease his tip with her nipples.

"I want to ask you a question," she said.

"Chantelle," he moaned as she continued stroking him until he thought he might explode.

"Tell me," she said, "what is your greatest fear?"

He closed his eyes and reached for her. "*Chère*."

"Open up to me."

"I don't know if I can," he gasped. *What is she doing to me? I want to fuck her or spank her. Or maybe both.*

She bent down and cupped his balls, making his sac grow taut against her fingers. She traced the thick veins of his cock with her tongue. "Tell me."

"Oh, *chére*, there are so many things," he moaned. *If I open up, then I can explore my fantasies.*

She dipped down and licked the head of his aching cock, catching the droplet of precum seeping from the slit. When she sucked on the tip, he gasped again and she stopped. "Tell me. I can tease you all night if I have to." She stroked his hot length, up and down, slowly.

"If I'm pleased with your answer, then I will make you come all the way to your toes." She took him in her mouth for one delicious moment then withdrew. He moaned again. He couldn't talk. What was she doing to him?

"Then I'll slide your big cock deep inside my wet pussy. I'll fuck you all night long." She squeezed the base of his cock and moved her head up and down his full length, in and out. Her warm, wet mouth was like heaven.

"*Mon ostie de saint-sacrament de câlice de crisse,*" he swore.

"Do you kiss your grandmother with that mouth?"

"I can do lots of things with this mouth." He snared her in his gaze. Swiftly, she clambered up and pressed her lips to his.

"Will you open up to me?"

He realised she wanted—needed—this. She had to know that he was hers and he would give her everything. "Yes," he said. "Anything you want."

She returned to his aching shaft, running her clever tongue from the base to the tip. "Talk to me." She waited.

"I need—everyone to think I'm in control. That I can protect them." He whooshed a breath in and out while she licked him again, up and down, cradling his swollen balls in her hand.

"You try to be everything for everybody," she said, feathering the purple tip with her tongue.

"I'm responsible for them." He gasped.

She flicked her tongue on his slit, then circled again around the head. He writhed under her, trying to stay in control and not come too soon.

"Yessss, I can't fail. They'll think I'm weak." He could hardly concentrate.

She sucked him for a moment, then pulled her warm, wet mouth away and looked in his eyes. Her hand stroked slowly up and down his shaft. "Vulnerability and love aren't weaknesses. They make you strong. Your family and clan are there to help. You don't have to carry that burden alone." She was right. He knew it, deep down. But still he resisted.

"I'll let them down."

Releasing her grasp, she moved up his body again to kiss his mouth with her lush lips. "I'm here too — just open up and share with me."

He paused, looking in her eyes, and shook his head. His heart raced. "Underneath the armour is blank space. I'm only walls and defences now, just pain and sorrow in the middle." *There. Now she knows.*

She claimed his lips with hers. "That's not true. There's a beautiful heart and soul inside those walls. Kind, caring and tough. Everything I love about you is in there."

He reached for her and she was gone again. Her wet, soft mouth enclosed his swollen member, sucking gently, moving along the shaft. He gasped as something shifted inside him. He felt lighter. Like he wasn't alone. He understood he had Chantelle and his pack and his family. He loved them all.

Her head bobbed up and down while she worked him with her mouth and tongue. It was exquisite. Thrusting back and forth, he moaned as he spiralled higher into ecstasy. He felt the ache and tightness in his balls as she sucked him harder, faster. Soon he was shooting his come into her beautiful mouth.

"So beautiful, so sexy, *chère*. I don't want anything else," he growled as he spent the last of his seed. She licked his cock clean, gave it a kiss then climbed up beside him. This was perfect. And they weren't done yet.

Chapter Twenty-Five

Charles' heart raced. When she kissed him again, he tasted himself and loved her for her generous gift. Once his breathing returned to normal, he sat up, adding some pillows to support his back. "Come here." He lifted her beautiful form into his lap. Tipping her face up with one hand, he snared her lips in a deep kiss. He was the luckiest man in the world. As he licked the slender column of her neck and grazed his teeth on her bare shoulder, his thick cock swelled against her soft buttocks. He skimmed a hand all the way down her smooth back, resting on the curve of her hip.

Wrapping her creamy legs around him, he rumbled low in his chest and she shivered. He ran a hand along the crease of her hip, caressing and tickling his way to her mound. When he reached her damp curls, he made little circles, playing and teasing. She gyrated her hips, moaning.

He grazed her lightly with one finger, tracing the outline of her quivering lips, down and up, stopping at the sensitive bundles of nerves. She squirmed and sighed on his neck as he held his finger a hair's breadth away from her clit. Her muscles tensed, taut as a wire. When he lightly brushed her swollen bud with his finger, she shuddered. He circled, applying light pressure to her sensitive spot. She whimpered at his touch and was rewarded with a stronger stroke, moving back and forth against her sensitive nub.

He grunted with satisfaction as she rubbed against him, feeling the pressure build. He rubbed his rough fingers along her damp folds and teased the slick entrance of her pussy. "You are so wet," he whispered in her ear. He shifted, lifting her up and onto his stiff, demanding cock. She moaned in pleasure as he gripped her hips and brought her slowly down on him, pressing in to his hilt. Her hot sheath tightened around his shaft, wet and perfect.

"This is my favourite position with you," he said, nuzzling her ear.

"I thought wolf-style was," she said as he pulled out then plunged deep.

"That does satisfy my primal urges. But there is something about this." He rode her slow and easy.

"Aaaah," she sighed. "What is it?" She gyrated her hips in slow circles, driving him higher.

"I can gather you up and hold you in my arms as close as I can get to you. I can feel you — you speak to my soul this way."

She ground into him faster as they started picking up the rhythm. His balls grew tight as his shaft pumped in and out. "Whenever you talk like this, I want to come all over you," she said.

"When I talk like what?" he asked, his shaky breath on her neck. He inhaled her scent and almost went over the edge.

"Mmm, anything really. It's like your words go so deep inside me. They reach right down. They drive me wild until I can't stand it anymore."

He kissed her and reached down and massaged her firm breasts. Running his thumbs over the nipples, he squeezed the pebbled tips. Moaning, she rocked against him, bringing him to the breaking point. "Come for me," he growled, grabbing her ass and squeezing the soft flesh. Her walls spasmed around him and he speared her over and over, trembling and quaking. His throbbing cock pulsed as her pussy milked every last drop of semen, sharing their pleasure together. The climax went on and on, like nothing he'd ever felt before, each fuelling the other's release. When they finally came down, they fell panting beside each other on the bed. He pulled her close as she settled against him. This was everything he had ever wanted. He knew they had surrendered to each other, finally given up the fear. They were no longer hiding – they just loved each other.

Charles kissed her on the head. "I love you so much. Move in with me when we get back?"

"I love you, too," Chantelle said. "This is a big step for me. I still don't know if I believe this whole Fated Mates thing."

"We are meant to be together," Charles growled. *I'm not letting her go. I can't.*

"What about my own life?

"Being Fated Mates doesn't mean you have to give up your own life. Sure, you'll have pack and clan responsibilities. But you can see your friends – I want them to be my friends, too." His chest expanded. Everything would be perfect.

"I'm going to get a drink of water. We can talk about it in a minute." She stood up and looked through her duffel bag. She pulled on a pair of sleep pants.

He sat up. "Are you upset?"

"No." She found a tee and put on fuzzy socks. "I just need a moment to think about everything." She smiled and left the room.

She's right. It is a big step. They'd just had the most amazing sex and he asked her to move in with him. *Am I ready? Or did I ask her in the heat of the moment?*

Chantelle slipped down the stairs. He was amazing, kind, loving, a leader. But things were going so fast. Were they really destined to be together? His people could be wrong. What if she said yes and a year later, they broke up? She didn't know if she could survive another horrible break-up.

But she couldn't let fear stop her from trying. She put her shoulders back and took a deep breath. She'd go back and talk it through after her glass of water.

Smiling, she reached the bottom of the staircase.

She heard a noise in the kitchen. Something must have fallen off a shelf. Rubbing her eyes, she walked towards the sound. As she entered the kitchen space, she saw a figure by the door, his back to her. It wasn't tall enough to be Derrick or Dominick. One of the other guards? He turned and saw her, his eyes widening.

Just as the stranger looked behind her, she felt a prick on her neck. Arms reached for her shoulder and waist, pulling her down. These people smelled funny, not like her men. What were they doing here? Were they René's people?

She tried to shout but nothing came out of her mouth. There was a hand over her mouth, but it didn't matter. She couldn't move or talk. She couldn't call on the security team or get to the walkie-talkie. She wondered if Derrick and Dominick were okay. Would they be on their way to her or were they knocked out in their chalet? She made a silent prayer that they were not injured.

She looked around the room. There were two, no, three, figures in the kitchen, all dressed in black. Two of them grabbed her arms and feet while the third opened the door. Her heart raced. When she reached for her magic, there was nothing there. She tried again. Nope. Whatever they'd injected her with must have also dampened her magic. A spell or potion, maybe? It didn't really matter, but the thought kept her mind busy as they carried her to a white van.

Where was Charles? Why didn't he wake up? A wave of dizziness passed over her. Was everyone dead? The black-clad men didn't say a word. They just wrapped her in a wool blanket and bundled her into the waiting van. When they got in—two in the front and one in the back with her—the driver spoke into wrist comms. "Package secured. You were right. The spelled pulse didn't affect her so we had to use the injection."

She must be the package. They weren't planning on killing her. At least not yet.

"Roger," came an answer. "Waiting for confirmation on Sleeping Beauty from A and C."

They must be René's men. The Trois-Rivières pack probably wanted to confront her, or maybe worse. The man beside her pulled out zip ties and secured her hands and feet, then pulled the blanket over her again before he lit a cigarette. A tear trickled down her cheek. She couldn't wipe it away.

The wrist comm crackled from the front. "All buildings confirmed. Trackers delivered. Six hours on the clock until Beast wakes up. Make the most of it."

"Roger," replied the driver. He put the car in gear, reversed then pulled forward. When they turned onto the road Chantelle tried to take some deep breaths. She prayed that her mate and her men were okay. She couldn't let anyone else die because of her.

Chapter Twenty-Six

Charles woke up and rolled out of bed. His neck ached and he was groggy. He must have slept in. The sun was already high in the sky. It was late. And too quiet.

Chantelle.

She'd gone downstairs for a drink of water. Why hadn't he followed her? He shook his head. When she didn't come back after a few minutes, he planned to go downstairs and to talk to her. Maybe she just needed some time.

He tried to stand up but he fell back on the bed. He was dizzy. Moving slowly, he stood up again. Holding on to walls and doorways, he made his way down the hall. When he got to the bottom of the stairs, he shook his head. He was still groggy.

"*Chère?*" he called. No answer. *Something is wrong.* Fear knotted his insides as he hurried into the kitchen. No Chantelle. The dinner dishes were still on the counter, and boxes of tea were on the floor. He struggled to keep the panic from taking over.

He tried the walkie-talkie but there was no answer from the concierge. Nobody answered the comms for the security team. Where were Dominick and Derrick? He had to check on the others and see if they knew what was going on. Pulling on boots and a coat, he opened the door. Footprints in the mud led away from the chalet. In the parking lot, he saw a set of tire tracks that hadn't been there yesterday. This was bad. His stomach flip-flopped. He had to get to Dominick and Derrick.

He leaned against the door frame as another wave of dizziness passed through him. He had to do something. Adrenaline kicked in and he raced to the chalet next door, stopping once to put his head between his knees. Reaching their room, he burst in. Both men were still in their beds.

"She's gone." He shook them awake. It was hard to say it out loud, but he knew he had to get them moving. They rubbed their eyes and sat up, holding on to their beds as their heads spun.

"She's gone," he repeated. His heart was racing as he struggled to keep calm. It wouldn't help if he panicked.

Dominick focused his eyes on him. "That's impossible!"

"What happened?" Derrick sat with his head in his hands.

"Get some clothes on. Whatever they did to us is still in our systems."

"We have to get moving before the trail is dead," said Dominick.

Charles tried to slow his breathing and wiped at his eyes. *Keep it together for her.* "A few more minutes won't matter. I need you both on top of your game. I'll go make coffee. Meet me in ten minutes."

The men gave curt nods. Charles asked them to check on the lodge staff and the security team before reporting to him. He staggered back to the chalet and turned on the coffee machine, cursing himself. They never should have gone away for the weekend. He thought it would be safe. But they had taken her. He was sure it was René's doing. He felt sick at the thought of something happening to her. René was a bully whose family tormented the weak and vulnerable. And now René had Chantelle, his mate. He had to stop him.

Dominick and Derrick stumbled into Charles' chalet, taking large mugs of coffee from him. They reported that the lodge staff was knocked out, but unconscious, not dead. That was a relief. He didn't know what he would have done if everyone had been killed. The rest of the security team was looking through the security footage.

"Guys —" Charles rubbed his face and fought his growing sense of panic.

"Don't even think about it. We'll get her back," Dominick said.

Charles couldn't speak as the emotions bubbled inside his chest. Wiping his eyes, he looked up and straightened his shoulders. He had to be strong, clear-headed. That was the only way to get her back. Derrick put two guns on the counter in front of him. He picked them up and nodded.

Dominick and Derrick took him to see the security footage. The security team counted ten to twelve intruders. The team was well organised. They'd managed to infiltrate the resort and take Chantelle without detection. Charles watched on the monitors as two stealth experts, dressed in night suits and headsets, hiked in and set up stakes at the corners of the property. On the stakes were some sort of charges. When the stakes were secured, the intruders set off the contraptions and brought in the rest of the team.

Jordan, their team lead, identified the charges as magical workings. "That's how they knocked us out without getting close enough to be caught." Jordan fast-forwarded through the footage. Some of the intruders went to the main lodge to cut the camera feeds. Three others went to Charles and Chantelle's chalet, carrying a small case and a blanket. Another two pairs approached the other chalets. The others waited in the parking lot with a white van until the camera feeds went off.

Charles' body tensed as his heart pounded. "Find her. And keep the three who touched her alive, for me."

The team nodded and got to work. Derrick and Dominick took Charles to the parking lot and got in one of the SUVs the security team had brought. They pulled out onto the road, following the tracks down the mountain. While Derrick drove, Dominick used the comms to connect with the security team. Then he opened the sat phone to talk to Juana and Michel back at the resort.

Charles sat in the back seat trying to calm his nerves. He took deep breaths. *It won't do her any good if you fall apart.*

Dominick turned to him, saying, "The helicopter is on its way. Henri and Michel are coming with Juana. Clem and Thomas will head up things back at the compound."

Dominick put Henri on speaker. "Bro, how are you holding up?" Henri asked.

Charles started, "I—" but couldn't continue. He pressed his lips together and buried his face in his hands. *Keep it together.* His wolf growled.

Dominick said, "He's here. He's in control but he needs you."

"We're on our way, bro. Hold on."

Charles clenched his fists as Dominick turned off the phone. His packmates would lend them their strength and keep him grounded. He just had to make it until they arrived. When they got to the bottom of the mountain, Dominick checked in on the sat phone. Clem had picked up a white van on CCTV at a nearby gas station north from their location. They had gassed up in the middle of the night. The footage showed the van turning onto another road in the foothills of a nearby mountain. They could start there.

Charles' wolf was close to the surface. He had to find his mate. This was killing him.

Derrick looked at Charles. "She's strong. That's one of the reasons you love her."

"She has to be okay. I can't lose her," he said. He struggled not to break down.

"The universe didn't bring your Fae Queen to you for her to go so soon," Dominick said, turning to look at him. "She's meant to help you slay your foes and stay with you until you're old and grey."

Charles hoped this was true. "You'll help me find her and bring her back?" He needed them.

"Or die trying." At Dominick's words, Derrick nodded grimly.

* * * *

Chantelle breathed, in and out, in and out, as they drove out of the gas station and started up another mountain. The men didn't talk unless something came over the comms. She still didn't know what they were planning to do. The pit in her stomach kept churning, but she gave thanks she was still alive.

When the adrenaline had worked its way through her system, she passed out from exhaustion. She jerked awake when the van stopped at the end of a little road. The men kept her wrapped in the blanket, even her head, so she couldn't see where they were. She thought it must be morning. Sounds of cars and machines surrounded her, voices shouting and laughing in the distance. Then they juggled her through a doorway. When the door shut behind them, it was quiet. They were still inside in a heated building, but it seemed large and airy. Footsteps on carpet. A warehouse, maybe?

They opened another door, heaved her up and deposited her on a bed of some sort. A cot, probably, small and uncomfortable. They pulled down the blanket and she looked around. A small office space, the cot instead of a desk, water on a little table. Her captors made no move to untie her hands and feet and promptly left her alone.

Would she be meeting René face to face soon? What did he want? Revenge, obviously. But what would it look like? And who would it involve? She couldn't stand to have anybody else's blood on her hands.

She looked inward and reached for her magic but it was still dulled. It felt like her abilities were muffled somehow. Her stomach flip-flopped. She had to reach Gwen or Pea. Or maybe she could connect with

Charles. They had a bond. Maybe it could cut through her muffled state.

A man returned and threw some clothes at her before leaving again. She looked down and realised she was still in her pyjamas. How was she supposed to put the jeans and sweatshirt on? She lay there sucking in deep breaths. *In and out, in and out.* Too bad she hadn't heeded her doctor's advice and practised more mindfulness for her ADHD. It could have come in handy now.

She worked on accessing her magic, but nothing changed. It could be from the injection still, or it was some kind of magical dampening field or object in the room. Maybe she could search the small space. At least it would keep her busy. She wriggled herself into a sitting position, but the zip ties made it awkward to get off the bed. Scooting to the edge of the bed, she looked around. Nothing but the cot and table.

She wondered where Charles was. Why did she get scared of moving in with him? They were practically living together already, so why would this be different? It meant accepting she was part of something bigger than herself.

If she got out of here, she was going to be braver. She would move in with him. He was her mate and she wanted to be with him. She didn't have to choose between him and her friends. They were all a part of her chosen family. When she was in the van, her heart had nearly jumped out of her throat when she heard that Derrick, Dominick and the others were not dead. She would fight to the death for them. For the whole pack.

That's when it hit her. They would do the same for her. Charles was right — this was what a pack did. They supported each other and would die for each other. If she was going to be a part of them, she had to accept this. It went both ways. A weight lifted from her chest to know that she wasn't alone anymore. This was what being in a family was all about.

The door opened with a clang and a strange woman dressed in black jeans and tee came forward. She was holding a small knife. Chantelle tensed up.

"Relax," the woman said roughly. "I'm just cutting the zip ties." She tugged and removed the bonds. She pointed at the clothes.

"Put these on. Then I'll take you to René."

Chantelle stood up, massaging her wrists and gingerly checking her ankles.

The woman pursed her lips. "What are you waiting for? You don't have anything I haven't seen before."

Chantelle turned her back, stripped and put on the jeans and sweatshirt. No underwear, no bra. She kept her fuzzy socks. When she turned around, the woman grabbed her and pushed her out of the room. Chantelle stumbled along a bare corridor to the end. The woman opened the door and took her down another hallway to the last door. This hallway looked different, more like a hotel than a prison. Carpet on the floor, beige-painted walls.

When the female guard pushed Chantelle into the door and closed it behind her, Chantelle almost fell on the ground. Struggling to stand up, she saw more carpet and wallpaper. A kitchenette, minibar and seating area with a big-screen TV. It looked like a hundred motels around the area. Bad prints of scantily-clad women on motorcycles adorned the walls. There was a faint smell of old cigarette smoke in the air.

Another door opened and René entered. She knew it was him even though they hadn't seen each other — in human form, at least — for ten years, maybe more. He was large and clumsy-looking, his hair slicked back. He wore a yellow track suit and sneakers. *He looks like a banana.* Chantelle took a step backward as he smiled menacingly.

"You remember me?" he asked.

"Yes," Chantelle said, suppressing a shiver.

"You look different now," he said, looking her over. "Still small and sexy. But a little tougher, a little less innocent." His eyes glinted and he smirked.

She put her shoulders back. "What do you want?"

"You, of course. What I've always wanted. And what you and that prick tried to stop us from taking."

"Us"? What did he mean? Had his pack been part of it?

"You don't —" she started.

He put up his hand. "Shut up. I've got a dress for you." He walked into the adjoining room, leaving the door open. On a bed were handcuffs, rope and duct tape. He came back out carrying garish red fabric and held it out to her. "Into the bedroom and put it on. Don't try anything."

She took the dress from him. When she got to the room, he closed the door partway and eyed her. The dress was form-fitting and bright red, cheap polyester and ruching that felt rough on her hands. The red colour was too orangey. She took off her clothes and quickly put the dress over her head. She pulled it down so it would cover her upper thighs but then her chest was exposed almost to her nipples. When she yanked it up, the bottom got dangerously close to her buttocks. *Tabernak, not enough fabric. Figures.*

When she exited the room, he was sitting on a couch with a plastic glass of brown liquor beside him and a gun in his lap. She moved slowly towards him, staying out of his reach and pasting a smile on her face. She tipped her chin up.

He looked her over, licking his lips. "That's perfect on you, just like I knew it would be."

She stifled another shudder. *Keep it together, girl.*

"Come closer," he leered, staring at her chest.

She sidled a couple steps closer, then cleared her throat. "What are you drinking?" She tried to look interested.

"Whisky. Do you want one?"

"Yes." She looked at the floor. *Keep pretending. Just hang on.* When he returned from the kitchenette and passed her a glass, she tried one of those smiles that models used — smile from your eyes, they said. She sat down on a chair — not the couch — and leaned back, crossing her legs. "Nice place." She took a sip of the foul liquor.

He crossed his arms and thrust out his chest. "Yeah, I decorated it myself. It's not permanent — we're just staying here until I bring you home, but I like to jazz things up wherever I am."

"You're bringing me to your home?" She tried to keep her face neutral, but it was hard.

"After I break you in a bit," he said, looking her up and down. Trying not to show her emotions on her face, she took a sip from her drink. There was a knock on the door.

A tall person in business attire entered, carrying a sat phone. "The bosses are on the line."

"They're not my bosses. They're my partners," René snapped. He stood up and grabbed the phone. "Hey, there." He moved towards the kitchenette but it was still easy to hear his side of the conversation. "Yeah, she's here. No problems. And we put the trackers on the others. Fifteen minutes ago they were still on their way here, following our trail of breadcrumbs. They're about an hour out." René listened. "Mmm-hmm. He's with them." The hairs on the back of Chantelle's neck stood up. He must mean Charles. "Both alive? You said I could kill him." René stalked around the room, clenching his free hand. The voice on the other end was still talking but she couldn't make out the words. "Okay. But I get her back when you're done with her." He listened. "Yeah, I won't be needing her mind, just her body. In fact, the weaker, the better." He cackled.

He's still a creep. He ended the phone call. Things were getting worse by the minute. She was being used as bait, then she and Charles were being turned over to someone else. What did these other people want?

She had to stall. "Come on, baby. You don't need to do that," she said, batting her eyelashes. She hoped it looked convincing. "I can be all yours."

His eyes narrowed. "Really?" he said.

"Yes. Charles is such a stick in the mud—all work, no play. I need a big strong man who will spend time with me. Make me feel like a woman," she said. She was going to make herself vomit.

He crossed the distance between them and lifted her chin with a finger. He was standing over her and it took all her strength not to tense up. He bent down and kissed her. It felt all wrong. He mashed his lips against hers so hard she thought she would have a bruise. His tongue felt like an invasion in her mouth and there was too much slobber—just like when he had licked her as a wolf.

He broke off the kiss and kept his face close to hers. Then he reached over and pulled her hair back so her throat was exposed to him. His nose sniffed at her jugular. "Don't lie to me. It's not going to change anything." He let go suddenly and stood up, towering over her, eyes glowing.

This is it, isn't it?

But he stepped back. Huffed, then crossed to the apartment door. Opening it, he called for the guard. "Take her back to her room and handcuff her. I don't need her until the Alpha gets here." He turned and sneered at her. "That's when the fun will start."

The woman entered, grabbed her arm and pulled her into the hallway.

Chapter Twenty-Seven

Charles bounced his legs as Derrick pulled into a run-down warehouse at the end of a windy mountain road. The warehouse was a sea of white plastic and metal. Beat-up trucks and abandoned cars were scattered through the parking lot. It looked abandoned but they knew better. They hadn't found out what company owned the property, but it hadn't been difficult to find the kidnappers once they knew the van and its plates.

Charles and Derrick and Dominick had rendezvoused with the chopper a couple miles out from the warehouse. The helicopter landed in a small clearing near the road. Thomas, Henri and Juana disembarked with a small security team. Several teams were driving in to join them, but it was going to take time for them to arrive. They had to assume that René would have extensive back-up nearby.

Charles had ensured that Thomas, his Lieutenant, was going in with him. Henri and Juana would coordinate the other team. Dominick and Derrick refused to be side-lined and were joining Charles, but he told them their job was to get Chantelle to safety. That came before anything else.

He debated with his pack about access points and strategies. He listened to their ideas and worked with them to formulate the plan. He fought the urge to storm in and kill the bastard who took his mate. Stop the Trois-Rivières pack once and for all, bring them down. Burn the whole thing to the ground.

The others used soothing tones with him, touching his shoulder, cajoling him. He was trying to listen to them. He knew they were taking it seriously but this was life and death for him and his mate. He couldn't go on without her.

If only he had let her talk about her apprehensions. It was a big step asking her to move in and he needed to give her some time. He just had to get her back and tell her what she meant to him.

He would do anything she asked. Anything.

* * * *

Chantelle shivered on the bed, trying to wrap the blanket around her. How much time until Charles arrived? He and her men would have a plan. They would get her out of this.

She took a deep breath and tried to move her wrists in the handcuffs. It was uncomfortable but not painful, just like the dress. René was a piece of work. Trying to make up for some kind of failed insult to his toxic masculinity. What a way to live.

Pop! She jumped when Peaseblossom appeared in the room with her. Relief coursed through her when she saw the sprite. Pea put their arms around her and hugged her tight.

"It's so good to see someone friendly," Chantelle said, sniffling.

"How are you?" Pea asked. "Have they hurt you a lot?" They looked her over, their pink eyebrows going up at the outfit.

Chantelle shook her head. "No, they're waiting until Charles gets here."

Pea seemed satisfied with the answer. "Okay, I've got something for you. Gwen says to take it now since it's going to take some time to work." Pea popped a pill into Chantelle's mouth and she swallowed it.

"What is it?" Chantelle asked.

"It should counteract the dampener they're using on your magic. It'll last for a few hours. I had to wait until Charles was almost here to give it to you. You'll need at least fifteen to thirty minutes until you'll feel it working."

"What do I do?" Chantelle already felt better knowing there was a plan. Her pack would make sure they survived.

"Gwen says don't let the bad guys know it's working. Wait until the signal. Then use your magical whammy to take down the guards in the room. Charles, Dominick and Derrick will help you take care of René."

"Thanks." She hugged Pea, the tension easing in her chest. "I'm sorry you had to put yourself in danger."

Peaseblossom smoothed down their pink hair, saying, "I volunteered. I'm a part of the clan."

"We both are," said Chantelle. Hope bubbled in her chest. "I always thought I'd be alone."

"And look at you now!" Pea grinned and popped away.

Chantelle took a deep breath. She was a Fae Queen and she had a clan to protect. She had a responsibility to make it out alive with Charles, Dominick, Derrick and everyone else. They were family. They were her clan.

* * * *

Charles stood with Dominick and Derrick at the warehouse doors. Thomas waited in the SUV. Once Charles was captured, then he would alert Juana and Henri and work his way inside. He would give them the signal when the time was right.

Derrick checked his guns and nodded. Charles threw open the main door and made a lot of noise as they charged down the halls. He was relying on René's guards to come running. And they did. Charles and the men took down a couple of the guards but didn't resist too much. They had to make sure they were captured and brought to Chantelle. The guards took them through the warehouse to an apartment. René was already there, drinking cheap whisky. Charles flared his nostrils as he tried to discern Chantelle's whereabouts. She'd been in this room but René had kept his distance. She was somewhere nearby, but that was all he could tell.

René sniggered as his men tied up Charles, Dominick and Derrick. They struggled on the floor. It was going to take all of Charles' willpower to stay down, but he had to make sure they brought Chantelle to the same room. He couldn't let them know there was a bigger plan.

René stood up, walked over and kicked him, saying, "Here's the big Alpha. Not so big now, eh?" Dominick and Derrick wriggled in their bonds, but stayed down. Charles kept his expression blank. He had to see Chantelle and make sure she was okay.

"My dad thinks you're hot stuff, but you aren't. I've always known that," René said.

"I kicked your ass before and I can do it again," Charles snarled. He kept his head down on the ground.

"That was a long time ago. I've hurt a lot of people since then — more powerful and more important people than you."

Charles growled and the guards pushed him down. René's arrogance would make this easy.

"And I'm going to hurt your little plaything now." He turned and snapped his fingers, saying, "Go and get the girl."

The guards at the door left quickly.

"I'm going to do what you stopped me from doing all those years ago."

Charles' blood pressure was rising but he tried to stay cool. René kicked at him again, connecting with his gut. He could take a lot more if he had to. As long as he could see his mate and know she was fine.

The door opened. The guards brought in Chantelle. She held her head high and strode in with confidence. She had a blanket wrapped around her, but René pulled it off and threw it to the guards. "No need for the extra layers. I want to see your dress," he said. When he leered, Charles held himself back, but a low growl erupted from his throat.

Chantelle stood tall and looked at Charles. Even in that ridiculous outfit, Charles thought she was the most beautiful woman in the world. When she started to walk towards Charles, René grabbed her by the hair and pulled her back.

"No. You stay with me," René sneered.

"You don't need him. You've got me. Just let him go and you can take me anywhere you want," Chantelle said.

Charles growled. He knew she didn't mean it but it didn't stop his wolf from reacting. He tried to break free from the ropes on his wrists and ankles.

René looked at Chantelle. "You have no idea what's going on here, do you? There's more at stake than you know."

"You want my territory. You don't need her," said Charles. "I'll fight you here and now. Winner takes all."

"Tempting offer," said René, letting go of Chantelle. "But I'm already getting it all. When I bring you two in, then my dad will give your territory to me. I decide who lives and dies. I'll get rid of the strong males and keep the women. I'll let the white children live, but not the mongrels you like to keep in your clan."

"You don't have to do this," Chantelle said. "There must be another way."

"You don't cross people like my partners. They're not human, not shifters. They don't care who they hurt or how they get what they want."

"They're the ones I saw in my vision, aren't they?" Chantelle asked.

René just laughed.

Charles tried to stand up again. "You don't need her. You need me. You want my clan. She's nothing. She can't help you."

"You're kidding, right?" René said. "You know what she did. What she can do."

Charles looked down, trying not to betray anything.

"It's so cute the way you stick up for each other. But don't worry, that won't last very long. Not when I get started." He smirked and crossed his arms across his chest.

Chapter Twenty-Eight

As René continued to rant, Chantelle felt the tingles of her magic spreading through her chest. It was coming back. She had to wait and not reveal it to René.

"Now come here," René said, grabbing Chantelle's handcuffs and pulling her to him. He ran his coarse fingers up her arm, across her shoulders, to her chin, making her shudder. "Mmm, this is going to be good. I've waited a long time."

Chantelle pushed him, but René yanked her close, chuckling. Charles started snarling, yellow flecks showing in his eyes. One of the guards pushed him down.

"Shut up," René said to Charles. "You can't do anything."

"And you, my little cock-teaser." René turned back to Chantelle. "This time someone else will hold you so I get to go first."

Chantelle's chest tightened. She didn't understand. "What are you talking about?"

"My brother isn't here, so it's just you and me. You know all about that, don't you?" René looked from Chantelle to Charles and paused. "Wait, what do you remember?"

"You attacked me," said Chantelle, thinking. "Charles pushed you off and you two fought."

"Your granny's memory spells were tricky. She must have layered the blocks, in case you broke through some of the barriers." He ran a hand over Chantelle's bare shoulder and she felt sick. "I wasn't the only one there that day. My older brother, Raoul. He was the one who said we should do it. He'd go first and show me how."

Charles snarled. "She was just a kid, for God's sake."

"Raoul said it was better that way. Then you get to show her what it's like." He ran his fingers down Chantelle's torso. Chantelle drew back, shivering. Charles roared and sat up, but the guards knocked him over again.

René turned to Charles. "You've had her first, but now you get to watch me."

Charles bared his teeth, pulling back his lips. "Don't touch her!" He struggled while the guards held him down.

René cackled.

Chantelle rubbed her temples, feeling something in the pit of her stomach. "Wait, I remember your brother now. He was big and mean. He pushed me to the ground and you grabbed my arms. He was on top of me when Charles found us."

"Yes, your little boyfriend ruined everything. Raoul was bigger and stronger but something happened." He shook his head. "I don't remember it all. Just bits and pieces. Your granny's spells were strong but the witch

I found poked holes in most of them," he said. "All I know is you two stopped my brother and me. And my brother got hurt."

Charles stopped struggling and blinked. He said, "I fought your brother. He shifted and clawed at my leg. I looked over and you were knocked out."

"I did that," said Chantelle, suddenly remembering.

René snarled and grabbed her handcuffs, yanking her to him. The smell of cheap whisky wafted to her nose. "Just like you shut down our team at the compound on Harvest Moon Night. We saw the footage."

"What happened to your brother?" Charles asked.

"You lashed out after he hurt you. Knocked him down. That bitch must have done something else to him because he was really sick after."

"Did he die?" Chantelle looked at the ground. *More blood on my hands.*

"My dad beat him when we got home. He got sick the next day. Internal bleeding. He died a few days later."

Chantelle looked at Charles, her eyes wide. Violence piled on violence in a never-ending cycle.

Charles said, "I'm sorry. We didn't mean for anything like that to happen."

"My dad said it served him right for getting caught. He taught us better than to get whipped by a couple of weaklings. But who's the weak one now?" He looked at Charles on the floor.

"You don't have to do this," said Chantelle. Wanting to stall, she put her hands on his chest, testing gingerly if she could feel any magic yet. Yes, there was a stirring or two. She clamped back down but it was too late.

René paused for a moment and looked at her. "What are you—"

She had made a mistake. He knew her powers were back. "Charles," she said.

Then everything exploded. Literally.

Chantelle heard the commotion outside. *That must be the signal.*

The explosions rocked the ground beneath them. Then rapid-fire gun shots blasted inside the warehouse. The guards flanking the apartment door turned to listen. The other guards holding Charles, Dominick and Derrick turned when they heard gunfire in the hallway. René stepped towards the door.

Chantelle met Charles' eyes and he nodded. She reached her arms out to the guards who were holding her mate and family. Closing her eyes, she pushed the pulse out, hitting them with the same blast she had used on the night of the Harvest Fête. It was almost too easy. This time she could control it and make sure nobody died. When they crumpled to the ground, Dominick gestured her over. She got out the knife he had hidden and cut off his rope ties. She moved to Charles and bent down. Dominick helped Derrick.

A rough hand grabbed her shoulder. It was René. "That was strong," he said. "But I planned for this. Got a ward."

Charles was still in the bindings but she was facing him. She put a hand on his chest, grounding herself, like they had practised with Gwen. Drawing from her centre, she took in all her rage and power. But these feelings were tempered by Charles' bond, making her magic—their magic—stronger, more focused, better. It took a split second to get the balance of defence and offense. Then she struck behind her.

René fell down. He crumpled to the ground and stayed there.

Chantelle stood, helping Charles up. She stalked over to their enemy. "How many defenceless women and children have you hurt in your life? How many immigrants? Indigenous women?" René's face was ashen. He looked around but his people were down. Derrick and Dominick closed in on him, too.

Chantelle had him in this moment. She could end it here. He would never hurt anyone again.

Then Charles touched her arm. "The Fae Queen protects and defends. You don't murder."

She paused. It would be so easy. Then it would be over.

The door opened. Henri and Juana rushed in with their team. They checked that the guards were incapacitated then hurried to Chantelle and Charles. The moment had passed as quickly as it had come. She knew her mate was right. She wouldn't kill him here. She felt the tension recede, leaving her with peace in her heart.

"What do we do with him?" Chantelle asked.

"He needs to be punished," said Charles.

"We bring him back and the clan decides."

"His father will retaliate, but we will face this together," Charles said. She put her arms around him. They would be strong together.

Charles waited impatiently as Dominick removed his restraints. Charles put his arms around Chantelle and kissed the top of her head. "I thought I lost you," he said, biting back his tears.

"Me too," she said, holding him like she would never let him go.

She fit perfectly in his arms. He put his hand on her chin and turned her face up to his. "Will you marry me? When you're ready. Not before. Then we can spend weekends at your place and weekdays at the compound. Or whatever you want to do."

She nodded. "Friday pizza and movie nights with Kat, Yvette, and Nadiya. Sundays with Grand-maman."

"We can bring your youth from the Art Club group to the ski village every week so they can be in the studio with you and our community artists."

"We can have dinner with them before we send them home."

"And you will stay by my side, through everything?" *Please say yes. I need you.*

"Yes."

He kissed her like there was nobody else there, like the warehouse wasn't falling down around them, like there weren't more dangers ahead. He kissed her like they were going to spend the rest of their lives together and he couldn't wait to get started.

Chapter Twenty-Nine

Chantelle was helping Thomas serve Sunday dinner at Grand-maman's.

"Where are you going for your honeymoon?" Thomas used Marie's rotary beaters on the pot of potatoes.

"We're looking at eco-resorts in Costa Rica. Or we could go to Prince Edward Island and relax at a beachside cottage." Chantelle dished the cooked carrots into the waiting bowl.

"Which do you prefer?"

"Nadiya wants us to go to PEI. She loves *Anne of Green Gables*. I told her if I went with Charles this year and we love it then we could bring her back next year with her mom."

"Sounds like the choice has been made for you," Thomas said, putting the potatoes in the casserole dish and picking it up. He and Chantelle brought the vegetables out to the large dining table and called everyone to eat.

Marie sat at the head of the table, Charles on one side with Chantelle beside him. On the other was Clem, with Thomas sitting at the end of the table. Family and friends filled in the remaining seats. Dominick sat beside Chantelle's friend Kat, chatting amiably. Yvette, Nadiya and Yvette's partner, Tanya, sat between Chantelle and Michel and Henri. Bertrand was with his latest date, and Derek and his partner had joined too.

Charles looked around as they passed the plates. "We might need a bigger table."

Chantelle smiled. "It's perfect." Her heart was so full. She had been lonely and afraid for so long that she had started to believe she would never find family. And now she was surrounded by love and laughter.

Charles called everyone to attention to say grace, then he told everyone how grateful he was to have the love and support of family and friends. After a hearty 'Amen,' they started eating. They filled Marie in on the company reorganisation plans. Charles would remain president but he would step down from the day-to-day operations. He would also chair the Elders' Council for the clan. The other management roles were almost decided.

Henri made a toast to his brother. "Finally, Charles, you came to your senses and are letting the rest of us take on more responsibility. You earned this. And I want some nieces and nephews soon — so you'd better plan on spending lots of quality time with your wife." Everyone laughed. "And, Chantelle, thank you for putting up with my big brother — nobody else can!"

As they ate, Clem asked Chantelle about the at-risk youth program.

"We're bussing them in to the community centre's studio. The seniors enjoy spending time with them and working on art projects together. Then the youth stay for cooking lessons and eat dinner in the dining hall," Chantelle said.

"Chantelle, would you like to head up a scholarship program for local youth?" said Thomas.

"Really? That would be amazing. I'm just finishing up the last story in my granny's notebook and then I can get started on that project."

"What's this story about?" Nadiya asked.

"It's different from the others. The Fae Queen meets her sisters. There are two more Fae Princesses, who are in hiding. They have to work together and defeat the corrupt friars who are hurting people in their kingdom."

"Can I be one of the Fae Princesses this time?"

"I'm not sure. I can see their faces, kind of. They aren't anybody I know," Chantelle said. "But you will definitely be in the story. What about being their Fairy Godmother?"

"Yeah! That would be cool." Nadiya reached for the homemade rolls and butter.

* * * *

Thomas sat at the end of the table. He asked Henri for an update on the warehouse search.

"We took some computers and sat phones," said Henri. "There wasn't much on them. But we found out that the property was owned by a shell company. We traced it back to the organisation that outbid us for the land, Frères Gris Consortium. We still don't know much about them. They seem to operate in the dark and they don't have a head office anywhere. But the sat phones we took from the scene made some calls to coordinates in Parc Mauricie in Trois-Rivières territory."

"Do you think that's where Frères Gris have their head office?"

Henri shrugged. "We'll send some people to investigate the Parc Mauricie location. We also have another lead through our R&D department. The Consortium has links to a Franciscan Society in New France a hundred and fifty years ago."

"What could that mean?"

"It's an old organisation. They could be immortals, or Fae."

"*Chu dans marde*, that's big trouble," Thomas said. "I have a contact at the University of Montreal's Archives. Why don't I see if I can find out about their early history? Maybe we can confirm their links to the current group, or at least rule this out."

"Are you ready if Roland comes after us?" asked Henri.

"If it comes down to it, I will challenge the Alpha one-on-one. And I want you to work with Juana to make sure everyone is up-to-date on their combat training. That includes all leaders, in case we need them."

Henri nodded. "There could be difficult times ahead."

"We'll face them together," said Thomas. "Like always."

Want to see more like this?
Here's a taster for you to enjoy!

Sin City Wolf: Howl
January Bain

Excerpt

I stared out at the night, the pull of the waxing moon yanking hard. Taking a gulp of my Dalmore 62, the finest single malt whisky ever produced, I raked a hand through my hair. The need to run free was building, growing stronger by the hour. I ached to let the clean, dry desert wind blow everything else away.

Blame it on the blood moon, an ominous portent to all my wild forbearers, scheduled to rise over Las Vegas's towering skyline in a matter of days. All my billions couldn't stop that trickster from wreaking havoc on my kind. Not that I would trade places with any otherworldly creature. *Nothing beats being a werewolf. Nothing.* Especially being a billionaire werewolf, with more money and possessions than any other wolf — and most humans — on the planet.

I savored the final gulp of the fragrant whisky with its drumroll and smooth finish. It would prove amusing to see what my rivals at the House of Ribelle had planned during the event, necessitating me showing those mongrels their low rank in the pecking order. My wolf bristled at the very idea, prepared to strike.

I dropped my glass onto the proofs of the recent interview I'd done for *Business Leader Quarterly*. The founding of the Royal Bank of Luceres and the recent expansion of our casino enterprises into several new countries was the stuff of legend and warranted a huge center spread in the magazine. Amusing really, humans being unable to see even that which what was right in front of their noses. My photo stared from the piece, all *GQ* to the public, but the slick surface hid a beast, one ready to burst forth at a moment's notice.

And that beast, bored and weary at the sameness of the days, needed a change. Where was the excitement? The new challenge? Having gathered all the riches the world had to offer didn't fill the deep void of longing, growing stronger by the day, of wanting something more. Only to myself would I admit that my life was lacking, that surrounded by so many, I was lonely.

Maybe it was time to choose a mate? Even if she wasn't the famed Forever Mate so valued by the pack, at least I would have company at night. Someone to share my victories with. *No.* I wanted the real thing. A true mate at my side, anointed as being the chosen one of destiny. I raised my head and closed my eyes, catching a sense of change on the wind. Something was coming…

Thud.

My office door slammed wide open, causing a low growl of warning to escape my throat before I caught sight of the intruder who'd broken my concentration. *Ah, Lucius. My identical twin.* He'd come bearing dubious gifts, by the look of it.

Two frightened young women preceded my brother inside the penthouse offices of the Glitter Palace casino. *They should be scared.* Lucius might have been named for the light, but his heart was filled with darkness.

"I caught this pair skulking about, asking the dealers questions about our operation and generally making a nuisance of themselves. I intervened when they bribed one of our staff into letting them into the restricted area…bribed with the promise of a free blow job."

"That's not fair," the taller of the pair objected. They were beautiful women, tall and blonde and done up in the stock-in-trade of those looking for a good time. *Or to provide one.* I raised a sardonic eyebrow at her as she continued her protest.

"I'm just a student of hotel management, trying to get some pointers from those working in the real world. My friend Brandi only came along for company. I'm Jill, by the way."

Even from twenty feet away I could smell the smoking lie that scented her skin. Normally I would tell them both to strip, to prove themselves innocent. Today, I found the idea abhorrent. Lucius gave me a strange look, waiting for my reaction. I nodded at him. *You want this, go ahead.*

"Strip."

They both stared at Lucius with huge doe-like eyes.

"What?" Jill asked, her gaze flitting back and forth between me and Lucius.

"You heard me. If you're innocent, strip," Lucius said.

"I'm not wearing a wire."

"Prove it. I'll let you leave if you're clean."

The one called Brandi shook her head. "I'm not doing this. You can't make me." She hugged both arms around her upper body.

"I can and I will. We're the only authority here at the Glit." Lucius used the shortened version of the Glitter Palace, our casino's name. His demands had aroused the taller one—her scent saturated the air with a sweet musk. My nose twitched, ambivalent about the odor.

"What's it to be, Jill? Strip or banishment?"

"So ban me. I don't care," Brandi said.

Jill looked my twin straight in the eyes, challenging him. She raised her arms in a graceful arc and undid the strings tied at the back of her neck, letting her short blue chiffon gown fall in a shimmer of fabric the length of her body to puddle on the floor. Underneath, she was naked except for a tiny pair of white lace panties. Her luscious double Ds were firm and upraised, the nipples tight and protruding out a good half inch, begging to be pinched and sucked. Apparently, Jill liked to be told what to do, like a long string of Jills before her. Bored now, my mind drifted. Even my wolf seemed to find the display less interesting than usual, just sitting back observing instead of wanting to play.

"See, no wire," she said. She twirled in a full circle, her long blonde hair cascading around her, her breasts swaying with the graceful ballet-like movements of her body.

"How about under those panties?" Lucius asked, the challenge clear. One thing we did agree on—there was nothing on earth more beautiful than the female body. But today, I sat and contemplated having another strong drink, drumming my fingers on my desktop.

She hooked her fingers into the elastic waistband and eased the panties down her long tan legs, exposing her complete Brazilian wax job. Then, slipping the lace over her four-inch platform heels, she threw them at Lucius. He caught them and took a deep whiff of their fragrant dampness. "Nice. Now you." He pointed at the other girl.

She shook her head. "No way."

I suddenly realized I'd prefer to go for a run than be here. The pent-up lust from the pull of the coming wolf moon made my skin ripple with the urge. If this female was reluctant, then banning her from the premises would suffice. Neither I nor Lucius would force a woman. Why should we, when they all came of their own accord? Not that I wouldn't mind a good chase for a change — as long as I won. *And I always win.*

"Fine. But be advised, a photo will be taken and shared with the staff," Lucius said. He was dragging this out and I wanted it over and done with. I tried to catch his eye to let him know.

The female hesitated, biting her bottom lip. I could see through the sham. I had to give it to them — the Ribelle dogs were attracting better-looking spies. Not brighter, perhaps, unless they were looking to be caught? They'd have to be checked over thoroughly before they could leave the premises. I'd leave those honors to my twin.

Lucius glanced my way, lust darkening his complexion. He, perhaps more than I, enjoyed our couplings with willing women in the immediate vicinity of the other. Our more studious younger twin brothers, currently in Rome, enjoyed having the *same* woman, but I did not imagine that ever being the case for me and Lucius, with me being alpha.

Spy number two shimmied out of her tight minidress, exposing another spectacular set of large breasts and a lack of underwear, her reluctance an obvious game. *And a lure.*

"I'll need to check you for bugs," Lucius said.

Jill, spy number one, offered herself to my brother, raising her hands high above her head in the surrender position. He caged her wrists between one of his hands, then ran his other hand through her hair, then down her supple flesh, tweaking her nipples before slipping his fingers down to her pussy. She arched her back.

From the corner of my eye, I caught the slight shimmer of the cosmic disturbance in the air around Lucius, his eyes flashing blue before returning to brown. He wanted the change. I got it. Business had been all-consuming of late, especially concluding the arrangements on the acquisition of the new bank.

A loud knock sounded at the door. "Come in," I called.

"Sorry to bother you, sire," Serge said with all due respect.

My right-hand man, second in line after Lucius and similar to a mafia don's *consigliere*, looked unusually agitated, though he was doing an admirable job of attempting to hide it. But *my* job was to miss nothing that might affect those I was in charge of. Every little nuance meant something.

"Yes?"

"Just advising you that the all-girl band, The Sirens, has arrived and is set up in Nero's." Serge was fully aware of my standing order to make sure I knew *everything* going on in my casino. The online contest we'd run for the chance to win three nights' playing at Nero's had drawn a lot of media attention—good for business, and good for the group that would benefit from the exposure.

I nodded. The sense of change in the wind tonight grew stronger. *Time to pay close attention*, it seemed to say.

The lights in the room dimmed. My twin was making preparations to fuck the women.

"Check their jewelry, Lucius. Remember the last time." Hiding a bug in an earring had worked until I'd had the penthouse swept for electronic devices.

I made a quick decision in the moment, born of my urge to get out of the office and check on the band that had drawn so much attention.

"Let's go," I said to Serge.

I led the way to my private elevator across the hall and punched the lobby number. We rode in silence, my wolf somewhat annoyed about losing out on the easy tail waiting upstairs in my office, now that I had chosen to move on. But my mind went back to thoughts of my own Forever Mate and what that would mean in my life.

I shook my head with finality, pushing the idea away. The chances of that happening after all this time were slim to none. But that didn't mean I couldn't enjoy the company of a female, under the right circumstances, to keep the urges at bay.

Moon madness is a bitch.

About the Author

Mimi B. Rose writes fantastic tales filled with steamy enchantment and tender-hearted fulfilment to thrill strong women. As a teen she read V.C. Andews's *Flowers in the Attic* and Anne Rice's *The Vampire Lestat* and she was hooked on fantasy romance and paranormal romance. Some of her favourite tv shows are *Sleepy Hollow, Grimm,* and *Once* — and the reboot of *Beauty and the Beast* starring Kirstin Kreuk (does anyone remember that series?).

She loves all kinds of shifters and vampires. Her all-time favourite authors are Faith Hunter, Ilona Andrews, Nalini Singh, and more recently Richelle Mead.

Mimi likes a sassy heroine who is independent but finds a strong hero who can keep up with her and treasure her for their uniqueness — including her flaws!

Mimi loves to hear from readers. You can find her contact information, website details and author profile page at https://www.totallybound.com

Home of Erotic Romance

Sign up for our newsletter and find out about all our romance book releases, eBook sales and promotions, sneak peeks and FREE romance books!